WORLDES DEID

A SAVERNAKE NOVEL

Copyright © 2023 Susanna M. Newstead
ISBN-13: 978-84-125953-5-2

M

MadeGlobal Publishing

For more information on
MadeGlobal Publishing, visit our website
www.madeglobal.com

Cover Design: Dmitry Yakhovsky

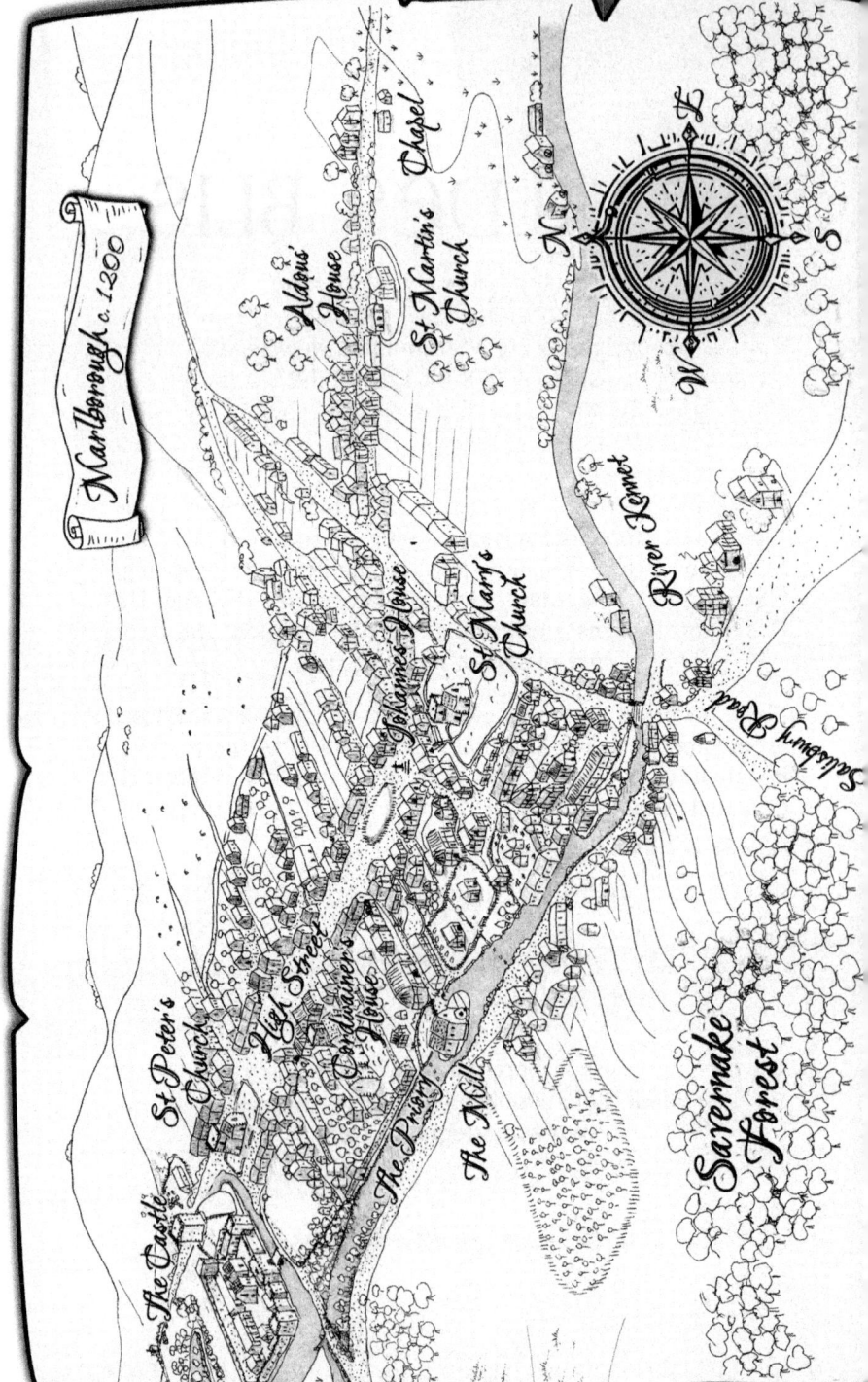

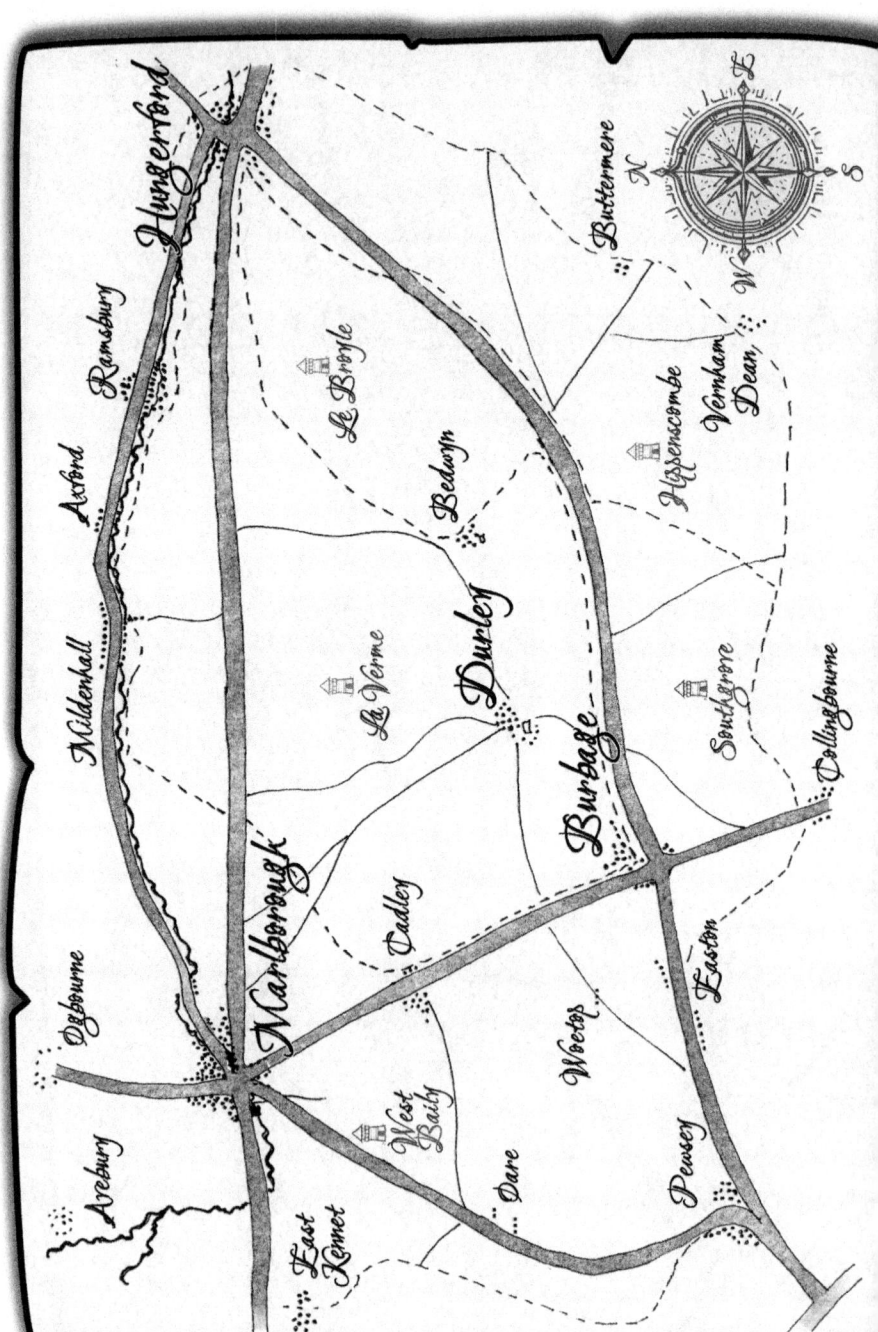

WORLDES BLIS

Susanna M. Newstead

A SCORCHING SUMMER.
A MELANCHOLIC MERCHANT.
A MYSTERIOUS MURDER.

For Michelle Miller - a true friend and supporter.

Worldes blis ne last no throwe;
It went and wit awey anon.
The langer that ich hit iknowe,
The lass ich finde pris tharon;
For al it is imeind mid care,
Mid serwen and mid evel fare,
And atte laste povre and bare
It lat man, wan it ginth agon.
Al the blis this heer and thare
Bilucth at ende weep and mon.

Wordly bliss last but a short time
It's here and then it's gone.
The longer I experience it,
The less I value it.
For it is shot through with care,
With sorrow and with failure
And at last, when it's gone
Man is left naked and poor.
All the bliss both here and there
Amounts in the end, to nothing
but weeping and moaning.

Part of an English song,
possibly 13th century.

Chapter One

"*T*HIS IS NO laughing matter, sir!" exclaims the man, his expression livid.

"I assure you, sir, the master..." begins his servant with a whine to his voice.

"Gentlemen, there is nothing I can do to aid you. Seek redress with your lawyers," I was saying.

Aldous Pitchcott, for he was the man, was breathing in angrily through his nose. I suspected he was not used to being denied.

"My Lord Belvoir, if you do not help me, before God, you may find yourself responsible for a murder."

"Oh, come Master Pitchcott. I think you exaggerate. Whose murder may I precipitate?" I remember I was laughing.

"My own, sir, my own!" he'd said.

Oh, Paul, my scribe... I am day-dreaming again... re-running the conversation I remember from that hot July day of 1208 in my head. You can write it down now you are back. Have you managed to find some more parchment? Good, then prime your pen.

What? It's not a murder? No, this time, we haven't begun with murder, but I promise you within a short time, we shall have one. We need to explain from the beginning, introduce our people and, of course, myself, and explain why I am writing these little tales. Who am I? Well, I am Aumary Belvoir, Lord of Durley, warden of the forest of Savernake, in the county of Wiltshire. My forest of Savernake was one hundred and fifty square miles of woodland with all its inhabitants and trades, close by the growing town of Marlborough in Wiltshire.

What's that? Oh yes, it's fewer miles now, isn't it? When I was a young man, it was the biggest it'd ever been. They felled many trees after the Charter of the Forest was issued in 1225. It's shrunken now, but it's still an impressive forest.

At this time, I was also the constable of the county and was responsible for the investigation of murders perpetrated on my soil. This was forty years ago, in the reign of the present king's father, John. I remember I was 34 in that year, and now I am an old man of 73 and unable to do much. I must live again through you and your pen, mustn't I? Yes, now I am old, but then, I was in my prime and... oh, I am repeating myself, am I? Well, I'm allowed to repeat myself, I'm seventy-two, you know... or is it seventy-three? I forget.

What I do remember is I was stripped to my shirt that July day in 1208; it was so hot. I wasn't, I have to say, the only one. I'd been out in the forest earlier and, as was my habit, wore my padded woollen gambeson for protection, not only against an attack by men but against the wayward blackberry bushes, the waving wild briar stems with their wicked thorns and the sharp spikes of the overhanging blackthorn bushes. It wasn't a bad protection either, against the biting flies which could plague the forest at this time of year. Now, I was as boiled as a fresh ham and pink in the face, and I gleefully threw it off and handed it to Henry, my steward. He, too, was stripped to his shirt and was sweating freely. He brushed my gambeson with his hand and lovingly touched the embroidered blazon on the breast: three small red flowers surrounded by oak leaves, the symbol of the Belvoirs of Savernake Forest.

"I'll hang it to dry off, sir, and put it in your chest."

"Thank you, Henry."

I lifted a fold of my shirt from my breast and wafted it to allow the breeze to reach me.

"It's damned hot!"

"It's hot enough without having to wear this," he said.

"You'd be glad of it if a desperate wolfshead were to come out of the forest at you, Henry. It would more than likely save your life."

Henry chuckled deep in his throat. "Remind me to stay in the safety of the manor then, sir!"

Henry didn't really enjoy venturing out into the forest, though naturally if he had to, he would.

Suddenly, we recalled the recent winter of 1207 when a band of murderers had attacked our village of Durley, and the stout manor walls had protected us from them. We remembered with a shudder how not all of us had been protected; not all of us had survived.

"Sir, you have a visitor."

"Ah, who's that then?"

I wondered if it was one of my neighbours paying me a visit.

"A man named Aldous, sir, Aldous of Pitchcott."

I screwed up my forehead. No, not a neighbour.

"Where is he, Henry?"

"In the hall, m'lord."

I nodded. "A moment only."

I drew the damp shirt over my head. "Can you fetch me another shirt, Henry? And I suppose I'd better have a cotte. No, on second thoughts, just a cotte."

"Yessir."

Henry disappeared into the screens passage and closed the office door.

I moved to the window, where I kept a bowl of water on a small table for washing my hands. I splashed my face, ruffled my damp curly black hair, and towelled myself dry. Henry returned.

"Who is he, this man of Pitchcott?"

"He tells me, my lord, that you *do* know him."

"I do?" Once more, I furrowed my brow. "Pitchcott? Where the devil is Pitchcott?"

"He tells me it is a small village in the county of Buckinghamshire, sir. Close by the larger village of Aylesbury."

"What the devil is he doing in Savernake, then?"

"I believe he's a merchant, sir."

"Oh!" I wracked my trammelled brain.

"Ah, yes!" I did remember him.

"Small chap with a widow's peak and a very lined forehead. Grey hair, not much of it. Has a small beard — a daft thing, nothing more than a grey spot on the chin?"

"Aye, sir, you have him."

"He lives in the town. He has a fine house and warehouse not far from The Green surrounded by a cob wall, a wall, I might add, almost as well built as that of the castle." I chuckled as I shrugged on my cotte. "I know him, but not well."

"I suspect you are about to get to know him better then, m'lord," said Henry with a grin.

I passed into the screens passage and stood for a moment looking into the hall.

Aldous of Pitchcott, as I had said to Henry, was a small man; a very small, compact man with, I noticed, tiny feet. The man had his back to me, his hands clasped behind him, and he was looking up at the solar stairs as if he were measuring each and every tread. His gaze travelled across the wall to the windows, and he noticed the glass in them. His face registered surprise and something else... envy perhaps?

I came forward, my heels clicking on the boards of the oaken floor.

He turned. I recognised him.

"Master Pitchcott. It is pleasant to see you again. I hope you have not been waiting too long?"

The man bowed. "No, no, my lord. Not long. Just long enough to begin to admire your lovely hall." He waved his hand around the space. "You will, of course, remember that I have a large house in the town..."

"Yes, I do. And I also think that congratulations are in order for you have been recently appointed to the town council, I hear."

The man nodded. "I have that honour, sir. The place on the council left by the death of Master Tyler some while ago."

"You have lived in Marlborough a few years now?"

"I have. I saw the possibilities and brought my business here in 1204 after the king saw fit to grant the town autonomy. I could see it was an expanding place, sir—a place of opportunity. The presence of the castle guarantees a man of business a good income, a steady revenue. Aylesbury is not such a vibrant place. It has a castle, of course, but it is much ruined now."

"And your business, Master Pitchcott?"

"Wine, sir, and not, as is every second man of means in this town, wool. Wine."

I nodded. I doubted that many of the council would agree with him. Several different trades were represented by the men of the town's council.

I moved to the table and offered the man wine. I wasn't surprised when he declined.

"What might I do for you, Master Pitchcott?"

It was then that I observed the other man in the room. He came up from my right-hand side, where he had been standing by the stairs to my private chapel.

"This is my assistant," said the merchant. "My man Agnew, Robert Agnew. He oversees my workers here in the town when I am called away. And other things." He waved his hand in the general direction of Master Agnew.

"My Lord Belvoir," The man bowed deeply.

"Master Agnew," I said, looking him over. Here was a small, wiry man with straight dark hair falling to his shoulders. His brows were black and bushy, which gave him a permanently peeved expression, though his mouth smiled. His complexion was swarthy and there was a strength in the man even though he looked quite effete at first glance.

Master Pitchcott came towards me.

"I'll not run around the subject, sir, and waste your time. If you are anything like myself, your time is precious."

"Yes, Master Pitchcott. I would appreciate that."

The man drew himself up to his full height, which, as I've said, was not great.

"I, sir, have been robbed."

"Robbed?"

"Yes, that is what I said."

I sat down on a bench at the side of the table we kept permanently in place at the bottom of the hall.

"Robbed of goods, or of gold?"

"Do you know anything about business, my lord?"

I blinked.

"I run the forest as a business for the king. It isn't simply his private land in which to hunt and play. It pays its way."

Pitchcott shook his head.

"No, no, no."

"And I admit to owning a thread business from the sheep which are grazed, Pitchcott, up on the downs."

"Do you understand investment, my lord?"

I could feel the presence of Master Agnew at my back.

He came forward. "With my master's permission, my lord, what he is meaning to say is that men of business, large and profitable businesses, such as that of Master Pitchcott, often have monies to spare. Rather than let this money do nothing but sit in a coffer, sir, we might invest it... by this, we mean lend it... to a business which, although of a good enough and profitable works, is in need of funds to expand. Thus we reap tenfold what we lay out."

Pitchcott nodded. "This, my Lord Belvoir, we call investment."

"Ah, I see." I did not need an explanation but nevertheless, I listened with amusement.

"I am being robbed."

"I take it you have invested in something and have not yet seen your reward. Why should you come to me?"

"It is a crime, sir. I come to you because you are the constable."

He was quite correct. The role had been bestowed upon

me in 1204 by no less a person than the king.

"Ah, Master Pitchcott. I am sorry. I deal with a different type of crime altogether. Surely this is a job for your lawyers or for the sheriff?"

The man made a strange gesture as if he was batting away a passing fly. "No, no, no."

"Sir," said Agnew again. "The master wishes you to investigate this crime and…"

I stood. "I'm sorry, gentlemen, I cannot help. I investigate murders. Crimes against the bodies of people. Those who have been unlawfully killed. Murders are reported to me, and I…"

"But do you not see, sir," said Pitchcott with a great deal of self-importance, "If you investigate, you may forestall a murder."

"Forestall?" I gave a small chuckle. "Are you thinking, Master Pitchcott, that you may become so incensed by this thieving person that you will deprive them of their life in a fit of pique?"

And now, Paul, we catch up with ourselves,
do we not? For this is where you came in.

"This is no laughing matter, sir!" exclaimed Pitchcott, his expression livid.

"I assure you sir, the master…" began Agnew.

"Gentlemen, there is nothing I can do to aid you. Seek redress with your lawyers."

Aldous Pitchcott breathed in angrily through his nose. I suspected he was not used to being denied.

"My Lord Belvoir, if you do not help me, before God, you may find yourself responsible for a murder."

"Oh, come, Master Pitchcott. I think you exaggerate. Whose murder may I precipitate?"

"My own, sir, my own!"

There was a small silence in which I heard Hal of Potterne, my senior man-at-arms, come clomping up the outer stairs; the sound of Hubert Alder's hammer ringing up from his forge in the courtyard and the children at play in the field behind the walled manor.

I gestured to the heavily breathing merchant Pitchcott for him to be seated, and I perched on the edge of the table.

Hal came and stood in the hall doorway.

"Master Pitchcott, you believe, quite apart from your monies being misused, that your life is in danger?"

Pitchcott threw a look at Hal and then sat slowly on a bench, lowering himself down as if it pained him. He passed a sleeve over his sweating forehead.

His assistant came to stand beside him.

"I have, it is true, not felt safe these past few weeks," said Pitchcott with authority.

"Why?" I asked. "Has something, in particular, happened that leads you to believe you are the target of a murderer?"

"Little things, my Lord Belvoir, little things."

Agnew made a small movement which was instantly stilled.

"Oh, but, sir. There was the matter of the block of stone," he said.

"Stone?" My heart lurched.

My five-year-old son Geoffrey had been brutally killed by a falling block of masonry some years ago, and even now, the mention of falling stone made me flinch.

"Aye, that and the fire in the warehouse."

"You have witnesses to attest to these things you say happened?" I asked.

"My Lord Belvoir, I am a respected man of the town. I do not make up stories to..."

"No, Pitchcott. I do not question the veracity of your words. I merely ask so that if I *were* to investigate, I have other people to question, other opinions to elicit, other recollections of events."

The man stared at me as if I were mad.

Agnew licked his lips.

"Master Pitchcott was passing his house, sir, on the road to Ramsbury and a block of stone was thrown from the rooftop. It missed him and his horse by an inch."

I nodded.

"Then we had a fire, easily contained, I must say, at the property, the warehouse out on St Martin's, but a fire nonetheless. The master just managed to get out before the smoke overcame him."

Pitchcott passed a trembling hand over his forehead.

"Two things, my lord. Two things only, but I do feel as if I am being watched. Observed. I feel… unsafe, yea, even in my own home."

I recollected the town house in which the man lived. It was like a fortress with a huge castle-like gate and high walls. If you couldn't feel safe there, you wouldn't feel safe anywhere.

"Do you have a name for this person you say has defrauded you?"

"I do, sir, indeed I do."

"And you think this man is the man who is trying to kill you?"

Pitchcott sat up straight. "I am a likeable man, my lord. I do not have a list of men wishing to get their hands around my throat and throttle me!"

"No business enemies?"

"I am good at what I do, sir. I have a good business. A very good business. Naturally, a man as successful as myself has detractors."

"Master, not one of them would wish to kill you," said Agnew.

"Envy, yes, some might be envious, but no, none would kill me to remove me from the competition."

"Competition?"

"The supply of wine to the castle."

"Ah, I see. You have the local contract to supply the king's table when he's here?"

Pitchcott stood up. He nodded his head in a little bow. "I do, sir. Hard-won, but I do have that honour."

"And the castle at other times, my lord," added Agnew proudly.

"It is good business, Pitchcott," I conceded. "I have drunk your wine myself."

I got up and walked around.

"This man, the man who took your money, who is he, and where can he be found?"

"The man is called Richard Deyning. He is a man of Marlborough who has a business close by the river, near the rope yards..."

"He's a furrier, sir," said Agnew.

I knew of the man. Not well, but I knew *of* him.

"I will speak to him, Master Pitchcott. That is all I can do."

"Arrest him, sir!" shouted Pitchcott. "He has taken my money, and I have not seen a penny of it back in a year."

"What does he say about it?"

"Pah! That it takes a while for these things to come to fruition, and that I must be patient, that I will see my investment grow with time."

"Can he provide you with any evidence of this?"

"No, sir. He most certainly cannot."

"Have you asked him for the monies you lent him to be returned?"

"Do you take me for a fool, my Lord Belvoir? Of course I have!"

"And his answer?"

"That he cannot give me my money for it is spent. Pah! Spent indeed! On his fine house and his vices, no doubt."

'Vices?"

"Horses, sir," said Agnew. "He loves horse racing."

"Ah…" He wasn't the first man to beggar himself over a horse.

I moved to the window where there was a breeze.

"And you think this man would kill you rather than return your money or honour the investment and pay you your profit?"

"What else can I think, sir? He is not a man of such high principles as myself," said Pitchcott haughtily.

"Then why did you trust him?"

A strange change came over Pitchcott. He squirmed and threw a crafty look at his assistant Agnew.

"I trusted him, sir, because I thought him an honourable man. He came with impeccable credentials and…"

"His word was good in the town, sir," interrupted Agnew.

"You took the word of your fellow councillors?"

Pitchcott filled his lungs with a laboured breath through his nose and snorted, exclaiming, "I did!"

I walked up to him and, as I did so, I watched him carefully.

There was more to this story, I was sure.

"And now, Master Pitchcott, you will tell me the rest of the tale. That part which you keep back."

Again the flick of a look to Agnew.

"The rest is unimportant."

"I wish to know the whole of it, or I will not speak to this man Deyning."

Pitchcott went red—almost the same red as his expensive murrey gown. I wasn't sure if it was embarrassment or anger.

"I... I..."

"The truth, sir."

He let out the breath he'd taken to form a denial.

"My daughter, my lord."

"Your... daughter...?"

"Everild."

"This Everild, your daughter, she has something to do with this matter?"

"She wishes to marry Deyning, my lord."

I pinched the bridge of my nose in frustration.

"And so now you are at loggerheads with her because you think her lover is a felon?"

"No, we are not yet come to feuding, sir. I think my daughter knows where her loyalties lie."

"But if you could prove this man Deyning to be a fraud and a cheat, sir, then your daughter would no longer..."

"That is my hope, my lord."

"I see..."

"I thought when I first met the young man that he was trustworthy and diligent. Now I have changed my opinion."

I narrowed my eyes. There was, I felt, still more to this.

"So if your daughter does not marry this Deyning the furrier, Pitchcott, have you plans afoot for her marriage - elsewhere?"

Pitchcott shrugged his gown onto his shoulders and jutted his chin.

"You have, sir, guessed my intention. You are quite correct."

"So where would you rather she bestowed her affections, sir?"

Pitchcott rose and, like a pedagogue of old drumming

his words into his students' heads, he walked about lecturing me on who, why and how his wishes were to be fulfilled.

Apparently, Everild was his adopted daughter. He and his wife had no children. Now his wife was dead and he did not feel inclined at his advanced age to marry again.

He'd had a ward for whom he had cared since the death of the ward's mother, Pitchcott's sister. This young man had lived with them for some years and the vintner wished him to come into the business. Sadly, this lad did not want to become a vintner and was trying to make his own way in the town in business, for he'd set up an armoury to supply the castle and other folk in the area.

Pitchcott had denied him funds with which to proceed.

The young man whose name was Farnell had abandoned his mentor's name and had taken the name Armer. He had moved out of the family home and had rented a small space in the town and was busy building up his business by working out of some old outbuildings at the back of the town ale house, The Green Man.

Recently he had introduced his uncle to a girl *he* wished to marry. She was not an instant success. Pitchcott had railed against him and threatened to cut him out of his will, for he naturally wanted to keep everything in the family and wished Farnell to marry his adopted daughter Everild.

My head was reeling with the complexities of it.

"So let me get this right, Master Pitchcott. You have several people with whom, in your own home, you argue about the future. You have made, if not enemies, then certainly not friends of your daughter, your ward and his beloved. You have a dispute with this man Deyning. And you tell me that no, you have no one who wishes you ill, except perhaps, Deyning?"

"It is him, my lord. I can smell it."

I sighed. "I will speak to Deyning, but that's all

I can do..."

Pitchcott pursed his mouth. He looked as if he were about to spit out grape pips.

"Thank you, my Lord Belvoir. I suppose it's all I can hope that your words frighten him enough that he abandons his suit of my daughter and returns my capital."

"Your adopted daughter is over twenty-one, I suppose?"

Pitchcott's eyes narrowed.

"You can't make 'em marry," said Hal from the doorway. "You can't force 'em."

Pitchcott gave Hal such a look as was intended to freeze him solid. It did not work on Hal of Potterne. He grinned nastily back.

"One cannot rely, sir, on worldly things. They forever disappoint," said Pitchcott gloomily.

"By this, I suppose you mean your young people, sir?"

"Everything one works for, all one's efforts come to naught."

"We must accept how it is, Master Pitchcott, not how we'd like it to be."

"I have not laboured this thirty years to see it all come to nothing, my lord."

"'You shall all relinquish here the possessions whereof you were lord; when you lie, man, upon the bier and sleep a very dreary sleep. You cannot have with you any company, but your life works on a heap,'" I said. "That is the word of a wise poet, sir."

The vintner scowled and bowed to me. He collected his gown around him.

"Come, Agnew," he said. "We have much to do. Good day, my lord. God keep you."

And he swept out, pushing past Hal, who was still leaning on the doorpost.

Hal came into the room, chuckling as I shook my head.

"Christ's bones," I muttered.

"There goes a disappointed man," he said. "'E'd come for a pound, and 'e's gone away with an 'alfpenny!"

"Odious little man," I said under my breath.

"Do you think it's true… that this man Deyning's got it in fer 'im?"

"I almost wish he had."

Hal laughed, "'Is face when you counted the folk that don't like 'im!"

I sighed, "And I have a feeling that's nowhere near the full number, Hal. I suppose I shall have to have a word with this Deyning man."

"Marlborough's getting a mite full of folk now, what with furriers and armourers. Not so long ago, we'd 'ave to go to Salisbury or Winchester for such things. Or London even."

I smiled. "You and I have seen this town blossom, Hal."

"Aye, that we 'ave."

Marlborough was a little town at the foot of the scarp of the downs on which lay the forest of Savernake. It nestled in the valley of the River Kennet and nuzzled the soft chalk downs of north Wiltshire.

When I was a lad, it had been some straggle of houses going from the church of St Mary in the East and the Green, to the castle in the west and a few cottages around the castle itself. A number of dwellings had been strung up the hill northward, and even fewer had wound down to the river in the south.

Now, the town was a thriving place with a twice-weekly market, a large fair in August, two bridges, many industries and a castle to rival several in the country.

With this came prosperity and expansion. All this Hal and I had seen in our lifetimes.

"You coming with me tomorrow, Hal? When I go to see

this Deyning the furrier?"

"I wouldn't miss it fer the world," said Hal. "I want to see 'is face too when you tell 'im that ol' Pitchcott had accused him of tryin' to kill 'im!"

Chapter Two

*W*E RODE OUT in a misty dawn the next day, which promised more hours of heat. The road under our horses' hooves was baked hard and rang out like a man striking a broken bell.

The man Deyning was not hard to find, for his property was on Barn Street at the end of the yard owned by Master Wayne, the waggon maker.

We entered a dark wooden building, and the smell inside was fearsome.

"Satan's bowels!" said Hal. "It's like the stink of 'ell in here!"

I screwed up my nose. "The skins, I suppose. Rather like those of our friend Master Tanner - the skins used here aren't too dissimilar to those manufactured in the tanning trade."

The warehouse, for so it proved to be, was strung with furs of all kinds, in various states of curing.

Hal stretched out a hand and lovingly stroked a pelt hanging from a beam.

"I don't know what this is, but it's lovely," he said.

"That," said a voice, "is martrons, sir."

A man came into view. "The fur of the pine marten. And the devil's stink is the smell of the stuff we use to preserve the fur, sir," he added with a smile.

He was modestly dressed, no fur for him, in a long cotte of dark brown with a sparkling white linen shirt underneath. His hair was cut to his ears and yellow blond. His eyes were a watery blue, and his face handsome but not stirringly so. He wore a bright blue belt with bronze decorations that dangled almost to the floor, and his thumbs were crooked into it.

"Master Deyning?"

"My Lord Belvoir, is it not?" He bowed.

"Of Savernake, yes. Good day to you. You have some fine furs here."

"Might I interest you in something, my lord? I have just the thing for a great man to line a cloak for the winter, though..." he scoffed, "At present, business is quiet. There is no call for warm furs in such a summer."

"Do not folk approach you now so you may create work ready for the winter?"

"They do." He shrugged, "but it is the most quiet of times right now in July."

"And forgive me if I'm wrong, but fur is becoming popular to wear on the outside of one's clothes, too, is it not? My wife tells me ladies of rank seek squirrel and weasel to trim their sleeves and necklines for the winter."

"Your lady wife is correct, m'lord," nodded Deyning. "We shall be taking advantage of this fashion here very soon."

I looked around.

"What might we help you with, my lord? Wolf or bear to line your winter cloak, perhaps? A caplet of beaver for the shoulders...?

"Ah, no, thank you, my good Master Deyning. I'm not here on the business of buying furs."

Deyning's face creased into a frown.

"I come at the instigation of Master Aldous of Pitchcott, master furrier. He tells me some unsavoury things about you. Might we have a word about the money he says he has allowed you as an investment in your business here?"

Deyning planted his feet wide and struck a pose, his arms folded across his chest.

"He will, I've told him, get his money once the business…"

"He's very unhappy with how you are working, it seems."

He made a moue. "The man is impossible."

"Tell me your side of the tale."

Deyning dropped his arms to his side.

"What is your interest, m'lord?

"He came to me because he is most unhappy and feels that you have defrauded him, sir, of his money. He tells me he asked you for the money back, but you refuse to return it."

"I cannot return what is not there. It's spent," said Deyning through gritted teeth. He sighed. "Please, my lord, come into my office at the back."

We followed him into a wooden made room at the back of the warehouse.

Deyning stood behind his table.

"I explained to Master Pitchcott, sir, when I first approached him for money."

"You approached him; he did not offer it?"

"No, sir. I needed more money to commission the hunters here and abroad to fetch me the pelts. This is a long-winded trade, sir. It cannot be done in the blink of an eye. Furs come from all over. Yes, many of them come from our own shores." He turned to Hal, "Like the pelt you admired, sir, but I import from Scotland, my lord, as far as the forests of the Holy Roman Emperor, the wastes of the frozen north. Things cannot be done quickly. I explained all this to the man."

I looked at Hal. "He knew then that this was a long drawn-out investment? That he would not get his reward within the year?"

"Yes, sir. He knew."

"So when do you think you will be in a position to reward him for his lending you the money?"

Deyning stuttered. "I cannot say with any certainty. I have had losses at sea lately. I shall make up the loss of that, there's no doubt, but you must see, sir, that it's a precarious business."

"Master Pitchcott knew how... precarious it might be? I hope you told him of the difficulties you might encounter?"

"I did indeed, sir."

The door behind me creaked and I turned to see a woman standing in the door hole.

"My Lord Belvoir, isn't it?" The woman curtsied.

"Yes."

I took in her good woollen bliaut and her soft reddish pink leather shoes which poked from the edge of her prettily decorated pink supertunic.

She was petite and good looking, with dark auburn hair braided down her back in a single plait.

"Have I the honour of addressing Mistress Everild of Pitchcott?"

The woman's perfectly plucked eyebrow lifted.

"Yes, sir, though how you..."

"Your father told me that you wished to marry Master Deyning here. I assumed since you are alone and had come to see him that you must be his affianced."

Mistress Pitchcott came into the room and daintily closed the door.

"We are not *quite* affianced yet, sir," she said sadly. "And

I would be very grateful if you didn't tell my father I had been here."

"Ah, no, no, he would be most displeased, wouldn't he?"

A look passed between Deyning and Everild.

"My Lord, we wish to be married, but Everild's father refuses to sanction it."

"So I have heard."

Everild's chin came up, and a sparkle was in her eye. "We shall do it as soon as Richard has made the money to pay my father back what he had lent him."

"I hear he wishes you to marry the young man he has cared for and adopted; his name is Farnell, I believe."

"Farnell and I grew up together. There is no way on earth I could marry him. He is like a brother to me."

I nodded.

Now it was my turn to cross my arms over my chest and look stern.

"Master Pitchcott tells me that he is being harassed, being followed and watched. He said he's in fear of his life." I paused. "Does this have anything to do with the money you owe him, Deyning, or the marriage you wish to contract between you, mistress?"

Everild gave a small nervous laugh. "My father is an over-imaginative man, my Lord Belvoir. We have never threatened him, nor made him uncomfortable. It is all in his mind."

"Everild is right," said Deyning, coming round the table and hooking his arm through the woman's. "There is no truth in anything Master Pitchcott says."

"Hmm."

"'E says there was a fire at 'is ware'ouse and that 'e narrowly escaped with 'is life when a boulder was thrown at 'im from a roof," said Hal. "No truth in that either, then?"

Everild Pitchcott sighed. "There is truth in that, yes.

It did happen. He *was* attacked. But it was nothing to do with us."

I stared the woman in the eye. She did not blink.

"Right." I turned to the door.

"Master Deyning, you had better make sure that the monies you owe Master Pitchcott are returned with the profit you promised within good time. I have advised him to take legal action should it not happen."

I held open the door. Hal passed through.

"I hope you can be married as soon as you wish and that nothing untoward befalls your over-imaginative father. I hope, too, that he may see the error of this belief in the marriage he wishes you to contract and that he does not disinherit you, mistress. It's a long fall from the daughter of a wealthy vintner to the wife of an impecunious furrier. My good wishes go with you for a speedy end to your trials, Mistress, Deyning."

A look passed between them once more. What it signified, I could not tell.

"My Lord!" said Everild breathily. "Love will conquer."

"Love, mistress, will not feed you, nor your children."

And I closed the door.

We walked slowly down to the road.

"There's somethin' up there," said Hal. "I don't think either of them is completely innocent."

"No. You're right. They really aren't bothered, are they? Either about their wished for marriage or the fact that her father is worried for his life."

I caught my lip with my teeth. "I have a mind, simply for completeness, to speak to the other party in this story. Let's see if we can find him."

"What, this armourer?"

"Aye, him. Let's see what he has to say."

We heard the man before we found his workshop, tucked at the back of The Green Man drinking house just off the High. The place had rented him a space in an outbuilding or two. Hammering and banging came from the shed, and we heard the rhythmic sound of the clipping of metal.

As we approached, a man came from the door, dropping a handful of links for a maille corselet from palm to palm and observing them closely in the sunlight as they fell.

He looked up.

This man wore a blue short-sleeved tunic over a brown shirt and over this, a long leather apron. His skin was smooth and the complexion perfect, though I judged him to be a man over twenty-five. His small beard and moustache were red-brown and his eyes brown like a conker.

These eyes lit first upon my sword, then my cotte, and only when he had seen how I was dressed did he look at my face. He then scrutinised Hal, giving every weapon Hal wore about him a long look.

"Good day, sirs," he said, bowing.

"Master Farnell Armer, Pitchcott as was...?" I asked.

The man turned inside the doorway and gave the links into an unseen hand.

"That is my name."

"I am Sir Aumary Belvoir, the warden of Savernake Forest."

Farnell Armer bowed again.

"My Lord, I am honoured that you should visit my humble establishment."

"How long have you been trading here? I don't remember you here last year when I had cause to come this way."

"Four months, sir. The landlord of The Green Man rents me the space and I live *there*." He pointed to a house across the alley way. "With the Widow Spynner."

"You left the house of your guardian?"

"Quite some years ago, sir. I travelled about meaning to learn the trade. I began with smithing and then..."

"It's an expensive trade to set up, Pitchcott, on your own."

"I had monies of my own, sir, and a patron. What is this? Are you interested in...?"

"I might be interested in commissioning you, should I think your work good enough."

The young man frowned, "I have spent eight years building up to this, my own business, sir. I have learned from the greatest masters in France and the Iberian lands. I know what I'm doing."

"I'd be interested in seeing what you can do, Armer," I smiled.

The man nodded seriously. "I think you will be satisfied with the quality we produce here, m'lord."

"Your guardian did not finance your business, then?"

A change came over the pleasant young man's face.

"That weasel!"

I chuckled. "I take it you do not see eye to eye with your relative, Armer?"

"Would you, my lord? The man who stole the very food from your mouth and the cloth from your back?"

"I was told that he succoured you as a child after the death of his sister, your mother. This isn't true?"

"Succoured? Pah! Who told you that?"

I saw Hal shift on his feet, but he said nothing.

"The man himself, Pitchcott."

"He lies, my Lord Belvoir. My mother had left me well provided for, and the grasping bastard took all under his wing when I was but a child. Ask how he became so wealthy in such a short time, sir. He took what was rightfully mine and spent it on his own schemes. Now when I want money to buy property in the town, the money is suddenly not there for me."

"I see. You have a reason to hate the man then?"

Armer's eyes narrowed. "Again, I ask you, sir, what is your interest?"

I looked up at the sun beating down on us.

"Might we go into your workshop, young man, and talk about this out of the sun's glare?"

The man extended an arm and with a slight bow, he passed into the gloom of the shed.

Here were three men at work. One forming, on a shirt of maille, the links Armer had been examining outside the shed; one sharpening a knife on a grindstone and the other hitting the glowing blade of a sword with a hammer.

"My interest, Armer, is merely a great curiosity at why the merchant Pitchcott, your erstwhile guardian, should come to me and ask me to arrest a man called Deyning for fraud, complaining that the man has harassed and attempted to murder him."

"Deyning?"

The man laughed out loud. "That is a very foolish notion. Richard may be an idiot, but he's not a murderous one."

"And yet he has every reason to hate the man Pitchcott."

Armer's eyes clouded. "Over Everild, you mean?"

"That and the money Pitchcott has advanced him."

"Ah, yes."

"I have spoken to the pair, and they admit that relations between Master Pitchcott and themselves are not good." I folded my arms. "And now you tell me that you, too, do not have any regard for the man."

Armer turned from me. "You may think what you like, my lord."

He began abstractedly to fiddle with the metal links

again and took up a pair of pliers with which to add them to the half-made corselet on the bench.

"I will have nothing to do with the old stoat."

"I'm told that your uncle wishes you to marry Everild."

Armer looked out into the gloom of his work shed.

"I will not. When I marry, it will be a girl of my own choosing. Besides..."

"I hear you have someone in mind?"

He turned back to me and threw down the pliers. "Aye, I have and that whistling toad can go and hang. I'll not go into his filthy business and I'll not marry Everild."

"*She*, sir, will not marry *you*."

"No! She's head over heels in love with Deyning."

"So, who are you head over heels in love with, Master Armer?"

Farnell sighed. "If you must know, I have asked the maid, Corlis Glover, sir, to be my wife. She has accepted and... and..."

I knew Corlis. She was the youngest daughter of Henry Glover. A bright sparkling girl with a sunny nature.

"And Master Glover?"

"Will come round in time, we think."

"Oh dear, your family is beset with problems, is it not, in matters of the heart? First Everild and her love, and then you and yours."

"Master Glover has not said we may *not* marry. It's all a matter of time. I need to get myself on my feet here with the business, and then, he's said that..."

"Tell me, Farnell, who is the beneficiary of the will of Master Pitchcott? Do you know?"

A small tic began in the corner of the eye of Master Farnell Armer.

"Last I heard, it was divided equally between myself and Everild."

"Hmm. No doubt a sum worth having for a struggling new business such as yours."

"I am not struggling..." he said, growing pink in the face. "It's merely a new venture and..."

Our conversation was interrupted by the sound of a woman yelling in the yard outside.

"Master Armer, might I have a word, sir... again? Master Armer... coooeee! It's about your rent."

"I must go, sir. Excuse me..."

He tried to push past me, but I held his arm.

"I think I must take seriously these allegations that Master Pitchcott has laid before me. These stories of murderous attempts on his life."

The door opened a crack and a shaft of sun spread over the dirt floor of the shed.

"Master Armer, sir. It's about your rent."

"Yes, Mistress Spynner, I'll get it for you," said Farnell in an irritated voice.

"It's just that I can't pay the baker if you don't..." the woman looked round.

"Oh, my Lord Belvoir, I'm so sorry to intrude. I didn't mean to..." She bobbed a curtsey.

"That's quite all right, Mistress Spynner. We are going now," I smiled.

I knew the woman for she was one of the people with whom I had dealings. She worked in the spinning trade of Marlborough town.

I saw one of the working men down his tools and look with narrow-eyed suspicion at the scene in front of the main door.

"It's just that you are two weeks in arrears, and I shall find it very difficult to..."

"I've said I'll get it!"

Farnell reached for the woman and hustled her out

of the shed.

I looked at Hal and then at the workman, who returned to his grinding.

We followed out into the bright sunshine.

"I don't think that young man," I pointed to his receding back, "Has a patron at all, or the backing he claims, Hal."

"'E might think it a good idea, you mean, to get rid of 'is uncle and suddenly get rich?"

"Enough to pay his rent and buy himself property from which to work, perhaps."

"And marry 'is lady love?"

"Indeed, Hal."

"Well..." Hal tucked his thumbs in his belt and rocked on his heels. "It's certainly a squirmy pile 'o eels. Or I'm a Welshman."

I had left Bayard, my roan gelding, at the castle, and Hal had left his favourite grey there, a big beast we called Grafton, so he and I wandered up the High Street nodding to folk we knew.

We were in no hurry and the day was glorious and not yet too warm.

We passed over the drawbridge and into the cool and dark of the gate arch.

My friend and master of the castle guard, Andrew Merriman, came clomping down the steps from the guardroom.

"Ah, just the person I want!" he said, wiping his neck on a cloth. He was dressed as usual in his full maille and was sweating freely.

"Andrew, good day. Why do you want me?"

"A man came in earlier. He was in a bit of a fluster.

Looking for you."

"Did you catch his name?"

"I did. Agnew."

"Master Pitchcott's man!"

"Where is 'e?" asked Hal.

"Gone back to the house. He said he lived on St Martin's."

"Did he say what he wanted?"

"Only that he had to speak to you. His master had sent him to find you, he said. Didn't say why, but like I say, he looked mightily displeased."

Hal and I looked at each other and made directly for the stables, where we collected Grafton and Bayard and rode for the other end of town.

As we approached the large house on St Martin's, the gates swung open, and two men ran to the stable to wait for us.

"We are expected, Hal," I said.

"You are to go into the hall straight away, m'lord," said the first groom, who took Bayard from me.

We walked into the hall and were met by Agnew who flew across the room wringing his hands.

"Oh, my lord, thank you for coming. Thank God the man passed on the message."

"You are lucky he caught us, Agnew, before we returned to the forest. What has happened?"

"Another attempt on my master's life, sir. The murderer failed."

"What this time?"

"An attempt at poisoning, m'lord."

"Poison?" said Hal and I together.

"The doctor is with him now."

"Dr Johannes?"

"Who else can be trusted in this town, sir?"

"Where is your master?"

"I'll take you to him."

He turned about, and as Hal tried to follow me, Agnew put out a hand.

"No, not you. You stay here."

"Like Hell, I will," said Hal truculently. "Where Sir Aumary goes, I go."

I smiled. "You will have to allow it, Agnew. Hal is my assistant in all I do. Without him, I do nothing."

Hal nodded once and firmly and pushed past the vintner's assistant.

We ascended some stairs and approached a private room situated at the far end of the hall.

"Johannes!"

"Ah, Aumary! I wondered how long it would take you to get here."

"Tell me all. Does Master Pitchcott still live?"

"He does. Oh, the man has been poisoned, of that, there is no doubt. He is very ill, but there was not enough of the stuff to kill him. I got most of it out of him, made him vomit before too much damage could be done anyway."

"Do we know what it is?"

Johannes shrugged. "As yet, no, not completely. My guess, and, of course, it's only a guess, is wolfsbane or aconite."

"Ah, one we have not had for quite some time."

"The dried leaves used, I think. Inexpertly done. Too little to be fatal, and we were called in time. Nasty all the same. The dried plant is not as efficacious as the new leaves."

We moved nearer to the bed where Master Pitchcott lay perspiring and breathing with difficulty, his eyes closed.

"Do we know how it was introduced?"

"Fed to him in his dinner, I believe, though naturally, I will have to go down to the kitchen and see what was prepared to eat today. They eat early in this household, I'm told."

I nodded.

I took Johannes by the shoulder and moved him to the window as far from the bed as possible. Master Agnew watched us warily from the bedside.

The doctor was a big man, tall, taller than me at over six foot and near to forty-five years of age. He had shoulder-length brown hair, scrupulously clean and shining, with just a hint of grey at the temples, which was tied back in a queue, and he was clean-shaven, contrary to current fashion, which dictated that men wore beards, as I did myself. His eyes were an amber brown, clear and direct of gaze.

He had been born in Oxford but had taken the name of the place he had learned his doctoring, Salerno in Sicily, the very best place in the world to learn the art of medicine, he told me. He was a very wealthy man, having made his money as a young man, soldiering in the Holy Lands with our previous king, Richard. Now he was giving back to the inhabitants of this little downland town.

He and I had a history of solving murders together and he was a very dear friend, not only a friend, since his niece Lydia was also my wife.

"The man came to me yesterday and asked for my help. I must admit to not really believing him. I've been in the town checking on one or two facts."

"There is no doubt it's an attempted murder, Aumary. A man doesn't accidentally take in the leaves of the wolfsbane with his dinner."

"No, indeed."

The plant abounded on the lanes of the chalk hills and

in the forest, for it loved the terrain hereabouts and was a plant which grew happily in the shade of the trees.

Hal came up and nodded to the doctor.

"First a fire, then a rock thrown at 'im, now a poisonin'. Someone is determined to get 'im, I think."

I whispered to Johannes and told him what I'd discovered today.

"He's not a popular man, Aumary."

"Not amongst his family, it seems."

"Nor in the town, really. He's haughty and proud, mean-spirited and avaricious, but he is efficient and gets things done."

"Hence his inclusion on the town council."

Johannes shrugged.

"My guess is he bullies things along."

Our sussurating whispers had been heard from the bed.

"My Lord Belvoir," said a weak voice. "Now you must believe me."

I strode to the bed.

"And you must arrest that man Deyning," said Agnew in a fierce tone. "The master knows it's him."

"I will arrest no man until I have the evidence to do it, masters. I will find out what has been happening."

"Take him… take him in and make him tell you…" said Pitchcott in the nastiest tone he could muster. He let out a huge breath and almost whispered. "He meant to kill me."

He tried to raise himself to his elbow from the pillow but fell back, weakened. "I am not safe, not safe."

"Rest well and recover, Master Pitchcott," I said. "Leave the investigations to me."

There was a pattering of feet on the stair and Mistress Everild Pitchcott came in through the door.

"What has happened? Thomas said that Father has been unwell."

Everild came slowly near to the bed and grimaced at the smell of vomit. She threw back her shoulders and advanced, giving me a sly sideways look as she passed me.

Johannes took her aside and there was a hurried whispering session where she was brought up to date with the facts.

"Your father is convinced that the culprit is Deyning," I said.

"It is not Richard!" she shouted. "Richard would not..."

"It's him, I tell you. He doesn't want to pay me the money and he wants to get his hands on you... oh not because as you think, you foolish girl, he loves you beyond all reason... but that with you comes my wealth!" said Pitchcott falling back exhausted.

"Don't be so foolish, Aldous," said Everild.

Ah, so now the man was spoken of by his first name and not 'Father'.

"Richard has been in his workshop all day."

Pitchcott lifted himself to his elbow with difficulty. "How do you know that, eh? How?"

Everild jutted her chin and pouted.

"How, you ungrateful child?"

"Master Pitchcott," warned Johannes. "This will do you no good." He reached for a cup and settled the old man on his pillows once more, holding the beaker to his lips.

"Drink and rest. Water is the cure, sir."

There was a slurping sound.

Everild looked away in disgust.

I stepped into the middle of the room.

"I will wish to speak to everyone involved later. I have just come from speaking to Master Farnell Armer. I will wish to quiz him again too."

"Farnell? What can he possibly have to do with this?" asked Everild.

"He, too, is none too happy with his ex-guardian. He also has a reason to want him dead."

"No!" said Everild suddenly. "That cannot be."

Master Pitchcott was listening to me but made no sound. I wondered why he did not deny or affirm the fact himself.

"He inherits a sum of money when your father dies, Mistress Everild. It is a good motive for murder."

Everild flounced off to look out of the window. Taking in a gasp of fresh air I heard her say, "Never!"

"Now," said Johannes. "The best thing we can do is leave Master Pitchcott to sleep."

"No, No! …Don't leave me alone! No!"

The man was wide-eyed and flushed, but with white rings around the eyes. His pupils were also dilated. No doubt a symptom of the poisoning, I thought.

"Hal of Potterne will stay here for a while."

Hal opened his mouth and lifted a hand as if to protest.

"Then, when you sleep, he will leave and lock the door behind him."

Pitchcott sighed.

"Does this meet with your approval, sir?"

"Leave the key with Agnew," he replied meekly, drawing the coverlet up to his chin.

"We shall."

Hal looked daggers at me.

"I will meet you in the castle later, Hal."

"Right you are, sir." This was one of his usual phrases, but today, it was delivered with an unusual amount of venomous dissatisfaction.

I grasped Johannes by the sleeve. "Can we leave him alone?"

"Aye, he'll sleep. I have given him a restorative."

We filed out of the room, and Hal, scowling, shut the door behind us. I heard the key turn in the lock.

"I'm for the kitchens," said the doctor.

"On my way to the castle, I shall drop in to talk to Nicholas. I want to know what *he* thinks of our Master Pitchcott."

Master Nicholas Barbflet was the town miller and its reeve. This meant he stood at the head of ten further men of worth who made sure of the smooth running of the town's business.

He was a wealthy man, but came from humble stock. When he was king, Richard, John's brother, had seen his potential and had granted him a licence for the town corn mill.

When the town achieved independence as such, from the crown with the granting of the charter in 1204, Nick was elected by the townsfolk to represent them. So popular was he that he'd been re-elected in 1206. Strange this, for millers were usually the most reviled of people. But Nicholas Barbflet was a straight and upright man. And he was an especial friend of mine.

I found him in the mill yard, watching his men operating the sluices which would fill the mill pond.

"Ah, Aumary. Yes, I heard about the attempts on Pitchcott's life. At first, like you, I think, I didn't believe it."

"Well, now we must. I have just come from his house. Johannes has brought him back from a severe case of poisoning."

Nick turned and faced me, leaning his lower back against the mill pond wall.

"Another attempt? Someone is determined to send him to his maker. He's a good councillor but not a popular man."

"So I hear."

"You have any idea who might have wanted him dead?"

"His family are not amongst his best friends."

"Ah no," said Nick with a slight chuckle, looking at his feet. "He has a brusque way with him. I can imagine that doesn't sit well with them. He seems to have annoyed most members of his family."

"More than that, it seems. I thought you might know a little about that family. I hear he's been here since 1204."

"Aye. The girl came with him then. The young lad, Farnell, was away abroad. He came back this year and set up in town."

"Why here if he didn't get on with his uncle?"

"I hear, but it's only hearsay, that there was some money and a parcel of land which the lad was expecting once he reached twenty-one. From his mother. As he was Pitchcott's ward, the land which belonged to the lad fell to the man. Now, the land is mysteriously in another's hands and Pitchcott richer by a few hundred pounds."

"He sold it over the lad's head?"

"Farnell came back here to claim what was rightfully his. It's in Buckinghamshire, I believe. That's two counties away." Nick shrugged and looked over his shoulder as the mill pond filled.

"Why doesn't Farnell take this to law?"

"Perhaps he will. Though to do so, he must first be able to pay the lawyers."

"So maybe he has taken it into his own hands and is dealing with it in… another way."

"You think him guilty of the attempted murder of his uncle?"

"Wouldn't be the first time a man has resorted to violence against a family member for money, would it?"

Nick put his arm across my shoulder and steered me towards his mill. "The girl is fairly feisty, too, I hear?"

"Yes, her and her lover. They, too, are in the running. What do you know of them?"

"Deyning is a Marlborough lad. His father was a tanner, and the son wanted to move upmarket into furs. He is making his way slowly, I hear. Though there was that story..."

"About the investment Pitchcott made in his business?"

"Ah, no. Though, yes, there's no love lost over that incident. No, this was all about Deyning's father."

"When was this?"

"You know, of course, that the house in which Pitchcott lives was once in the Deyning family?"

"No, I didn't."

"Ah, yes, well. Deyning senior had to sell. He had fallen ill and it was just before he died that he sold it to Pitchcott. His son was not pleased, I can tell you."

"But he must have inherited the money?"

"Deyning senior had been ill a long time. Most of it went on paying debts and lawyers. That is why the son, Richard, had to start all over."

"Ah. There really is no love lost between them, is there?" I frowned. "If Richard Deyning wasn't happy about Pitchcott living in what he sees as his house, why would he ask the man for money to invest in his business?"

Nick slapped me on the back. "Makes you wonder if it's not some kind of ruse on the part of Richard Deyning. 'You took all I had, now I shall take what you have.'"

"And his adopted daughter, to boot!"

"Ah yes, take her too," he said.

"And with her he gets back the money?"

"One way of doing it."

"Maybe he can't wait. Perhaps he too has thought to take all into his own hands."

"Murder, you mean?"

"Pitchcott wants me to arrest him on suspicion of trying to kill him."

Nick laughed out loud.

"He's not dead yet!" he said.

Hal came grumbling into the castle at vespers, and we resigned ourselves to a castle supper and bedding down in the guest house.

"All safe?" I asked

"That place is tied up tighter than a miser's purse. No one will get 'im in there."

"There are folk sleeping in the hall... servants. No one could creep past them. The door to the solar is locked. The door to the house is locked, not to mention the great outside door and the stout walls."

"'E'll be safe then."

But we were wrong.

Half way through the night, there came a great banging on the castle gate.

Bunce, who was on duty, slid back the wicket peephole and peered out.

"Who's making all that racket out there? Don't you know folks are trying to sleep?"

"Bunce... Bunce... it's me, Agnew!"

Agnew was known at the castle. He oversaw the wine deliveries to the castle cellarer, Ansell, now and again.

Bunce opened the wicket gate and Agnew fell in.

He was out of breath after running the length of the High Street.

"M'lord Belvoir? Is he here?"

"Aye, Agnew, I'm here," I said, striding through the gloom of the bailey whilst buckling on my sword belt. "What's amiss?" I'd heard the banging from my bed in the guestroom.

"Master Pitchcott, sir."

"He has taken a turn for the worse?"

"No, sir. He was recovering well..."

"So?"

"Someone has tried to strangle him, sir."

Chapter Three

*H*AL CAME UP behind me. I noticed Andrew, bleary-eyed and tousled, open the door of his small room on the south wall. In his hand, he had his sword belt.

"Tried and failed, Agnew?"

"His daughter, Mistress Everild, sir. She was roused and heard the noise. She came running and then so did I. The would-be murderer got away."

"What did you see?"

"Nothing. No one."

"What time is it, for the love of God?" said Hal.

"Moments past vigils, sir."

"Bloody middle of the night!"

"We shall come now."

"Oh, thank you, sir," said a nervy Agnew hopping from foot to foot.

"We shall walk… no point in disturbing the grooms, and Bayard won't be happy being saddled at this time of night."

Hal harrumphed, "Damned inconvenient. I was 'aving a lovely dream about a large 'are roasted with…"

I laughed. "Come on. The sooner we get there, the sooner we can understand what's happened and be back in our beds, and you can continue your gastronomic dream, Hal."

No one could tell us exactly what had happened at first.

We ascended the solar stairs, and Master Pitchcott lay on his bed as he had when we'd left him, and Hal had seen him sleeping, leaving and locking the door behind him.

"I gave the key into 'is 'ands, sir," said Hal, pointing at Agnew. "As instructed by 'is master."

"Then what?"

"Everyone bedded down," said Agnew. "I have a little sleeping room just there." He pointed down the stairs to a small door halfway up the steps. "It's under this room, the master's."

"Hmm. Who was here, in the hall?"

Two men put up their hands. "We were, sir."

These were one manservant and a groom. The other groom slept in the stable with the horses.

"I was in my room, sir," said Thomas, the steward.

"Where were you, Mistress Everild?"

"I have a room over the pantry there on the next floor." She pointed to the other end of the hall. "Some servants sleep in the hall, others live out, except the cook, who is in the kitchen." She gestured outside. "The steward Thomas has a room at this end. The stair is in the passage."

"Who heard the noise first?"

"I think I did," said Everild.

"You heard the noise? What did you hear?"

"A garbled screaming and yelling. I was still up and dressed, so I ran out into the hall."

"Down those steps and into the hall?"

"Yes."

"Mistress, you are probably the furthest person away from your father's room, yet you heard the noise first."

"I was awake, I tell you, my lord. The others were asleep."

"Aye, we were, sir. Sound asleep. Though at the mistress's shout, we all came awake pretty quick, I can say," said the groom, whose name was John.

"You sounded an alarm?"

"I did," said Everild.

"Hue and cry?" I asked.

" I… it…" Everild sighed. "Truthfully, it was some time before we sounded the hue and cry, for we were unsure what had happened, what was going on."

"Then the lads went out into the street and chased about, but the man was long gone," said Agnew.

"Did no one see anything?"

"No, sir."

"What then?"

"I went into the hall. The boys were there, as I said. We heard the commotion in Master Pitchcott's room. I ran up the stairs. Agnew was at the top of the stairs," said Everild

"I came quickly on the scene, sir. For the noises woke me, and I sleep just there and close by." He pointed again to the small room underneath the solar.

"The door was locked," said Everild. "Master Agnew had to use the key on his belt to get in."

"Locked from the outside?"

"Yes."

"Hal… you *did* lock the door when you left?"

"That I did. And gave the key…"

"Ah, yes. So, Master Agnew, you opened the door. Where was your key?"

"On my belt with the rest of them, sir."

"Where was your belt?"

"In my hand. I picked it up when I heard the noise, for my knife is on there, and I was afraid and thought I might need it."

"What did you see?"

"It was pitch black. The master was gurgling on his bed. Mistress followed me in and she lit a candle."

"The room was empty, sir, empty of anyone but my father."

Suddenly there was a banging on the outer door.

"That will be the doctor, m'lord," said Agnew, and he nodded to one of the other men to answer it.

Johannes came yawning into the room.

"What's this then, Parfitt? The master has..." Johannes caught sight of me in the gloom.

"Oh, Sir Aumary!"

"Another attempt on the life of Master Pitchcott, Johannes."

"Aye, I hear. What now?"

"A strangling, sir," said the steward Johannes had addressed as Parfitt.

"Well, I'll give this murderer his due. He tries every method he can and is never predictable!" He went to the bed to give attention to his patient.

"Hal, what can you make of it?" I asked.

"Well, sir. The room is locked. The man's in his bed. He yells 'cos someone's got their hands around 'is throat... sounds to me like the man's been dreamin'."

"Ah no, Hal," said Johannes from the bed. "Here we *do* have the signs of a pair of hands; fingerprints on the throat of Master Pitchcott. Someone *has* tried to strangle him all right."

"Well, I'll be bugg... buried in Burbage!"

"More light, please," I said.

Further candles were lit.

Master Pitchcott was still gurgling on his bed.

I looked at the shutters folded over the windows, barred from the inside. Opening one of them, I looked out. The gap was a mere twenty-four inches across. It was a completely black world beyond. I looked down and waved a candle as far out as I could. We were over twenty feet from the ground. No ladder would easily reach here, and it would be very difficult to enter and even more of a challenge to exit swiftly, but not impossible.

I closed the shutters.

Pitchcott was now calmer. Johannes had got him to drink some ale and it was going down quite well.

"What did you see?" I asked the vintner when he had swallowed the liquid.

"See? Are you mad?" he croaked. "I was fast asleep. I had a sleeping draught, remember? I opened my eyes to complete darkness and to feel a pair of strong hands around my throat. I yelled and thrashed, and reached out. The man left me and disappeared."

"Where did he go? Can you tell me?"

"No, I was gasping for breath."

"You did not see who attacked you?"

"No, but it will have been that bastard Deyning. I swear on the Bible it will be him," he croaked.

"NO!" cried Everild. "It can't have been him, he was..."

I looked over at her, but she clamped her lip with her teeth and fell silent.

I stifled a yawn.

"There is nothing to be seen till dawn now."

"But my lord!" began Agnew.

"Your master lives. The murderer will not be back tonight. The morning will be early enough for more questions."

I motioned to the steward and the groom. "Both of you will stay inside this room until the morning. You may bed down on the floor. No one is allowed to enter. I shall return after dawn."

They looked at each other but nodded reluctantly.

Johannes tied up his pack. "Your throat is bruised, but in truth, you got away lightly, Pitchcott. There will be no lasting damage. Just ensure you drink enough and try not to speak too much."

I saw Everild Pitchcott smile at that.

She turned briskly on her heel and went down the stairs taking one of the candles with her.

The gloom deepened as she left. Hal took up another candle to light us down the stairs. Agnew took another. One was left for the two servants. They leapt down the stairs, collected their beds and ran up again, dragging their mattresses. Agnew followed and locked the door.

I was half way across the hall floor when I heard Pitchcott cry out, "'Twas Deyning, I tell you... he's a murderer!"

His voice broke and he collapsed into a fit of coughing. Johannes, following behind me, shook his head.

We exited the house, made our way in the darkness through the yard and out onto St Martin's. Agnew followed and locked all the doors.

I stood there in silence for a while, listening.

"Well?" whispered Johannes.

"Well," I answered. "Unless someone was let into the house and out of it again..."

"Deyning?" asked Hal.

"Perhaps. We must ask what Mistress Everild was doing up at this hour, fully dressed."

"Lettin' that man in an' out of the 'ouse?"

"Perhaps."

"Or?" said Johannes.

"Someone in that house, behind locked doors, is a would-be murderer."

Morning came too soon for my liking. Hal and I rose bleary-eyed into the dawn of another beautiful day.

The heat was already building as we walked up the High Street, laboured up Kingsbury hill, along Silver Street and onto St Martin's.

The swallows were twittering to each other above us as we passed through the gate, opened for us by one of the grooms, and up to the house.

"We laying odds," said Hal, "as to whether ol' misery guts is still alive then?"

I chuckled, and we passed through into the hall.

Of course, Master Pitchcott was still alive. Agnew opened the door to the solar and a wall of heat hit us as we entered, along with that stale smell of warm bodies shut up in a hot room overnight.

I opened two of the window shutters. Light flooded the room and Hal repeated my action on the further wall.

I thanked the groom and the steward and they clattered down the steps and off to their duties.

Master Pitchcott wriggled himself up in his bed and adjusted his cap.

"Have you got him?"

"Got who?"

"Deyning, of course."

"No, Master Pitchcott, I have not got him. Neither will I get him. I shall today make inquiries of all the people involved in this..."

"All the people? What do you mean... all the people?"

I took in a breath and counted to five slowly, letting out a frustrated sigh.

"Pitchcott, there are several people with whom you have had dealings who might wish, it seems, to part your soul from your body."

"Indeed, there are not!"

"And I shall speak to them all. What is more, I shall inquire further about the town to ascertain if the list of folk is longer than that of which I am presently aware." I glared at him.

The man harrumphed. "You are a hard man, m'lord Belvoir."

"Meanwhile, I think that we must get you a bodyguard."

The merchant looked horrified. "Oh, no, no, I can't sanction that. I can't have a man trailing around after me all day. No, no, no."

"Then take your chances."

"Even with a bodyguard, Deyning might get to me. He's a madman. A madman, I tell you."

"If he made an attempt, he would be seen and apprehended."

"Noooh, he'd find a way." Pitchcott sneered and his eyes wore a sneaky expression. "I know what he's like. He'll get to me regardless of a bodyguard. I need somewhere where no one can get at me."

Agnew took me aside.

"Sir, ...might...might the castle be a good place?" he asked.

"The castle? Hmmm." I thought about it for a moment and then turned back to Pitchcott.

"Then our only choice is to remove you to the castle," I said.

"The castle?"

"It's the safest place I know."

Pitchott's eyes grew large. "The castle."

"Guards on the gate who will have instructions to let no one in to you by day that are not themselves accompanied by a guard. You will be locked in at night. A stout door, forty foot of six-foot thick stone wall between you and harm. A moat of twenty feet between you and the road.

The windows are tiny. No man may scale the wall and creep through. It will not be as comfortable as you're used to, but I think to save your life, until we find the culprit…"

"The castle…? Hmmm." Pitchcott, pulling his face awry, scratched his chin.

I really did not think the man would accept my offer, and I was very surprised when he said, "I'll do it. But you must watch Deyning and get the truth from him. He'll give himself away in time."

I sighed. "Collect what you need. You may use my room as a place of business and Agnew will do your bidding during the day."

"Aye, aye, I will."

I nodded. "No one will be allowed in unaccompanied. Not even your family."

"Oh, they won't want to come and see me," Pitchcott answered tetchily.

"Your daughter Everild…"

"I doubt it. She's besotted with that fellow Deyning. She won't bother with me until I can unmask him, prove that he's a villain, a murderous bastard. Ha! And then she'll eat her words, eh?"

I sighed again. "I'll return for you as the bell at St Mary's strikes for terce."

That gave the man enough time to collect his business parchments and personal effects together.

I marched off to organise our truculent guest's accommodation with Master Peterkin Gayle, the keeper of the gaol and master of the treasury at the castle, and Andrew, my friend, who was to be on duty that day.

Hal growled as we walked out of the gate.

"I'm glad he didn't want a bodyguard. I could see where that was leading."

I looked sidelong at him.

"You don't like him do you?"

"Do you?"

"Erm…"

"Anyway, I don't wanna be cooped up with that ol' grunter all day."

"Oh?"

"He's got terrible wind. Farts like a farrier, he does!"

Pitchcott rode down the High Street later that morning on his high-stepping palfrey, eyes darting everywhere. There was no sign of Deyning.

Agnew followed, clutching the parchments his master felt necessary to carry on business from his new office.

Andrew accompanied them into my office, which I had allowed to be the temporary residence of the vintner until we could unmask the villain threatening his life.

Merriman locked both the merchant and Agnew in the room and went about his own occupation.

At dinner, the door would be unlocked and food passed to them. Agnew would return to the house on St Martin's for supper and Pitchcott would be fed from the castle kitchen. He would then be locked in for the night. Alone.

Hal and I made our way to the furrier's workshop again. The man was annoyingly away from his premises.

We turned about and walked to the armourer's.

"Master Armer!" I yelled as we approached the workshop. Various metallic clinkings and ringings were coming from inside.

I pushed open the door.

"Oooh!"

"Oh, forgive me, mistress, I didn't mean to…" I had bumped the door into the back of a girl who had been standing quite close to it.

She righted herself and turned, and I realised it was Corlis Glover and that she'd been in an amorous embrace with Farnell Armer.

They jumped a yard apart.

"Oh, my Lord Belvoir," said Corlis, embarrassment colouring her pale face. "I'm sorry." She patted down her rust-coloured dress.

"No, girl, it's I who am sorry. Did I hurt you?"

"No, no, not at all, m'lord."

I smiled. "It's nice to see you again."

Corlis simpered and blinked her long dark eyelashes. She was a pretty girl of twenty with dark wavy hair and light hazel eyes. I sometimes saw her when I visited the glover's premises on the London Road.

She smoothed her hair over her forehead into the plait, which was fashionably wound at the back of her head and kept in place by a net.

She curtsied, rustling her good woollen gown. "It's good to see you again, too, m'lord," she said.

"I hear that you have accepted a proposal of matrimony from this young man here. I hope you'll be very happy."

The smile left her face. "Oh, my Lord Belvoir," she whispered. "It's not to be widely known. Not yet. If you could just..."

"Then I have heard absolutely nothing about it, Corlis." I smiled and put my finger to my lips.

"As I said yesterday, we've a way to go yet, sir, before we can be married. I'll not claim Corlis as my wife until I have a proper place of which she can be mistress and a business which will keep her in comfort," said Farnell.

"Ah yes, I have heard more about this little problem of yours, Farnell. I hear that you are owed a great deal of money by Master Pitchcott, and there seems to be some trouble about a parcel of land which is... erm... missing. I think you came back from your studies abroad to find it gone. You expected an inheritance, did you not?"

Corlis looked quickly at her beloved.

"I told you yesterday, sir, that Master Pitchcott, my guardian and uncle, had stolen the land and sold it."

"Now I have had it confirmed by another."

Farnell Armer's eyes became wary. "You didn't believe me, sir?"

I shrugged. "If I believed everything everyone told me, Armer, I'd be knee-deep in deceit."

Hal sniggered behind me.

"The Lord Belvoir likes t' confirm what folks tell 'im. It's all part of the process of investigation, see."

"What investigation?" asked Corlis.

I ignored her question.

"So, Master Armer, where were you at about the third hour of darkness last night? Past the matins hour almost at vigils?"

Farnell Armer frowned. "Where all decent men are, sir, in my bed. Why?"

"At the Widow Spynner's?"

"Aye, there."

"I suppose the widow will vouch for you?"

"I wasn't in bed with the widow, sir," said Armer flippantly.

Corlis giggled. I looked stern.

"She will be able to say roughly what time you came into the house and when you retired?"

Armer still looked puzzled. "Aye, sir. I've no doubt. Why?"

"And you didn't leave the house at all?"

"No, sir!"

'It's no great 'op from 'ere to the Pitchcott 'ouse, sir," said Hal.

"Why would I go there? I can't stand the man."

"That might be why you DID go!" said Hal.

"Oh..." said Corlis, perhaps suddenly realising what her lover had not yet grasped.

"I heard that the old skinflint was attacked in his bed last night. Aebbe told me early this morning."

"Aebbe?"

"Aebbe is the girl who works as their maid, sir. Her sister is a friend, and I saw them in the street as I came up."

"Ah."

Farnell Armer folded his arms. "I didn't attack him."

Corlis put her hand on her lover's arm.

"M'lord. The man is a devil. He's a thief and a liar. I think others besides Farnell would wish him harm."

"Master Deyning for one?"

"I have no wish to point the finger, sir. I'm just saying Farnell isn't the only one who hates him."

Farnell came forward and took Corlis's arm.

"Master Pitchcott was very cruel to Corlis when I introduced him to her. There was no need for the things he said nor the names he called her."

"He's a monster of a man, sir and I hate him," said Corlis. "I really do. He wants Farnell to marry Everild, but..."

"Everild wants to marry Deyning. Yes, I know."

"Everild and I will do as we damn well please," said Farnell, his teeth clenched.

I saw Corlis squeeze his hand.

"I will do anything sir, so that I can marry my Farnell. I'll not let that fat old miser come between us and our happiness, sir."

"I would keep that to yourself, mistress," I said.

The woman stared at me with an open mouth.

"So Farnell, how will you recover this money you say he owes you?"

Armer stuck out his square jaw.

"I will take him to court. As yet, I am unable, but when I have the backing I expect from my patron…"

"And who is this? This patron who will allow you money to take a wealthy and influential town councillor to court?"

Farnell clamped his jaw shut.

Corlis looked at him with a puzzled expression.

"Ah, well, I am sure it will all work out well for you eventually."

I nodded to them both and we exited, pulling the door closed. "God keep you."

As we walked away, I heard Corlis say, "The easiest way we *could* get our hands on the money is for the old devil to die, as the Lord Belvoir thinks."

"If I am in his will as I hear," said Farnell. "Then I should get what's rightfully mine."

I stood still and listened.

"Why should you be in his will, Farnell?" asked Corlis, "I thought…"

"The old man told me I could have the money when he's gone. It was the last time I spoke to him. I told him I needed it now, but, no, he must hold onto it now."

"He's old, he'll die soon."

"Or sooner if someone does get to him, as the Lord Belvoir thinks."

"It wasn't you, was it, Farnell?" said Corlis in almost a whisper.

"No, my love, it wasn't me."

And then there was silence.

Hal chuckled all the way to the road.

"Another one who 'ates 'im."

"Corlis?"

"Who else is there, eh?"

"We must find Master Deyning and ask him where he

was at the hour of midnight last night."

"You 'ave a feelin' he weren't where 'e should'a bin?"

"As do you ol' Hal. As do you." And I put my arm over his shoulder as we walked along.

Deyning had still not returned to his premises in the waggon yard, so we decided to try the place where he lived, which I was told was on Chantry Lane, a road running up the hill from the High Street. It was on our way back to the castle.

Deyning was at home and came down to the hall of his house when roused by his servant.

He looked as if he'd had a very busy night and had been late to bed.

"Master Deyning, we are sorry to intrude. We looked for you at your place of business, but your man said you'd not yet been to the workplace."

"No. I am feeling unwell today..."

"Oh, I'm unhappy to hear it."

"Skinful was it?" said Hal grinning. "Bad wine per'aps?"

"Merely a late night."

"Ah. A night when perhaps you did not reach your bed until well after midnight?"

"I cannot remember rightly when I reached my bed."

"You were alone, were you?"

"Of course I was alone, sir."

"Is there anyone here who can verify that you were here, perhaps, after midnight?"

"Why should they? I'm not a child who must be in my bed before midnight."

"Out too late and the devils'll get you," said Hal.

Master Deyning looked at Hal with a strange glare.

"That's what my ol' mam used to say when I was a child. A-course, I never took any notice."

I smiled. "A servant let you in, perhaps?"

"I let myself in, my lord."

"Ah, now that is awkward."

"How so? What is this about?"

"It's about the attempt on the life of Master Pitchcott in the early hours of this morning."

Deyning's face paled.

"I didn't know…"

"I think you perhaps left the Pitchcott house just before the alarm was raised."

"What?"

"You were there, weren't you?"

"No, I was most certainly *not* there. I was in my office working late." Deyning's lips were a hard line.

"Ah, so Mistress Pitchcott was entertaining another gentleman late last night in her part of the house?"

The lips clamped even tighter. Then he said angrily, "Mistress Pitchcott is a principled woman, m'lord. A woman of good character. She would never, as you so crudely put it, entertain a man in her own room after dark. Nor at any other time. Certainly not alone."

"As you say, she would not. No one with whom she was not very familiar," I answered.

Deyning wiped the sweat from his upper lip.

"Is that all, my lord, or is there more of the same?"

"No, Deyning. That will do for the moment. But please think on it."

I opened the outer door.

"Aldous Pitchcott was accosted last night in his own home as he lay in his bed. He swears that you are the culprit. I would think carefully about where you were and what you were doing, sir, when the man was being strangled."

"Strangled?" spluttered Deyning.

"The hour after midnight. I hope I don't have to arrest you, Master Deyning. I think it would be a great shame. Not only for you but for your beloved too."

Hal smiled widely at the man as we shut the door. We collected our mounts and rode for home.

A change in the weather and there was a light rain pattering delicately on leaf and fern, frond and flower as we made our way back to Marlborough the next morning.

It was still very warm, but there was now a little freshness to the air and a light breeze lifted the tremulous silver-lined leaves of the aspen trees which grew on the roadside before the bridge.

We decided to turn onto the Newbury Road rather than go through the town for it was market day, and the High Street would be teeming with people buying and selling.

"What say you we do some practice this morning, Hal, here in the castle bailey?" I asked.

"Aye, it's been a while since we 'ad a go 'ere in the castle. Maybe Sir Andrew would like to make a threesome, sir?"

"You're feeling so full of life then, Hal?"

Hal was my sparring partner, and we often practised with sword and buckler in the courtyard at Durley to keep up our fighting skills and to maintain our muscles. One never knew when one might need to defend oneself.

The bailey of the castle was quiet very early and we thought it a good place to practise fight.

I stripped to my shirt and Hal took off his gambeson and fought in his tunic.

"Not too vigorous, ol' man," I said. "The sun will strengthen soon and it will get too hot."

"Ah, this is nothin'," said Hal, flexing his knees. "When we were in the lands of the 'eathen, the sun would scorch the eyebrows off yer face at dawn."

I laughed.

Hal had been a foot soldier in the army of Henry II, but had never seen action in the Holy lands.

I suddenly remembered that the blunted swords we used for practising were kept in my office.

"Ah, Hal. I shall have to go to the office and fetch the swords."

"But you gave your key to Sir Andrew, sir."

"Ah, yes, I did. Well, nothing for it. We must fight with these."

"Pullin' our strikes then?"

I smiled. "*We* aren't trying to kill each other, Hal!"

"Right you are then, sir."

And so we began to circle.

A couple of the guards on the wall walks turned to look down on us. A few of the masons working on the westernmost walls downed their tools and took the opportunity to rest, mop their brows and swig their ale.

We kept well apart as is right and proper and traded a few blows but nothing particularly spectacular.

Hal got under my guard and, at the last minute, deflected his point.

"Got you!" he cried. "You're nicked on the 'ip."

We laughed and circled again. Now it was my turn. "And you're pricked on the pate!"

Suddenly there was the most awful scream. It rang around the stone of the bailey with an awesome echo.

Momentarily startled, Hal drove his sword at my leg and turned at the last moment to stagger sideways.

"What the 'ell?"

The edge of my sword nicked his waist and tore a slit in

the bright yellow of the saffron wool.

"God's almighty balls!" he yelled.

"No harm, Hal?" I shouted, worried I'd nicked him with the sharpness of my blade.

"No harm to me, but..." Hal wiggled his finger in the hole in his tunic.

Andrew came running past. "Your office, Aumary," he yelled as he ran off, buckling on his sword belt.

I wiped my arm over my sweaty forehead.

"We'd better follow."

Andrew was now at the door of my office, looking in. Another piercing shriek rent the air and reverberated around the hard surfaces of the stone courtyard.

"Alysoun..." I heard him say. "Come away."

I reached the door as a young woman of about twelve backed out of the room and ran for the kitchen, crying.

"Andrew?"

"I unlocked the door for Alysoun to take ale and bread to Master Pitchcott to break his fast, and then I thought he'd need to go to the privy, perhaps."

I looked into my room. It was dark, and I could see nothing after the glare of the sunlit courtyard.

I pushed past Andrew.

There was the tray the girl had dropped to the floor. Bread and ale lay spilt on the flagstones.

"I didn't come in to look. I just opened the door and then came back to you. I was about to join you when..." said Andrew.

"Aye, I saw you out of the corner of my eye."

I marched over to one of the window shutters and opened it wide. Light flooded in.

I turned.

On the small pallet bed which had been brought in for Master Pitchcott to sleep on, lay the merchant.

Partly on the bed and partly off, the man lay slumped, totally naked but for a cap upon his head.

I rushed up to him. Hal came in after me and Andrew blocked the door.

There was no sign of life.

Master Aldous Pitchcott was very dead.

I grabbed a handful of my curly black hair and pulled in frustration.

"HOW?" I yelled.

Hal leaned over the dead man.

"Dead a while. 'E's quite cold."

"What killed him, Aumary?" asked Andrew from the door.

"I can see nothing," I said honestly.

Hal pulled the man over.

"No knife wound. Not bashed on the 'ead."

"Looks like there's no sickness or other effect of poison, though we shall have to ask Johannes."

"No stranglin' but what he received the other night."

I looked carefully around my room.

"No one can get in, Hal. The key has been with you the whole time, Andrew?"

"All night. I also lock my own door. The key is in your lock now, but I put it there just heartbeats ago."

"Nowhere to hide."

"This is rather like that locked room murder you had up there," said Andrew throwing his thumb up at the keep.

He referred to the murder of two people in a locked room at the top of the keep, which Johannes and I had solved four years before: bodies in a locked room. There the similarity ended. This was one despised elderly man, not a girl and a young man about to be married.

"Cover him," I said to Hal. "And I'll send news to the house."

"And a runner to Johannes?" asked Andrew.

"That too, please."

Andrew turned and left, closing the door.

I sat on my chair and stared about me.

How on earth had the murderer gained access?

I scrutinised the door and the windows - there were two windows, one opened out onto the drawbridge side and one onto the easternmost moat.

I searched the ceiling. Nothing there but rafters and stones of the wall walk above.

The floor was solid stone.

The door had not been forced. The key, my key, the one I'd given to Andrew for safekeeping, was still in the lock on the outside, as he'd said.

I looked down once more at Aldous of Pitchcott. His lank grey hair fell on either side of his face, which was quite serene and composed.

His nightcap was slightly awry on his head, the sparse hair poking out from the sides; everywhere else, he was practically bald, except for that ridiculous peak of hair above his forehead. The strings which kept the cap on his head dangled loosely under his chin.

Most folk, especially on nights as hot as the last one had been, slept naked.

I thought back to the night before when I'd seen the man in his own room. Yes, under the sheets, he'd been naked then, with this silly cap upon his head.

His clothes were piled upon my chest in the corner.

His parchments littered my table. I could see nothing here which was going to help me.

"Shall I go to the 'ouse?" asked Hal, wiping his forehead

with a fold of his now spoiled saffron tunic.

"No, send Peter Devizes. He'll do the job." Peter was one of my men-at-arms whom I kept at the castle against the day my king might want me to follow him to war.

"Peter is good at sympathy."

Hal scoffed. "They won't need sympathy... none of 'em," he said.

"No, I suppose not."

"Don't seem right."

"What?"

"The ol' man. He was by all accounts a bit of a bugger, but don't seem right fer 'im to go this way."

"No, Hal. I do feel I've failed him."

"You did everything you could'a done."

He'd now donned his gambeson again and was buckling on his sword belt. He slammed his sword back into its scabbard angrily. I realised mine lay on my table where I'd laid it down upon entering the room.

"Someone's done fer 'im, and I'll be buried in Burbage 'fore I know how they'm done it," he said.

Chapter Four

*J*OHANNES ARRIVED at the same time as Master Agnew.

No news had reached the house, for Agnew had set out early to get to his master before our messenger could be dispatched.

When told about his master's death, he reeled against the outer wall of the guardhouse and slid down to his haunches, the parchments held under his arm in a leather scrip discarded in the roadway.

"God's teeth. Dead... dead? But how? In God's name, how?"

"That is something we must do our utmost to find out," I said.

Agnew looked up.

"Somehow, Deyning must have got in there. He's the very devil, the devil himself. He can walk through a locked door, he must have..."

"There will be a sensible explanation, and I will find it," I said. "Meanwhile, nothing must be moved or touched."

"But there are documents inside the room that I must..."

"No! All must be as it is for the coroner to see, and I have asked Dr Johannes to come here to look at the body and see if he can ascertain what killed your master. After this, you may have any documents you require. Then you may take the body for burial."

He looked up and shook his head. "This is such a shock. We almost expected it, but now, it's actually happened…"

"Aye. I'm sorry I wasn't able to protect him."

"He warned you, m'lord, he warned you."

He lifted himself from the castle wall.

"I will go and tell his daughter Everild. She must know."

"That would be helpful and kind, Master Agnew," I said.

The man wiped his hand across his nose.

"And I'll tell the priest and the master's lawyers also."

"And I think that Master Armer, Farnell Pitchcott, must also be told, for he is a relation too."

Agnew sneered. "He will learn, but it won't be from me." He retrieved his pouch, turned on his heel, and slouched across the castle bridge.

"Oh dear," said Johannes. "The animosity runs across family boundaries."

"By that, you mean that Aldous Pitchcott is dead but that his right-hand man is carrying on the feud between the vintner and his erstwhile ward Farnell?"

"I mean exactly that. Ah, well, let us go and look at this mysterious body of yours, Aumary."

Johannes hunkered down by the pallet upon which lay the body of the vintner and ran his eye up and down its nakedness.

"Found just like this?"

"Hal moved him to see if there were any hidden wounds, but when we could discover none, we arranged him as we found him again."

Johannes looked around my little office. It was a room twelve feet by sixteen with two windows which had shutters, the bolts of which could be dropped across into metal brackets. There was one stout oaken door and no other. In the room were a chair, two stools, a chest, and a side table, rather like a pot board, one large table and one small one. Behind the door was a hook for my cloak. In the winter, a brazier would be wheeled in to supplement the very small fireplace with a flue which led up to the roof. This was the latest addition with the new building work and was very welcome in cold and damp weather.

Johannes eased his head up the chimney.

"Ah, nothing here," his voice echoed

There was a small tumble of soot, and he coughed as he extricated himself.

I paddled his shoulders of soot. It was a good job that his robe was of a dark blue today, so the smudge wouldn't show.

He smoothed his hair, held back in its queue.

"No man could get down the chimney."

I shook my head. "Nor through the window."

"And besides, we are fifteen or more feet up in the air. The land drops below us here to the moat." Johannes stood above the body again.

"If this is how he fell, what was he doing when he died?"

"I hate to ask this, Johannes, but might he have died of apoplexy or congestion of the heart? Something natural."

"The man was as fit as a fiddling fly, Aumary. As far as I remember, he was a man of fifty, and he had the constitution of a thirty-year-old."

"But it's not impossible, is it?"

"I shall look for the signs."

He began by taking off his robe and laying it on the table. We opened the shutters wide so that as much light as possible came into the room.

I also lit two candles.

Again, Johannes hunkered down and lifted the dead man's arm. "Stiffening," he said.

"Aye, I looked at 'im and thought it was somewhere around the darkest hour when 'e met 'is end," said Hal. "Judging by what you told me before about bodies, doctor."

"He was locked in just after vespers when it was still light," I said.

"And we found 'im not quite two hours after dawn," added Hal.

"No one will have been let in to see him, but someone might have known when no light could be seen through the windows or round the door. We might then make a guess when he retired."

"Bunce was on duty last night. I'll ask 'im," said Hal as he disappeared through the door.

Johannes removed the man's coif and examined his face. He lifted the lids, peered carefully into the man's staring eyes, tried to close them and failed because of the rigour. Then he looked in the slightly open mouth and sniffed the lips.

"Not poison. He took nothing in his mouth which killed him… nothing I'm familiar with, at any rate."

"No wounds that Hal or I could see."

As Johannes began to look at the rest of the merchant's body, I walked around my room, checking for things which, perhaps, should not be there.

I hadn't left anything personal in the room.

The practice swords were still locked in one of the chests, along with some spare clothes, a pair of ankle boots and some parchment.

"Here, Aumary, look!" said Johannes suddenly.

He was holding the merchant up, and with the rigour beginning to establish, it was quite difficult to make him sit straight.

"Blood?"

"Very little. A dribble, really, down the side of his neck under his hair."

"What can that be from?"

"Did he cut himself shaving?"

"I left him my polished steel with which to manage that operation should he wish to maintain his beard, if one can call that ridiculous smudge a beard."

I gestured to the top of the pot board, where I kept a circle of polished steel propped up against the back of a shelf.

It was missing.

"There," pointed Johannes as he laid the merchant down again.

The piece of metal had fallen from the board and had come to rest between the door and the edge of the piece of furniture.

I bent to pick it up and replaced it on the pot board.

Peering at it, I said, "It's dented."

"Damaged when it fell," said the doctor.

I came back to Johannes squatting over the body on the pallet.

"Hold him for me." I reached down and held the body steady whilst Johannes lifted the man's sparse hair.

I saw him frown.

"What?"

"Wait a moment." He reached for the pack he'd left on the floor and fiddled until he came out with a metal probe about six inches long. I'd seen him use something like this before.

"Hold him very steady."

There was a moment of silence whilst I held and Johannes prodded. I heard the guard at the gate challenge someone, and that person answer. Then there was some laughter: Hal and Bunce.

"There! Wait again."

Johannes straightened and retrieved a small pair of tweezers from his bag.

"Yes. There we are."

I let the body down to the pallet again.

"What is it?"

Johannes strode to the window and held up the tweezers.

There, at the end of them, was a small ball made of metal.

"A little bloodied, but I think you can see."

"A small metal ball? That killed him?"

"I think so, yes. It passed through the skull where the bone is the thinnest. Here see, just before the ear." He pointed to his own skull. "And where the cap did not reach. It's cut away just there. And the man is bald."

"No wonder it was hard to spot."

"As I say, the bone is very thin there, and if someone is hit there, they die after a while from a bleed to their brain. It can't be seen but if you look into the skull…"

"Which we aren't allowed to do…"

The church forbade any kind of dissection of the body.

"No. Then we see that the bone which lies here adjoins another, and the join is very vulnerable; if it is ruptured, it often results in death."

"And that is what has happened to Pitchcott?"

"I suspect so, yes."

"But how did the little metal ball get into his head?"

Johannes dropped the little ball into a piece of linen he'd fished from his pack and set it deliberately on the table.

"Ah, I have told you *what*, and now it's your job to work out *how*," he chuckled.

I stood in the middle of the room.

"Well, I can only think of a slingshot."

We looked at each other, aware that we were both thinking the same thoughts. It had been the first day Johannes of Salerno and I had met all those years ago. He had been called to look at my first wife, Cecily, who had been hit on the head with a stone flung from a sling.

"In here?"

"There's no room to swing it."

"And wouldn't the man try to avoid it?" asked the doctor.

"And call for help, maybe?"

"Quite apart from the fact the merchant was locked in. How did the assailant get in?"

I scratched my head.

Hal came back through the door.

"Bunce said that 'e was standing out there when the chapel bell at the priory was ringin' for vigils." The Gilbertine canons were exempt, it seemed, from the prohibition of the Pope's interdict.

"So – midnight, yes?"

"And there was no light coming from round the door then."

"So our man was asleep or at least in his bed at midnight," I said.

"What made him get up?"

"Did 'e?" asked Hal

"He must have risen because he was draped across his bed as if he'd been standing and then fallen sideways."

Hal looked down at the body again.

"Someone called from the door, and he gets up to talk to them."

"Ah, yes, Hal, you don't know about our little pellet, do you?"

I told my man-at-arms about the small metal ball which we'd found in Pitchcott's head.

"God's cods!" he exclaimed. "That can't 'ave got there through a locked door, can it?"

We were all silent as we looked down at the body again.

"Aumary," said Johannes. "Can you be the merchant and lie on the bed, or close by? Hal, go outside and shout through the door. Aumary will... ah, no... we still have the problem of how the assailant got in."

"Was 'e already 'ere and hiding when the merchant was locked in?" said Hal.

"And the man didn't notice him for... how many hours?"

"Ah, no," said Johannes.

"No chest big enough to 'ide in," said Hal.

"Then the door must have been unlocked somehow."

We all peered at the lock on the door. There were no scratches, no evidence of forcing. I turned the key in the lock.

"I don't think it's been tampered with. It moves sweetly enough, and Andrew had the key."

"There must be another key," said Johannes.

"Hmm, not to my knowledge," I said.

Silence descended once more.

I heard the sound of horses coming in through the gateway and looked around the corner.

"The coroner. He must have been in the town for him to come so quickly. Now the fun and games begin," I said.

I argued with the coroner about the little metal pellet. He wanted to keep it. I needed it, I explained, as evidence. I wanted to show it around, see if anyone recognised it. I eventually prevailed upon the man, Hugo of Ramsbury, to let me keep it.

The body was removed to the house on St Martin's, for since the Interdict, no man could be laid before the altar of his church, and then began the process of laying him out for burial elsewhere.

Master Pitchcott could not be buried with all the rights the church would normally afford him, for the ban on church services meant that no mass could be said for him, and no prayer might help his soul to Heaven. He would not lie in the churchyard with prayers said for the rest of his soul.

The men who had been in the guardroom through the night were now going off duty, and I waylaid them as they filed out of the gatehouse and made for their room across the courtyard.

"Bunce, Davison, Hardcastle, good morrow to you."

They all bowed.

"Have you any idea how the man locked into my room last night might have been murdered?"

They all three looked at each other.

"Woe sakes, sir," said Davison. "If it wasn't the devil walking through a locked door, then…"

"If it was a devil, Nick, then it was a human one," said Hardcastle. "No, sir, Sir Andrew had the key in his room. He locked himself in as he does every night he's not on duty. None had the opportunity to steal it."

"Is there another key, do you know?"

They all three shook their heads.

"Unless someone has made a duplicate," said Hardcastle. "And why would they? Only someone from the castle might get access to it."

"It's with me all the time," I said.

"That's right, sir," said Bunce. "There ain't no one's gonna' get 'old of it to make another."

"No time, sir," added Hardcastle. "You brought in the merchant man yesterday. The key was given to Sir Andrew. By midnight, we're told, the vintner was dead. Who's going to get a key made in that short time?"

I shook my head.

"None of you saw or heard anything?"

None of them had.

Johannes returned to his house, and Hal and I walked into town to speak to the man who, at first thought, had the wherewithal to have made the little metal pellet.

I found Master Armer bending over his corselet of mail. Many more links had now been added. It was a painstaking process which took some months. He was concentrating so hard upon his work, he didn't hear us enter.

"Master Armer, good day."

He looked up quickly and straightened, throwing down his pliers and making the little rings sitting on his wooden bench jump.

"You are very busy, it seems, today?"

"I have a few ongoing commissions and I am experimenting with some new ideas which I think will make my work stand head and shoulders above the work of the mere ordinary arms smith, sir." He bowed.

"Ah, and that is?"

"Ah, no, m'lord, I cannot say. It would be foolish of me to tell." He smiled. "My secrets must remain my secrets."

"And do you have any other secrets, master armourer? Like where you were around midnight last night."

The man threw down the handful of rings he'd held in his palm. "Not again, my lord!"

"I really do need to know where you were."

"As I told you last time, in my bed at the Widow Spynner's."

"You were not at the castle?"

"Why would I be at the castle at night?"

I waited.

"If I go to the castle, it's in the day."

I fished in my purse.

"Do you know what this is, Master Armer?"

I held his hand and placed the little metal ball into his palm.

He caught it up and, with an exasperated look at me, moved to the light of the door.

"No."

He tried to give it back to me.

"I would have a very good look at it if I were you."

He sighed in vexation and flipped out his hand again.

"It's a metal ball."

"It's the weapon which killed the man Aldous of Pitchcott last night."

A strange look came over the armourer's face.

He looked down at the ball sitting on his palm.

"The man is dead?"

"As last Christmas," said Hal.

"And because I make metal things, you think that I made this with which to kill him?"

"Did you?"

"How can a tiny thing like this kill a man? It's preposterous!"

"Nevertheless, it did."

Hal drew off as I talked to the man and poked around on the benches dotted about. The two men we'd seen on the first day we'd come to the workshop were missing.

I took the ball back from him. "This tiny thing penetrated the skull of Master Pitchcott and killed him as surely as if an axe had been taken to his head."

Farnell Armer laughed. "I'm sorry, sir, but it's something that I find hard to believe."

"Perhaps you'd better talk to Doctor Johannes of Salerno, Armer. He was the one who fished the thing out of

Pitchcott's skull. If he says it killed him, it killed him."

"But how would it get into his head? Did he swallow it?"

"Master Armer, somehow it was thrown at him."

Farnell Armer laughed aloud again. "Oh, my lord, that can't be. No man is strong enough to throw such a thing to kill someone."

"A slingshot, Armer?"

"A child's plaything?"

"Lethal when a stone hits a bird or a coney."

Armer swallowed.

He turned from me.

"Last I heard, you had the man locked up in the castle as tight as a tick, my lord. How could anyone with a catapult get in to him?"

"Ah, so you know about that, do you?"

"I know. I have friends at the castle."

Hal looked up from his task of scrutinising the benches. "Oh, you do, do you?"

"From them, I heard you'd locked him up in your office."

"You even knew where he was. Oh, Master Armer, it really isn't looking good for you."

Armer swallowed again.

"What's in here then?" asked Hal, tipping a barrel on its basal rim.

"Sand, for polishing mail."

"Ah, yes. Stops the rust, doesn't it, so they say?"

"Yes, it's very efficient."

"This looks interesting. What's this?" asked Hal again, moving another barrel to reveal a wooden structure about six feet high.

"That is something I am working on."

"Hmm."

Hal began to move the barrel back in front of the structure. As he turned it, it made a metallic clanking sound, rather like many pebbles being sucked by the tide.

Farnell Armer bounded to Hal's side and took the barrel from his hands, rolling it gently back into place.

"Please. I don't want anything broken."

"Fair 'nuff." Hal sniffed. "Only lookin'."

"Well," I said conversationally, "We'll just go and have a word with your Widow Spynner, see what she has to say, and then we'll leave you in peace."

"A-course, you'll be happy now the ol' skinflint's gone, won't you?" said Hal with a wide grin. "You'll inherit, and then everything will be spices and roses for you and yer lady love, won't it?"

"I will admit that life will be easier, yes. But that doesn't mean I killed him."

Hal just continued to grin at him.

"Good day, Master Armer," I said.

"Damn, damn, I was sure it was 'im," said Hal a little while later when we were walking away from the house of the Widow Spynner.

"He can still have got out of the house and back, Hal."

"Yeah! S'pose so. Even if the Mistress Spynner vouches for him."

"She told us he retired after supper, but that doesn't mean he stayed at home."

"No, 'e might've hopped outta door or summat."

"And back in."

We walked along in silence.

"We goin'a talk to that other fella?"

"We are. Let's see if he's heard the news, or how he seems when we tell him the news, if he says he doesn't know."

Master Deyning reeled backwards stiffly when we told

him that Master Pitchcott was dead.

"Dead? No, I... I didn't know."

He sought a seat and sat down heavily. "How did it happen? Did he fall from his horse, or was it apoplexy?"

He gestured for us to be seated.

"Ah, Master Deyning, you know that there have been several attempts on the man's life and yet you immediately assume that the cause of his death is accidental."

"I cannot believe..."

"Even though the man was convinced that you were trying to kill him?"

"I most certainly was not... did... not."

"Where were you at about vigils, around midnight last night?"

"I was at home."

"Again, I am afraid I must ask you if anyone can verify that. A servant, perhaps?"

"My lord, I keep only one servant who lives with me. He sleeps at the back of my house. You may ask him where he thinks I was, but..."

"You didn't go out once you'd reached home and eaten your supper?'

"No, sir, I didn't. Osbert will be able to tell you that I retired to my room, but after he, too, went to his room in the roof, we neither of us could tell if we each had exited the house again."

"Such is the configuration of your dwelling?"

"We have very separate quarters, my lord."

"Hmm."

Deyning breathed noisily through his nose. "Sir, I would not kill Master Pitchcott. Quite apart from him being a fellow human being, I could not deprive a man of his life no matter how repulsive he seemed; he is my beloved's adopted father and I could not cause her grief."

"You think the death of Master Pitchcott would cause Everild grief, Deyning? That is not my reading of the situation."

"Whatever the man was, he was her father for many years."

"So now..." began Hal, "the debt which you owe the man will not need to..."

"Oh, but it will, sir. I will make sure that Everild is paid back every penny with profit when she becomes my wife."

"That will not be necessary, will it, Master Deyning?" I said.

"What?"

"You and your Everild can be married, can't you now, with no opposition from the 'ol vintner," said Hal, chuckling. "An' all 'is lovely money..."

"No, Hal. As I say, I don't think that will be necessary."

"Eh?"

The door to the furrier's work place opened, and Mistress Everild Pitchcott slid through the gap.

"Richard?"

Deyning leapt forward and took the girl in an embrace.

"My love, the constable has just come to tell me the news that Master Pitchcott is dead. I am so sorry, sweetheart."

Everild allowed herself to be embraced for a moment and then broke away.

"Does the constable still think you are responsible for his death, Richard?" She gave me a quick sidelong look through lowered lashes.

"My condolences, Mistress Pitchcott, upon the death of your father. I am sorry I was not able to keep him alive."

The woman sniffed. "As you know, there was little love left between us. He liked to control, sir. I do not react well to control. He was a somewhat repulsive man, my lord, and became more so the longer he lived."

"Will no one mourn him?"

"Not me. Maybe his equally odious little clerk will do so. I cannot tell."

I fished in my purse and brought out the little metal ball.

"Have either of you seen this before?"

"What is it?" asked Everild, standing on tiptoe.

I gave it into her hand.

"It's heavy," she said. "I ask again, what is it?"

"It is the thing which killed your father, mistress. It was fished from his head by Doctor Johannes of Salerno."

Everild Pitchcott dropped the ball as if it were red hot.

"Oh…"

Hal picked it up.

"It is a small metal ball. Probably iron," said Master Deyning. "I don't know what it might have been made for."

"Neither of you have seen it before?"

They shook their heads.

"Richard, I came to ask you to come to the house. The lawyer will be there soon, and I do not want to be alone. You will understand all that goes on… I do not… I'd rather not be alone with that horrible man Agnew."

"Certainly, Everild," said Deyning. "If the constable has no further need of me."

I nodded. "I may wish to speak to you again, but I am finished with you for now."

Richard Deyning took Everild by the elbow.

She curtsied, and he bowed.

"Good day, m'lord."

"Good day, Master Deyning, Mistress Deyning."

I saw the woman's back stiffen, but she said nothing and walked through the door, her head held high.

Hal took off his coif and scratched his head.

"I can't fathom 'er y'know."

I chuckled.

"And you just made a mistake callin' 'er Mistress Deynin' She i'nt that yet."

"Ah, Hal, that's just where you're wrong," I said.

Chapter Five

*W*E LEFT THE FURRIER'S WORKSHOP and watched as one of his men came from another building and locked the door behind us.

"Where to now?" asked Hal.

"The lawyer is very quick upon the death of Master Pitchcott, don't you think, Hal?"

"Well, it does seem a bit unseemly to me to be so quick about getting the lawyers in. It's normal to 'ave buried the man before you start to talk about the will, in't it?"

"I wonder who called them?"

"That man Agnew said he was going to tell them di'n't 'e?"

"Hmm. Yes, now I recall. He did."

I rubbed my nose.

"Why the haste, I wonder?"

We walked to the junction of the main road and watched as Everild and Richard climbed the hill arm in arm.

"I think we must go and see what all the hurry is about." I turned and winked at my man-at-arms. "Don't you?"

"Mistress Pitchcott don't like that chap, Agnew, does she?"

"No, not a scrap. I wonder if he, too, will gain from the will of Aldous Pitchcott."

We followed the couple slowly up the hill and onto St Martin's.

Hal and I stayed for a moment to allow them to enter the house well before us and then followed them into the courtyard.

The same servant as before let us in.

Two black-garbed lawyers stood in the hall speaking with Master Agnew. He turned to see us, and I swear his step faltered.

Outside we could hear the sound of thunder in the distance.

"Aw!" grumbled Hal quietly, "We're gonna get wet."

"Let's hope it's just a passing shower," I said.

Agnew came up to us and bowed.

"My lord, can I help you further with anything? I have much to do... I..."

"Yes, Agnew. You can begin by telling us what you were doing at about midnight last night."

The man put his hand on his breast.

"Me?"

"And where were you when your master was attacked on the first two occasions? With the rock and the fire."

"Here, sir, in my room asleep. And on the first occasion, I believe I was in the counting-house, and I saw the rock fall from the roof, so I..."

"Vigils were being sung in the chapel of the priory, I believe, when your master died last night."

"Ah, well then, yes, I was in my room, up there." He pointed to the room halfway up the stairs at the other end of the hall. "I was asleep, I expect."

"Is there anyone who might vouch for you?"

"Vouch for me, my lord?"

"Is there anyone who can say that is where you were?"

"Well, erm, I suppose there might be." He giggled like a girl. "I normally sleep alone, you see."

"Normally?"

"There is a woman…" he whispered.

"But last night you were alone?"

"I saw him retire," said a voice.

Mistress Pitchcott, now in a different dress, came down the stairs at the other end of the room and we noticed she now had her hair covered.

When we last saw her in Deyning's workshop, she'd worn a dark blue bliaut over a pale yellow tunic. Now her dress was pale yellow wool of the finest weave, and blue bands of embroidery stood out at the neck and half way up the hem. Her hair was tied back in a light-coloured net and caught in a white barbette; a thin silken veil was laid over it with a deep crown of stiff white linen.

I nodded to her. It was an odd choice of colour to wear as mourning, but I'd heard other countries wore yellow at such a time.

"Mistress Deyning."

The woman smiled.

"Little escapes you, does it, m'lord?"

"You say you can confirm that Master Agnew went up the stairs and was in his room at midnight?"

"I can confirm that he left the hall after supper and walked up the stairs. Why would he leave again?"

"Why is this so clear in your memory, madam?"

"Because it was just before…"

"Before she let me in," said yet another voice.

"Well, I'll be…" I heard Hal say under his breath.

Richard Deyning came down the stairs behind Everild. He, too, had changed his clothes. Now he wore a long cotte of undyed wool and the beautiful long blue leather belt I had seen him wear on the first occasion I met him.

"My Lord, you know our history, so we shall not dissemble."

Everild stretched out her hand and Deyning took it in his, bringing it up to his lips to kiss her fingers.

As she lifted her hand, I saw the bright new ring upon her finger.

"I think congratulations are in order?"

"Thank you, m'lord," said Deyning smiling.

"What? What?" shouted Agnew. "What do you mean congratulations?"

"Mistress Pitchcott and Master Deyning have married," I said. "They are man and wife."

The two lawyers looked at each other blankly.

Agnew spluttered.

Hal chuckled.

"I think they have been married for some time," I said.

"Holy...!"

"Matrimony... yes," I said with a chortle as Agnew continued to splutter.

"It must, of course, have been before marriage was prohibited by the Interdict of the pope."

"As far back as March, sir?" said Hal.

I nodded.

I turned a quizzical eye on Deyning.

"We were married in early March, sir, in London."

"That was why you were here when Master Pitchcott's life was attempted the night someone tried to strangle him."

"I was with my wife in her room, yes."

"And she let you out of the house just before the alarm was raised."

"I left not knowing about the attempt on Pitchcott's life."

"Of course, a wife may not testify for or against her husband but, madam, I must ask you: did your husband stay with you the whole time he was here?"

"My Lord Belvoir," said Everild unabashed. "It was the very first night we could stay together as man and wife. Would you have left your wife's side on your wedding night if you hadn't needed to?"

I smiled.

"But I must say that it would not stop both of you from colluding and perhaps you, madam, keeping watch whilst you, Deyning, went into the room of Master Pitchcott and attempted to strangle him, failing only because he was too strong for you and made too much noise."

Deyning smiled. "No, sir. We did not, as you put it, collude."

He came down the remaining stairs leading his wife.

"We were in Everild's room until the early hours of the morning, and then I left. As you say, just before the hue and cry was raised."

"Fortunate for you," I said.

Agnew was apoplectic.

"Married? Married without the knowledge of your father?"

Everild Deyning tossed up her head. "And what is it to do with you?"

Agnew's eyes narrowed.

Then his shoulders slumped.

He stammered something and then said officiously,

"We are waiting for one other and then we shall see to the reading of the will."

"What's the great hurry, Agnew?" I asked. "Could it not have waited until the poor merchant was in his grave?"

"There are many ends which must be tied, sir. They

cannot be allowed to float away. The business, for example, cannot be neglected and allowed to drift for want of a strong hand."

The thunder grumbled louder and nearer and the two lawyers looked nervously to the windows of the hall.

"Close the shutters against the rain," said Everild. The servant who had let us in grudgingly went to do her bidding.

As he stepped up to the window, there was an almighty flash of lightning.

Everyone waited for the roll of thunder.

As yet, there was no rain.

The crash came a heartbeat later.

Lights were procured and candles lit, for the day had suddenly become very dark.

A banging was heard at the front door, and the man-servant was dispatched to open it.

Master Armer fell in through the screens passage door.

"Heavens! It's like the end of days out there. So dark," he said, pulling off his cloak.

"I think it will rain like the devil in a moment."

Everild Deyning came up to Armer and kissed him on the cheek.

"I'm glad you have come home, Farnell," she said.

The young man beamed. "It's good to see you, coz."

Deyning nodded to Armer, "Farnell."

Farnell smiled back. "Nice to be here with you at last, without that poisonous toad, Aldous, setting us all awry."

Then Master Armer caught sight of me. He paled.

"My lord, what do you do here?" He bowed at last.

"I came to ask a few questions, Armer, but please, lady, gentlemen, do not let me distract you from your business."

The two lawyers made for the large oak table in the middle of the room and pulled candles towards them.

Now it really was very dark.

One more huge bolt of lightning sizzled, the light falling amongst us from the gaps in the shutters. A clap of the thunder followed quickly on its heels.

I noticed that documents had been taken from a large leather case and put on the board.

One clerk sat while the other maintained his stance, slightly stooping over the table, and began.

"Here we have the last will and testament of Aldous of Pitchcott, a village in the county of Buckinghamshire, but a man who had been resident in the town of Marlborough, Wiltshire, since the year of Our Lord, 1204. The will was drawn up and sealed in August of the year 1205."

Hal and I sat ourselves at the furthest end of the table and watched and listened.

"He was, as you all know, a wealthy man with properties in that county of Buckinghamshire."

Farnell Armer scoffed and sat back in his seat.

The clerk ignored him.

"With a warehouse in Bristol, properties, too, here in the town, including this house and a business of which you are all aware. He was, I repeat, a wealthy man."

The lawyer unrolled the parchment and put his pen case, fetched from his bag, on the top.

"Now. He leaves his estate almost in its entirety to his adopted daughter, Everild Pitchcott."

Everild took hold of her new husband's hand.

"He leaves the buildings in Pitchcott and the land there to his nephew and ward Farnell Pitchcott along with a sum of money."

"How much?" said Farnell suddenly.

The lawyer blinked, and there was another flash of lightning and a huge peal of thunder which grumbled away. The dark room was suddenly bathed in light even though the shutters were closed. Then began the rain.

It teemed suddenly onto the thirsty ground with a deafening hiss and bounced, clattering on the tiles of the house roof.

The lawyer had to raise his voice to be heard. However, even though he did, I didn't hear the amount Farnell was to receive.

"A bequest to Robert Agnew, manager of the business, is also stipulated."

It was not insubstantial.

Agnew grinned.

"I knew he wouldn't forget me. I knew he valued me." He preened himself and seemed generally very well pleased with himself.

Everild pouted and scowled.

The lawyer looked up and directed his gaze to me.

"However..."

Everyone looked up, puzzled and worried.

"However, I am instructed by Master Pitchcott..."

"He's dead, man!" shouted Farnell. "He can't instruct you in anything now."

"I was instructed some days ago, sir, by my client, that if anything untoward were to befall him, I was to speak to the Lord Belvoir, who, I believe, is, by great fortune, present."

"I am." I sat forward.

The lawyer bowed to me.

"Master Pitchcott, sir, spoke to me on Tuesday. He told me that his life was in danger and that you were investigating in order to unmask the perpetrator and lead him to justice."

"That is correct."

"My client, only as recently as a week last Thursday, sir, made a new will."

The company was hushed.

Thunder growled in the distance.

"He wished you to witness it. He also felt that in the light of what he had told you, you would understand and act 'accordingly' — whatever that means. Does that mean something to you, my lord?"

I pictured the little man standing in my hall at Durley, and I thought carefully.

"I think I know what he means —yes, I think I know."

"The will was changed from its previous form."

"A different will, master clerk?" asked Deyning.

"Indeed, sir."

"What does it say, for Heaven's sake?" shouted Farnell again.

"This will, as you can see, my lord, is much changed."

The man picked up a second parchment and walked with it to the end of the table where I sat. Bowing, he gave it into my hands.

The clerkly Latin was difficult to follow and the light was not good, but I think I managed to get the gist of it.

"Ah," I looked around the assembly. They all held their breath.

"This will, made so recently, makes the whole of the estate of Aldous of Pitchcott, upon his death, to no other person but Farnell Pitchcott, his nephew and once his ward."

There was a small silence accompanied by the sound of the drumming rain and then Everild cried out "NO!"

"I have a feeling, madam, that your father must have got wind of your marriage to Master Deyning."

"NO!"

Deyning was the sickly colour of butter.

"No! That can't be right," said Farnell rising to his feet. "It was always going to be divided between Everild and me. Always."

I smiled at him.

"However, please be seated, Master Armer. That is not

the end of it."

I gave the parchment back to the clerk.

"Please carry on, sir." I nodded.

The clerk walked slowly back to the head of the table.

He put down the parchment.

"There is just one problem with this," said the clerk.

Farnell sat down, his face pasty white, his brow sweaty.

"The second will is not signed and witnessed," I interrupted. "Someone desperately needed to kill him before it *was* signed. And they did."

The clap of thunder which followed my words was the loudest yet, and it rattled the very fabric of the building.

We left them to their arguing and speculating and walked down the High Street. The world was bright and sparkling with raindrops. Gone was the heaviness of the past few days.

However, the road underfoot was puddled and muddy and still running with water.

People had dived for the cover of awnings and shops. Master Philbert Fleshmonger, the meat merchant, had an awning in front of his business premises half way down the right-hand side of the High Street at the northern side. He poked upwards with a stick and the whole puddle of rainwater which had pooled there in the storm came down with a woosh and landed on two elderly matrons who had decided to come out from their hiding place at that very moment.

There was a shriek, followed by some restrained swearing and an earnest apology from Fleshmonger.

Hal chuckled. "I thought as they were goin'a do something about this rainwater in the High," he said.

"Ah, yes. That was at first Master Glover's job on the town council and then latterly, Master Pitchcott's."

"Hmm. Won't be done now, will it?"

I shrugged, and we walked on.

Gilbert Cordwainer came out from his shop by the priory.

Master Cordwainer was an avuncular man with a large round red face, thick brown hair and a permanent grin.

I knew him well, for he had made my boots and shoes since I was a lad and could first walk in them, firstly as a journeyman, then as his own master. His house, workplace and shop were next to the entrance of the Priory of St Margaret of Antioch, and there was no doubt he benefited from being in such a spot. No pilgrim or visitor, secular or clerical, could pass by into the priory without first casting their eyes over his wares.

Over the years, he had become a special friend of mine, despite the gulf between our stations in life.

He was also an excellent source of town gossip and that was always to the good.

"Ah, my Lord Belvoir," said Gilbert, moving his head left and right from the door of his shop. I caught the whiff of leather and glue emanating from the building.

He looked down at my feet. "Boots still good on yer feet, are they?"

"A trifle damp, Gil, but, yes, they are still very comfortable."

I'd had a new pair of riding boots from him in the spring.

"Hello, Hal."

"Gil," nodded Hal.

Gilbert looked up to the Heavens. "That was some storm we just had."

"Freshened the air nicely."

"Yes, indeed. It was getting a mite too close."

Gilbert looked up the street and watched the people

returning to the marketplace.

"Have you the time for a cup of my best, sir?"

I looked at Hal and he grinned.

"I don't see why not, Gil."

Gilbert reached under the counter of his little shop and brought out three leather cups and a leather flagon.

"Soooo, I hear that Ol' Master Pitchcott has gone to meet his maker despite your best efforts to foil the attempts on his life, m'lord."

"I feel rather bad about that, Gilbert," I said, scratching the side of my nose. "I really did think I'd done it by locking him in the castle."

I sipped the ale which Gil handed me in his homemade leather cup.

"A-course, Aldous was all for getting things done in the town. I can't say as he was a likeable man, but he did get things done. I'll say that for him."

"What things, Gil?" asked Hal.

"Well, the ditch for the rainwater, for one thing. You know how we at the southern side of the High suffer with the rain running down from the northern side?"

"You have been complaining about it since Adam was a lad, Gil," I chuckled.

"Ah, well. Master Glover was supposed to get something done. But then he got himself a young and pretty second wife, so that work went the way of all flesh," he laughed.

"And Pitchcott? He took over the job?"

"Aye, he did. It was all supposed to start being dug next week."

"Surely the town council will honour the contract?"

Gil shrugged. "I dunno."

He took a sip of his ale and smacked his lips. "And then he was going to get some good folk to come for the fair. Entertainers, he called them, sir."

"That doesn't sound like the man I knew," I said.

"Aw, no doubt there was something in it for 'im," said Hal, smoothing down his moustache.

I laughed, "Ah, yes, no doubt. If I know Pitchcott."

"Well, a-course it wasn't Master Pitchcott completely himself. It was that man of his."

"Agnew?"

"Aye, that's his name."

"What was it to do with him?"

"Apparently, he knew where some folk could be found, some good tumblers and jugglers and musicians and the like."

"Did he now?"

"Who'd come to the fair for a fee, of course, and entertain the crowds."

"Well, that'll be a first," said Hal. "Except we had that bear the other year."

"Ah yes, Isabella," I said.

We all fell silent as we remembered the bear that had been at the centre of a particularly nasty series of murders in the town.

"She never got to do any tricks, though, did she?" said Gilbert.

"No, the king took her off to London." I looked down into my cup and swilled the ale around.

"Do we know where Agnew hails from?" I asked.

"Same place as his master, I don't doubt."

"Aylesbury village, or rather Pitchcott, Buckinghamshire?"

"Maybe he knows these tumblers and such from there. He's a bit of a musician himself, you know."

"Is he?"

"What's he play?" asked Hal.

"Flute, I'm told. Never heard him, but Grace has." Grace

was Gilbert's wife. "She says he's really good."

"Well, 'e may need a new job any day now. I think Mistress Pitchcott will be kicking 'im out on 'is ar... backside soon," said Hal. "He can take up pipin'."

"I can't think she'll do it too soon. He's too useful. Who else will know about the running of the wine business?" I said.

"That young man of hers, he'll no doubt be a useful fella" said Gilbert.

"Deyning."

"Hmmm, him."

I smiled. "Maybe."

There was a little silence and then Gilbert shifted on his seat.

"I got some news, my lord."

"Ah, have you, Ol' Gil?" I said, laughing. "Will we like it?"

"You know my journeyman Harry is finished with his learning and all that?"

Harry Glazer was, firstly, Gilbert's apprentice and then his journeyman. Harry had completed his masterpiece and was now considered a fully-fledged shoe maker.

"Now he's a master..."

"Oh, Gil, he isn't going to leave you?"

"Ah, no, not at all. He shall be staying as a partner." Gilbert puffed out his chest.

"He came up to me last week and asked if he and Gytha could be married?"

"Oh, that *is* good news."

We always knew that Harry would marry Gytha, the cordwainer's elder daughter. It was just a matter of when.

"Gytha's a mite young yet to be goin' off and running her own house, says her mam, an' they'd have to find somewhere to live, so they have agreed to wait a while. But they're engaged, handfasted. Just a matter of time. Of course, it's awkward with the church being closed an' all."

"Oh, I am very pleased about that," I said. "Harry is a fine young man and a worthy partner for you."

"Always wanted a son," said Gilbert in an embarrassed tone. "Now I got one."

"'E's been your son near on this nine years, Gilbert Cordwainer," said Hal. "Ever since you first 'ad 'im as an apprentice."

"Aye, well. That's true, I suppose. Grace is that pleased…"

"You must be pleased too that Gytha is going to such a good young man and that Harry isn't moving away."

Gilbert beamed. "One big happy family."

We all smiled.

"Unlike those up at St Martin's," said Hal.

"Aye, they're always at each other's throats. Always have bin. Ever since they got 'ere."

"Well, we must be going. I had better poke my nose in at the castle," I said.

"Those masons done with that south wall yet, sir?" asked Gilbert. "It seems to be taking forever."

"There's a lot of building work to do, Gil, but yes, they've finished there. They're on the western wall now."

"The king must'a spent a fortune on the castle already?"

"He has indeed. And more work is to be done, I'm told."

I stood up. "In fact, I have neglected the masons of late. I suppose I better go and say hello to them."

"Ha!" said Hal "They knows what they're doin' that lot. They don't need any help from us."

"No, I know, but I Iike to keep abreast of what they're up to."

We exited the cordwainer's shop.

"Give our love to the family and congratulations to the youngsters."

The noise on the western wall was deafening.

Masons were shouting to each other. There was the noise of the carpenters who made the scaffolding, sawing and banging, and the din of the men who were demolishing the old crumbling blocks while whistling to themselves as they went about their noisy business.

There was a general grinding of stone, a slapping of mortar and a creaking of the winches used to get the blocks up to the highest parts of the wall.

I stood on the wall walk and looked over the parapet.

Not long before, a woman had fallen to her death here. I saw her body in my mind's eye, half in, half out of the moat, her hair spreading out like weed into the water. I shook away the memory.

"Ah, Gervase, how does the building go?"

"It goes well, my Lord Belvoir," said the master mason. The carpenters are just now finishing with the scaffolding, and we can begin to shore up the wall and lay new blocks."

"Good."

"We shall need to make sure that no one comes this way. I was about to come and talk to you, sir, about the wall walk. We shall need to demolish it in part, and so the guards who patrol must stop short there, sir," he said, gesturing to the corner where the steps led up to the parapet.

"I shall make it known, Gervase."

"Thank you, sir."

Once again, I leaned out over the edge.

"You must have such a good head for heights, Gervase, to be a mason."

"Aye, sir. There's one thing you must be. Unafraid of heights. Why, some of the buildings I've worked on, you wouldn't believe the distance to the ground."

"And the carpenters who make the scaffolding. They, too, must have strong stomachs and a good sense of balance."

"Aye, they build as they go up, roping the poles together. Little to save them from falling but a few flimsy bits of tree trunk." He laughed, "They're all touched they are, sir. Every man of them."

I looked over to where a couple of the carpenters who raised the scaffolding were bending over their structure. One man on the next level down, was throwing a pole up to the man above him, who caught it deftly in a gloved hand and laid it just where he wanted it on his level. He took some rope and had it in place and steady in a heartbeat. I watched as the process was repeated. Then planks were laid over the beams and the process began again.

"At least as a mason, we're entrusting our lives to good solid stone. These scaffolders, they're a reckless lot. Nothing but a bit o' wood and string."

Suddenly, something struck me. I frowned.

"Excuse me, Gervase."

I ran around the wall walk, dodging the guards, passing through the towers beginning to rise at the corners of the walls. The south-easternmost tower was complete. I leaned over the new parapet and scanned the eastern wall.

"Ah, no," I said to myself. "It's not so."

I had thought that maybe some of the scaffolding was still in place on the eastern wall where my office lay. That might have allowed an intruder access to the little window in my office wall. But no, all the scaffolding had gone.

I slowly returned to the western wall, where the master mason was in conference with two or three of his stone workers.

"Gervase, might I have a word?"

"Certainly, my lord."

I took his arm and steered him to the wall.

"I have a mind to build a porch to the church at Durley.

We have good builders in the village but are in want of a man to design and oversee it. Of course, our men don't build in stone."

"You'd like me to come and have a look at it, sir?"

"Aye, I would, Gervase. If you can spare the time."

"I'm sure I can, my Lord Belvoir."

Gervase Mason removed his linen coif and scratched his grey hair.

"I expect I could find some men to help too."

"I've good carpenters in the village."

"Good to know, sir."

"They aren't perhaps used to building in the same way as your men, but I'm sure we could get them to build us some scaffolding."

Gervase smiled, and his leathered face creased into a myriad of folds.

"Are they as touched as my men, sir?" he chuckled. "Well, if they are, I'm sure they'll do very well."

We shook on it.

Later, Hal and I made for the stables and were about to collect our horses for the ride back to Durley when I heard my name called.

"Ah, Master Agnew!"

He puffed up to me. "My Lord," he bowed.

"Might I ask if I can get into the room now for the correspondence left there, the parchments I need, sir?"

The coroner had been, and Johannes and I had given him our report. The first finder, the young kitchen girl Alysoun, had been questioned, the body of the merchant had been collected.

"I don't see why not, Agnew," I said.

He followed me across the bailey and I unlocked and opened the door of my office. He stepped gingerly inside.

His eyes strayed over every inch of the room.

"Do you know what happened, sir?" he asked, shuffling his parchments on the table.

"It's a mystery, Agnew, but we shall come upon the answer soon, I've no doubt."

He smiled. "A demon conjured up by Master Deyning, sir. That's what happened. It makes my blood boil to think that the man has profited by his wicked deed, it does."

Hal sighed. "It was no demon but a two-legged human one."

"A demon who could scurry up the wall or pass through the door." He shuddered. "It fair makes me cringe to think about it."

The bell of the chapel in the priory tolled for nones, the third hour of the afternoon.

"Oh! I must away," said Agnew, gathering up his work and stuffing it into a leather bag.

"You have some pressing business, Master Agnew?"

"Just that I promised to be at the Barbflet house before the fourth hour."

"What do you do there?"

He puffed out his chest, "I am teaching, m'lord, teaching the young ones to play the flute. The other girl comes from the Snap household. They sit together for me to tutor them."

Nicholas had a girl, and Richard, Lord of Snap, had another, both of an age to learn music. They lived only doors away from each other on the High Street.

"I heard you were very good."

"Oh..." Agnew proudly threw up his head. "Where did you hear that, m'lord?"

"From my friend the cordwainer. His wife Grace has heard you play."

"Ah, yes. She was at the Barbflet house when Master Nicholas asked me to demonstrate my skill and engaged me."

"Perhaps you'll come and play for us one day."

Agnew tightened one of the buckles of the leather bag. "I would be honoured, m'lord." He bowed again.

"Oh, Agnew,"

"Yessir?"

"We did not finish our conversation yesterday."

"We didn't?"

"You were about to tell me where you were when your master was being killed in this very room."

Once more, his eyes travelled around the space.

The day was warm but I swear he shivered.

"I was about to tell you, m'lord, that I was away playing at a party."

"Where, Agnew?"

"At the Chapman house, sir."

"And you returned, when?"

"I stayed, sir, the whole night."

"Ah, yes. And you were also about to tell me you might have had company some nights?"

Agnew's expression changed. "At midnight, sir? Y... yes, I have had company some nights."

"Mistress Deyning says you went to your room alone. She saw you."

A sly look came over Agnew's face. "Well, yes, sir. That is what we like *her* to think."

"It would not reflect well on you, were it known that you entertained a woman in your room, under the roof of your patron and employer, would it?"

"You are quite right, sir."

"Who is this lady, Agnew?"

Agnew shuffled his feet.

"It's... it is... the cook at the house, sir. She has a place in the kitchen, but is often with me of a night. She goes back there before dawn."

"Ah. And she joins you in your room late at night so that your master and mistress do not find out?"

"Everild Pitchcott is not my mistress, sir. She is the adopted daughter of my employer."

"And on that subject, Agnew, do tell me, what do you know of the history of that lady?"

"History, sir?"

"She is, as you say, adopted. Why did Master Pitchcott adopt the girl when he already had a nephew in Farnell, his sister's son, living with him?"

"I cannot say what his motive was, sir, but," the man licked his lips. "I do know that Master Pitchcott had two sisters."

"Ah?"

"And that Everild was what is called, sir, a love child of his younger sister."

"Farnell was the son of his elder sister?"

"Yessir, and forgive me, m'lord, a bastard."

"What happened to this younger sister?"

"She, too, died, sir, shortly after the child was two. Master Pitchcott kindly took her in, though he didn't have to."

"The child's father couldn't be found?"

There was a little silence.

"No, sir, I believe not."

"Hmm. She, too, was born out of wedlock then?"

I saw the man flinch as if I'd struck him.

"Some might like to think so."

"Hmm."

"Though I do know that he was a clerk of some kind, so perhaps he was unable to marry."

"Being in Holy Orders, you mean?" Many priests were

indeed married, but it was beginning to be frowned upon by the church.

"Maybe, sir."

"Thank you for that. I shall, perhaps tomorrow, speak to your lady love, the cook, and verify your word that you were both in your room when you say you were."

He bowed again. "Yes, sir. Her name is Margery."

He made for the door. Suddenly, the leather bag in his hand slipped from his grasp and he uttered a cry of surprise.

"Oh! How clumsy of me!"

He bent and picked it up. It had landed on the floor by the pot board, almost where my disturbed polished steel had rested. He scrabbled on the floor, recovered the parchments and fastened the buckle.

"Thank you, sir." He bowed once more and was gone.

Within the time it took to lock the office door, buckle our saddle bags and lead out our horses, we, too, were gone from the castle.

We rode through the forest of Savernake as the late afternoon light filtered through the trees, dappling the ground with yellow patterns.

"Warm again, Hal, even after the thunder."

"Aye, sticky again. It'll be another uncomfortable night, I warrant."

We left our mounts with the grooms at the stables and made our way to the hall.

Henry Steward was sitting at the table in conversation with Crispin, our village priest.

Do you think I should explain, Paul, my
scribe, about the Interdict? How the king had

so annoyed the pope that in March 1208, the pontiff had pronounced a punishment upon the king, his country and his subjects by disallowing church services to be held in the church building?

You do.

Well, then, we need to write down that no one could be married… and this was why Harry and Gytha were being forced into a long engagement, though a handfasting such as they'd entered into was binding and if they had wished they could have lived as man and wife.

No mass might be said in the church on Sunday, though a sort of gathering was allowed, and the priest might make a blessing. No one could be buried with proper rights. No man except the priest, I believe, might enter the church.

It was a period of great uncertainty, but as time went on, we all got used to it.

Crispin, our priest, had felt the loss of his role keenly. We wrote about that in our last tale, didn't we, Paul?

Henry and Father Crispin, who was one of my childhood friends, were deep in debate.

Henry rose as I entered and nodded to me.

"My lord, welcome home."

"Thank you, Henry."

Crispin took his boots from the bench and swung himself round.

"Father, I have today asked Master Gervase Mason to come and see about beginning the porch to the church. He will no doubt come to the village soon and take measurements and begin his drawings."

"That's good, Sir Aumary," said our priest with a smile. "I thought you'd forgotten about it."

"No, not at all. I just needed to turn it over in my head a little before I came to ask him. Will you speak to him about what you'd like?"

I heard Hal grunt in a sort of laugh as he made for the pot board and the jug of ale, which always sat there.

"You know how I like to think these things out. Make sure I'm doing the right thing."

Henry smiled. "I suppose you'll be doing the same, m'lord, with this next murder of yours, as you normally do?"

"Oh, you've heard, have you? News travels like wildfire."

Henry followed Hal to the pot board and picked up the jug of wine, which also sat there. He brought me a cup and poured for me.

"It came back to Durley with John Brenthall... the news. We naturally take an interest, sir, because we met the man."

"I remember you introduced him, Henry, but when did *you* meet him, Crispin?"

"A little while ago. In town. He knew that I was priest here and caught me when I was visiting in Marlborough with Father Torold, priest of St Mary's."

"Why?"

"He was asking questions of us both, Aumary. He'd heard I had worked for the Bishop of Salisbury."

"Ah, he tried to sell you wine for Eucharist?" I chuckled.

Crispin laughed. "He was asking questions about marriage."

"Marriage? He wasn't thinking of getting married, was he?"

"Not from what I could gather. He wanted to know if a marriage which had been enacted without the sanction of the church could be legally valid."

"Ah, yes. His daughter Everild married her lover Richard

Deyning without his knowledge, and Pitchcott got wind of it after the event. He then made a new will which cut her off without a penny. He was killed before he could sign it and make it legal."

"And so what happens now?"

"The old will still stands. She inherits half his wealth."

"They *were* married then?"

"Perfectly legally and in church before the prohibition, in London."

"She has a powerful motive then for killing her guardian, sir," said Henry.

"And so does Deyning. The money will be most welcome, I think."

"Well, now Pitchcott's gone."

"Are you any nearer knowing what killed him?" asked Crispin

"Johannes dug a tiny pellet from his skull just behind his ear." I fished in my scrip and came out with the ball.

"It lodged in his brain and the doctor says it interfered with the blood lines going up from his neck."

Henry took it in his hand. "This little thing?"

"Aye, that little thing."

Crispin peered at it over Henry's shoulder.

"What is it?"

"I have to say, I haven't the faintest idea," I said, and with a wave to the three of them, I made my way up to the solar to be with my wife and children.

"Aumary, have you found out if this young lady... what's her name?"

"Everild?"

"Everild, such a pretty name, Everild, if she actually

cared for her father at all?" asked Lydia, my wife, busying about with our young son Phillip.

"I am afraid there really wasn't much feeling for him, no."

"And yet surely there must be *some* feeling, for the girl was adopted by him? Even if it only comes down to gratitude. Where would the girl be else?"

"Hmmm."

"And have you also asked her if she knows where her real father is and, better still, who he is?"

"How could she know, Lydia? She was but two when her mother died."

"Someone might know."

"Someone might have told her, you mean?"

She shrugged her shoulders. "She might know."

"And then...?"

"Family skeletons have a way of rearing their ugly bones when inheritance, particularly money, is in the offing, Aumary."

"Aye - you of all people should know that."

Lydia had been made homeless when her first husband's son by his first wife decided to take the manor, which was his inheritance.

"You have, of course, asked her where she was when her father was being killed?"

"I have. She was not at the castle."

"Ah."

"She was in her own room with her new husband."

"And he can confirm that I suppose?"

"He can, and she can also confirm that Master Agnew was in his room on the stairs at other times. He was playing the flute for a party the night his master was killed. So none of them could have been at the castle then."

"Except the armourer and his lady friend."

"Corlis."

"It seems you have fewer people as suspects now, Aumary."

"There may be someone entirely unknown to us as yet who wished Master Pitchcott dead... they may be the culprit."

Lydia looked up at me with her large violet-blue eyes.

"But how will you find them?"

"Gossip, my love, gossip. And I must think. I must sit in the quiet and think."

"Here again, my Lord Belvoir?" said Agnew with obvious irritation as we once more walked up the hall in the house on St Martin's.

"I am sorry to keep bothering you like this, Master Agnew."

The man flapped his hands. He seemed very agitated.

"I have *so* much to do. With the master gone, I must ensure everything is in order for... for Mistress Deyning and... and... Master Deyning... to take over the business." His distaste at saying the words was obvious.

"I have come to talk to the cook, Agnew."

"Ah, she will be in the kitchen. I will take you there."

"Margery! Margery!" called Agnew as he crossed the small courtyard which separated the main building from the kitchen.

He pushed open the door.

There was a scurrying, and the kitchen girl, who had been filling her face at the main work table, jumped up and tried to stuff the last of the crumb of bread into her mouth.

"She i'n't 'ere," she mumbled.

"What?"

The girl chewed. "I i'n't seen 'er."

"That much is obvious, my girl. Get about your chores now."

"I i'n't got no chores."

"What do you mean you haven't got any jobs to do? You always have jobs to do," said Agnew irritably.

"Cook i'n't told me what I gotta do."

"Ooh!" said Agnew, most annoyed. "I cannot imagine where she's got to."

Just then, there was a terrible frightened scream from inside the house. High-pitched and ululating, the scream went on and on.

Hal bounded back the way we'd come and ran up the solar stairs.

"Sir!" he yelled from one of the middle steps. The door to Agnew's room was open.

Running after, I followed him in. Master Agnew ambled after me.

"That's Aebbe. She does the linen and the cleaning and looks after Mistress..."

I reached the door just as Hal was enveloping in his arms a young girl who stood in the room crying. He turned her away from the mess on the bed.

"Come on, lass..." he said. "Let's get you down the stairs." He nodded to me as he passed.

"Keep her there, Hal. I'll want a word in a while."

Master Agnew came into his room.

"Oh, my Lord! Oh, by all the saints! Oh, Margery! Oh, Jesu!" He crossed himself.

I held out my arm to bar the way.

"No, Agnew. Do not approach. I need no fouling of the area of the bed place before I examine it so that I might know what has happened here."

"But, sir, it's obvious what has happened." Agnew put

his hand to his mouth. "Excuse me, my lord, but I think I am going to be…" and he fled down the stairs, and, after a heartbeat, I heard the front door bang.

Margery, the cook, lay on her back. Her pale eyes stared unhappily at the roof beams.

The bed was rumpled and unmade. She lay partly covered by the sheet - there was only one, for it had been another warm night as Hal had predicted and no one needed blankets on nights as hot as the last one.

She was stark naked. Her large bosoms dangled to the side of the frame of her chest. One arm was dangling over the bed's edge. The other was clamped to her bloody throat, which was a gaping hole. There was blood everywhere. Someone had very efficiently cut the throat of Margery the cook.

Chapter Six

AS WE DESCENDED the stairs, Mistress Everild Deyning was coming down the hall from the other end.

"Madam, might we send to the coroner and the priest at St Mary's? We must also bring the doctor up to the house from the bottom of Kingsbury Hill."

"Whatever was that awful screaming, my lord?"

"It was your maid, madam."

The maid had been taken outside by Hal. They stood with Agnew, for she, too, was vomiting up her morning ale.

"It is my sorry duty to tell you that your cook…"

"Margery?"

"Is dead."

"Dead, my lord? Oh, that's ridiculous. Margery was perfectly well last night when…"

"Her throat has been cut."

The woman paled and reached for the tabletop where she stood, leaning for a heartbeat, taking in my terrible words.

"Your maid found her."

"Who, Aebbe?"

"It was she whom you heard screaming."

"Where is she now?"

"The maid is outside with my man-at-arms and Robert Agnew. The murdered woman is in Master Agnew's bed."

As if the mention of his name had fetched him in, Master Agnew came through the outer door wiping his mouth with his hand.

"In his bed?" Mistress Deyning's eyes grew large and round. "What is she doing in his bed?"

I saw Agnew falter. He looked sidelong at me quickly. In that look, I thought I saw a plea not to tell of the relationship between the cook and himself.

Interestingly the woman did not first ask *why* she might have been murdered.

"Agnew, tell me, at what time did you rise from your bed?" I asked.

Agnew closed his eyes and took in a deep breath.

"Just before dawn, sir."

"I take it Margery had gone by then?"

Another swift look at Everild Deyning.

"She did not come up to me last night, sir."

"Agnew," said Everild with a scowl. "What is this?" Then I heard her say under her breath, "I knew it."

"Then why is she in your bed over two hours into the day, Agnew?"

"I cannot say, sir. She was not there when I rose."

The manservant now arrived, putting on his outer tunic.

"Go down to the doctor opposite the high cross. Ask him to come up here. Then go on to the church and ask Father Torold to come. Will you then go to Master Barbflet, the town reeve, and get him to inform the coroner that we have a body for him to view? Run."

"Yessir."

The door banged after him as he left.

"Agnew, answer me. What is all this about?"

asked Everild.

Robert Agnew ignored the woman and turned to me.

"I swear to you, my lord, that the woman was not in my bed when I left it. Why would someone put a body in my bed?"

"Why would anyone want to kill Margery?" said Everild, her voice almost a whisper.

"She could give Master Agnew an alibi for the time your father was attacked."

Her eyes narrowed. "Agnew?"

Still, the man did not attempt to explain.

"We are unsure, as yet, when the woman died, but it must have been between dawn when you rose, Agnew, and a moment ago, when," I turned to face Everild Deyning. "Your maid, madam, found the body."

Everild scowled at Agnew.

"The doctor will be able to put a time to the murder as he understands how the body behaves after death, mistress."

"How can he do that, m'lord?" asked Agnew quickly.

"The body cools and the doctor will be able to tell by the amount of warmth and stiffening how long the woman has been dead."

Agnew's eyes enlarged momentarily. "He can be so sure about it?"

"Give or take a couple of hours. He is very experienced in these matters."

"Why? Why?" said the man. "Why Margery? She's done nothing, nothing wrong."

"Agnew, I cannot now, of course, confirm your story that Margery was with you when your employer was killed at the castle."

"No, sir. Very unfortunate. Very unfortunate." He shook his head sadly.

"Tell me, Master Agnew... when we were in my office, I noticed that when you dropped your pouch of papers, the ones you collected from my desk, as you recovered them, you picked up something from the floor."

"I did, sir?"

"You did, Agnew."

The man looked puzzled.

"Oh, yes, now I remember." He undid the laces of his purse and rummaged around.

"It was this, sir. I believe it belongs to... to Master Deyning."

He looked across into the face of his employer's daughter.

"I was going to give it back to him... to save you any... embarrassment, madam."

He placed the small thing in my hand.

It was a belt strap end, the sort of thing which protects the final piece of the leather as it is threaded through the buckle.

Everild leaned forward. "It's from Richard's belt."

"I have seen this myself, mistress. Does it not belong on the end of his fine blue leather belt?" I asked.

Everild Deyning licked her lips. "I cannot deny it. Where do you say it was found?"

"In the room of my Lord Belvoir at the castle. The room where..." Agnew faltered. "Where your father met his end."

"Richard has never been in that room! I swear it. As far as I know, he has never even been into the castle."

"And yet his belt has been broken, and the end has fallen off in my office, madam," I said.

"I cannot say how it got there."

I shrugged. "We must ask him."

We waited a little longer, and a few more questions were asked and facts discussed, long enough for Johannes to come running up the hill and along St Martin's with the priest following closely on his heels.

We allowed Father Torold up into the room before we examined the body. He would do no damage to the evidence with his ministrations.

I prepared the doctor for the scene.

"Johannes, the woman's throat is cut. I think she thrashed about in her death throes, for the bed is very disordered."

After he'd finished, we met the good father halfway down the stairs into the hall as the priest Torold, white-faced and trembling, collected the items he'd brought to help the woman's soul into Heaven and put them into a bag. This was, I was told, the only service a priest might render those who had died unexpectedly whilst the Interdict was in force.

"Her priest is Father Godric..."

"Aye, of St Martin's."

"But I am more than pleased to help, sir. I did know her, but only slightly."

"Thank you, Father Torold. It's not a pretty sight."

"No. Death is never pretty - but that... the poor woman. She didn't deserve that."

"A donation will be made to St Mary's," said Everild, rising from her place at the head of the large table. "I much appreciate what you have done, Father Torold."

He nodded and was gone.

Johannes, as was his custom, looked down at the body for the time it takes to say a Paternoster.

"What's this?"

He picked up a piece of material on the end of his long metal probe.

I grasped it and pulled.

"It's a man's shirt," he said.

"Agnew's? He must have tossed it on the bed as he left this morning."

"It is very bloody."

"It will be, it was under the body."

Johannes peered into the woman's eyes and mouth.

"No one saw her this morning?"

"Not Agnew, not Mistress Deyning. The servant says he did not see her, nor did the kitchen maid. I think the house maid's first sight of her today was her dead body."

"Deyning?"

"Out at his work."

"It's a very efficient cut and done from behind. Grab the chin, pull up and swipe with a sharp knife."

"And done here in the bed."

"Yes, I would say so by the amount of blood here and how it has sprayed and pooled. The weapon? Have you searched?"

"I have. Nothing."

"I cannot say what kind of knife it was, other than it was very sharp."

"When do you think she was killed?"

"Any time leading up to dawn or just after."

"Hmm."

"Does that help you?"

"Done here and at dawn... no, not really," I said.

"If this man Agnew had gone downstairs... where was he? Did he lock his room?" asked Johannes.

"Why did the woman come up here at dawn? Why would she come up here alone, and who would lie in wait for her here?"

"I do not lock my room. I have nothing of any great value there," Agnew said moments later when we tackled him. "And as to where I went, I broke my fast on some ale I had in the office. That's where I was, in the office until you came, sir."

"Why might Margery be in your room if you say you hadn't seen her last night?"

"I have no idea, my lord."

I rubbed my forehead in frustration.

"So now I must speak to Master Deyning about his belt.

"It must be him. I told you, sir, that it was him all along. The master told you it was him."

"Why would Deyning wish to murder the cook here in this house, Agnew?"

"What did she know about him, sir? Did she see him try to murder the master?"

"Did Margery say anything to you?"

"About Deyning, m'lord?"

"Did she say that she had, for example, seen him arguing with Master Pitchcott, or threatening him perhaps?"

"Richard would never do that," said Mistress Deyning, suddenly coming into the room. The door clicked shut. She sat down with a flourish of her grey skirts. As they lifted, I noticed that her little blue shoes with side laces were muddied at the pointed toe.

"He was nothing but politeness and tolerance to Aldous. I do not know why. Aldous would goad him unmercifully. He was most unkind, and Richard would take it all upon himself as if it didn't matter to him."

"The quarrel between them, when did it begin?" I asked.

"It went back to when Aldous bought this house from Richard's father. It was just a short while before he died."

"Did Richard keenly feel the snub from his father?"

"Richard was already successful in business, m'lord. He is an only child. His father was a very sick man. He sold this house to Aldous, and the money, I believe, was transferred to the priory, for Richard's father was to live out his last days as a corrodian there."

"Ah, so the priory was the beneficiary of the sale, not his son."

"Most of it, yes."

"So why was there such bad blood between them besides the quarrel over the money Pitchcott says your husband owed him for his investment?"

"Aldous was a quarrelsome man, sir. I cannot count the people with whom he has been involved in litigation over the years."

"Some folk are just so... they must be at someone else's throat over money," I chuckled.

"That was Aldous of Pitchcott, sir."

"Why did he lend Deyning the money? I cannot understand that, if he had such a poor opinion of him?"

"At first, he was quite good to Richard. Aldous was avaricious. He could indeed see that it was a good investment. What he could not see was the time it would take for his money to double. He had no patience. He wanted an instant reward. Also, when Richard and I became... involved, Aldous became more opposed to him."

"Ah, so it was a case of jealousy."

The woman lowered her eyes. "Perhaps. I never felt myself truly his daughter and I think he started to become quite possessive of me. If I was not going to behave like a devoted and obedient daughter to him then I could not be married to Richard."

"It was as simple as that?"

"He wanted me to marry my cousin Farnell to keep all in the family... oh, how often did we hear him say, keeping it in the family."

"But you two are full cousins—son and daughter of sisters. The church would prohibit your union. There is too close a relation..."

"Nothing that Aldous felt he could not buy his way around, sir."

"Money is rarely the answer, madam."

"It was something both Farnell and I used to tell him, but he would not listen to us. Farnell left eight years ago to begin his studies and his apprenticeship. He got out. I could not leave. Then I met Richard."

I nodded.

Hal came back in with the little maid.

"Aebbe, isn't it?"

The girl sniffled and nodded.

Hal sat her down and offered her a beaker of ale. She shook her head and looked up at her mistress through lowered lashes.

"Tell me, girl, what did you see when you entered the room of Master Agnew this morning?" I asked.

Again the servant looked to Mistress Deyning.

"Speak, girl. The constable is asking you, not me."

The girl's voice was weak and trembling.

"I never seed such a thing in m'life."

"Yes, it must have been very unpleasant to come upon something like that. Especially when you know the woman well, Aebbe."

"Yes, my lord. It was awful."

"Did you see anyone else close by when you discovered the cook?"

"No, sir. No one. I went to make the beds and tidy up. Fetch some washing from the rooms. I'd got the laundress coming round later and..."

I studied the other two, Everild and Agnew, as they

watched the girl twisting her hands together in her lap. Their faces were blank.

"I opened the door, and there was this awful smell."

"Smell?"

"Like the killing time just before Christmas, sir."

"Ah, yes, when the animals are slaughtered. Blood."

"So much of it. Everywhere."

"Then you screamed?"

"Aye, I did."

"There was enough light to see by?"

"Aye, sir, there was," sniffled Aebbe.

"The shutters were open?"

"They were, sir."

Everild Deyning sighed and stood up. "We shall need a new cook."

I frowned at her.

"Agnew, see that one is engaged."

"I beg your pardon, Mistress Deyning, but that is not my job."

Everild pouted. "Then tell Thomas Parfitt, the steward. I'll not have the smooth running of this house upset for want of a cook for the kitchen."

"I shall need to speak to your steward too, madam."

"Speak to whom you wish, m'lord."

She turned to leave.

"Madam?"

"Yes, my lord?"

"Where were you when your cook was being killed?"

"Where do you think, my lord? In my bed, with my husband. Sleeping."

My eyebrow lifted.

"At dawn, we were sleeping."

Hal guffawed quietly in the corner.

I saw Johannes' face crease in a suppressed smile.

"Isn't that what everyone does… at dawn… in bed?"

And she marched down the hall and disappeared through the door by which she had entered.

Hal tapped his fingers on his sword hilt.

"That woman! She 'as no care for anyone but 'erself."

"She certainly doesn't care about her cook," said Johannes.

I saw Agnew, out of the corner of my eye, raise an eyebrow and sigh.

"Oh, you mustn't judge her too harshly. Living with my master all these years… it's made her a little… detached from things, a little cold. She isn't really all that bad. She is a very sweet lady."

"She needs to know who she is," said Hal. "She's not the fine lady she thinks she is."

I turned to my man-at-arms in surprise.

"Well! The way she speaks to you, sir. It i'n't right. You'd think she was a noble woman. An' she i'n't."

I chuckled. Hal was so loyal to me.

"No. She is the bastard daughter of Pitchcott's youngest sister. That's all," he finished.

Agnew took in a sharp breath. "That's a little cruel, Master Hal."

"S'true!"

"Well, whatever she is," I said. "We need to see if Master Deyning, now her husband, can confirm that the woman was with him all night."

"An' you think 'e won't?" scoffed Hal. " A-course 'e will. Let's 'im off too, doesn't it?"

I shrugged. "Let's see what he says when we show him what Master Agnew has found."

I threw up the belt strap end and caught it again.

"Now what?" asked Hal as we stood outside the house.

"I have a mind to look around the outside, Hal."

"Outside? Ah, I see."

"Perhaps someone came up the wall? It isn't far up to Agnew's room, not as far up as Master Pitchcott's, and I don't know if you've noticed, but at the base of the wall, there's a plinth of stone upon which the building stands, about eighteen inches high. Someone might have climbed up on it and gained entry to the window."

"The windows are quite large, big enough for someone small to squeeze through."

"Just my thought, Hal," I said.

We rounded the building and stood looking at the gable end of the house. There was Master Pitchcott's room; the window overlooked the yard and the high outer wall. Under it, by about seven feet, was another window. I noticed the shutters were open inside.

"Hal, stand on that block and see if you can get anywhere near the window."

Hal hoisted himself upon the base plate of the wall. He clung on with his finger ends and flattened himself to the whitewashed surface of the gable end, standing on tiptoe.

"Yes, I can hoist myself up from here," he said in a tortured voice, his arms above his head.

"Do you think you might be able to get into the window?"

"Aye, I think so."

He jumped down and brushed down his cotte. "I could, especially if I had a bit o' 'elp."

He looked up. "What're you doin', sir?"

"Looking for... ah, yes, here."

Under the window were a few weeds, and some flowers had been planted though they had not been well looked after. I parted the plants. Apart from the rain in the night and the thunderstorm, they'd seen no water for weeks.

"See here, Hal. A footprint."

"A dainty footprint."

"Did you notice that Mistress Deyning's shoes were muddied this morning when she entered the hall?"

"No, no, I didn't, but I s'pose you saw them."

"I did, and I wondered what might have taken her out into the mud so early."

"It rained in the night, di'n't it?"

"It did," I answered. "A little."

"Right where we need the footprints to be. Under Agnew's window."

"It would certainly account for no one seeing anyone entering or leaving the room."

"Mistress Deyning gave 'er 'usband a leg up, do you think, sir?"

"Perhaps."

Suddenly history repeated itself and there was a terrified screaming.

"Aw, not again!" shouted Hal as he tore off in the direction of the kitchen at the back of the house.

We were the first to arrive.

Young Aebbe was staring at the kitchen table.

"Aebbe, what's the matter, girl?" asked Agnew, quickly on our heels.

Hal once more took hold of the girl. She crumpled into his arms, muttering.

I took a step towards the table.

"Mercy." Agnew crossed himself. "Almighty God and all his angels!"

"That wasn't there when the kitchen girl was 'ere earlier," said Hal.

"It has appeared since. I would have noticed it," I said.

"No, it definitely wasn't 'ere."

"No, don't touch it."

I lifted a cloth which was lying by a pail of water on the table and took up the bloodied knife, for a knife it was which had set poor Aebbe crying again.

"It's the kitchen knife, sir," blubbered Aebbe. "One we do skinning and the like with."

"It's the knife which killed Margery Cook."

"Oooh," said Aebbe faintly.

"Hal, take her out and find the kitchen girl."

"Her name's Otille, sir," said Agnew.

"Right you are, sir," said Hal.

Mistress Deyning came breathlessly into the kitchen.

"What now?"

She looked back as Hal helped Aebbe out of the outer door into the garden.

"What's the matter with her now?"

"She has just found the knife which took the life of Margery Cook, madam."

Everild's face went white.

"It was one of ours?"

"A kitchen knife, and it has been returned to the kitchen by the murderer," I said as I laid it down again on the table top.

"The coroner will have to be informed."

Mistress Deyning collapsed onto a stool. "Oh, this is too much."

She looked up at me.

"Who sir... who will be next?"

"I didn't even know it was missing," said Richard Deyning.

"You wore the belt last time I saw you. Was it whole then?"

"I have never been in that room, my lord. Never!"

"How do you account for it being found in my office where the dead man lay?"

"I cannot, my lord."

"You do not wear it today, Deyning."

"No sir, today I wear a brown belt as you can plainly see."

"You did not pay a visit to Aldous Pitchcott to discuss the money he said you owed him."

Deyning's mouth set in a hard line, then he said, "No, I most certainly did not, m'lord. I have kept away from the man as much as I could."

"And yet you were sleeping under his roof on the night he died."

Deyning put down the small sample of fur he had been examining.

"Everild and I put off being together as man and wife for quite a while, sir. She was concerned that her guardian would cause a major argument if it were revealed immediately that we had married."

"But, Master Deyning, somehow Aldous Pitchcott *did* find out you were already man and wife," I said.

"No, sir. How can he? We were very discreet."

"He was in the process of changing his will to disinherit Everild. All monies were to have gone to her cousin."

Deyning scoffed. "That I find very hard to believe. He could not abide the young man because Farnell accused him of theft. Farnell left the house rather than suffer further abuse at Aldous' hand, m'lord."

"And yet, his lawyers tell me—I have had the paper in my hand, I've read it—that Pitchcott was about to sign a new will which left all his monies to Farnell, the armourer. You were there, you heard."

"It must be a forgery."

I sighed.

"No, I think not. I think the man was killed to prevent him from signing it. Now Master Deyning, who might have the best motive for killing Master Pitchcott, do you think?"

Deyning stared at me. "I did not kill Aldous of Pitchcott and neither did my wife."

I held out my hand. "I would like the belt end back, please."

Deyning dismissively dropped it into my hand.

He turned back to his work. "If I were you, my lord, I would look to some of those people with whom Pitchcott dealt in his business. There may be someone there who holds a grudge. He was, I hear, the most litigious of people and most unpopular."

"Do you know of anyone, Deyning?"

"No, I don't, but Master Agnew might. After all, he had the complete confidence of his master."

Hal leaned on the wall and I saw Deyning flick him a glance.

"What do you know about Master Agnew, Deyning?"

Richard Deyning lifted his head and scowled.

"The man is a complete fawning flatterer. He would do anything to gain the approval of his employer."

"You don't call that kind of behaviour - loyalty, Deyning?"

"Not that amount of subservience, so much servility, no. Naturally, Pitchcott loved it. He expected the same from his niece, his adopted daughter. Everild is made of different stuff, my lord."

"So you met Everild when?"

"Shortly after they bought the house, I had cause to go back there to speak to Pitchcott and Everild was there. It was a while before we contrived a meeting between us."

"And Agnew?"

"The man was there, scraping and licking Pitchcott's boots. Agnew came with Pitchcott from Buckinghamshire,

I believe. I know he has worked for Pitchcott for twenty years or more."

"So, from a young man?"

"Yes, I believe he was about twenty when he got into his employ."

"Will he be kept on to run the business?"

"Not if I can help it. Repulsive creature."

"He knows about the wine trade."

"Nothing I can't learn there."

"You would do well to keep him on and learn from him."

"Oh, I will... and then he'll be out on his ear."

I saw Hal stand up straight from his slouching position by the wall.

"That's a mite unkind, don't you think? After all 'e's done."

"It's business," said Deyning.

Hal and I exchanged glances.

"You have heard no doubt that the cook at the house is dead?"

"Thomas came down to tell me earlier. Everild sent him."

"What do you think about that?"

"I have no idea why anyone would wish to kill the woman. She was a servant."

"Where were you when she was killed?"

"What time have you decided that was, sir?"

"Dr Johannes thinks it was around the last hour of darkness or the first light morning hour."

"I was asleep in my bed and heard nothing. I arose at about dawn and came down here."

I looked around his workshop.

"Your wife will corroborate what you say, Deyning?"

"She will."

"She was awake when you left?"

"She arose with me," he said confidently.

"Then what happened?"

"Then, sir?"

"What happened after you rose?"

"I came to the workshop and drank my morning ale here. Everild will have gone to the kitchen to find something to drink, I expect, and to discuss the day's food with the cook. That was her usual routine."

"She did not notice that the cook was missing?"

Deyning shrugged. "Perhaps she didn't go to the kitchen after all."

"So, Master Deyning, you get to live in your old house again?"

"I can assure you, sir, that it was not of my making, this return to Deyning House."

Hal snuffled a laugh.

"Still, it's a mite convenient, i'n't it?" he said.

I smiled at Deyning.

"I noticed this morning after you left that there are some footprints by the wall directly under Agnew's window. It rained in the night. Someone will have muddy shoes."

Deyning's face creased in puzzlement. He folded his arms across his chest.

"What would anyone be doing under the window?"

"You have not heard that the cook was found in Agnew's bed?"

His arms dropped. "No, no, I didn't know that."

"The footprints may be those of the murderer. They may have gained access to the room by climbing up the wall. Hal here has tried it. It's quite easy."

"Fer a fit man, a man none too large. A man who's nimble, sir," said Hal stroking the twin peaks of his long grey beard, worn in imitation of his Viking ancestors.

"Climbed the wall… into the window? That's ridiculous."

"It *can* be done, sir," finished Hal.

"The person will have been very bloodied, for the woman's throat was cut. We shall be looking for some bloodstained clothing."

Deyning grimaced.

"Then you'll find none of mine nor my wife's."

"What was your wife, Mistress Deyning, doing out by the window after the rain?"

Richard Deyning took in a quick breath.

"I believe the footprints to be hers."

"She lives there. She may walk around her house any time she likes."

"Of course, there may be a perfectly good explanation," said Hal with a slight edge to his voice.

Deyning scowled. "You'll have to ask her."

"We shall."

I walked to the door.

"So, Master Deyning, you won't be leaving Marlborough any time soon, will you?"

"No, my Lord Belvoir. I'm here and here I shall stay. I have business in other towns and in London now and again, but Marlborough will remain my home. I am not leaving."

"Good. See that you don't."

"The more I know 'im, the less I like 'im," said Hal as we left the workshop.

"They're well matched, I think," I answered, chuckling under my breath.

"'E's worried," said my old retainer.

I chuckled again. "It does no harm to let people stew a little, Hal."

"Like an ol' boiling fowl."

I looked down at the belt strap end which had been

clutched in my hand all this while.

I looked again.

"Hal, look at this and tell me what you see."

Hal took the piece of metal from me and turned it to the light.

"It's not fallen off."

"No."

"No, it 'asn't," he said. "There's a bit o' the leather still crimped in it."

He looked up at me with a serious face.

"It's bin cut off!"

Chapter Seven

WE STOOD LOOKING DOWN at the belt end in Hal's palm.

"What's that all about then?"

"Someone wants to make us think Deyning was in my room?"

"But 'oo put it there?"

"I presume the person who killed Pitchcott."

"That Corlis Glover came to see you, didn't she? She was pretty adamant about ol' Pitchcott not getting in their way. She's bin in yer office."

I had forgotten that Farnell's beloved had come up to the castle to see me just after the murder of the merchant and after the body had been taken away. She had been there such a short time, it barely registered in my memory.

She had come to see me, she'd said, because she was worried that I'd thought badly of Farnell and that she didn't want me to think that he had killed his uncle.

"And why would I think that?" I'd asked.

"Because, my lord, he can be a little fiery and his temper sometimes gets the better of him. I tell you this now, in case you hear of it from someone else and think him the culprit."

"Why? What has he done that might make me think he is not in control of his temper? Has he threatened his uncle?"

Corlis had run her hand along the edge of my table and looked coyly at me under her long eyelashes.

"He did threaten once to kill him, yes, sir. But it was just words, my lord, just words. It was only I who heard him and, of course, Master Pitchcott. Oh, and the two men who work for Farnell."

"You believe he couldn't carry those words through to deeds?"

"Oh no, sir. He couldn't do that."

"Most men can be goaded into a foul deed if pricked often and deep enough," said Hal. "You say that his uncle was foul to 'im and you too?"

"He was, sir, but Farnell wanted to make his way without the help of his uncle, and so his good opinion meant nothing really. His uncle's words were just that... foul words, and words cannot kill you. They traded insults and that was that."

There was more of the same and the girl had left.

"And yet Master Pitchcott made a will in his favour?" I said to Hal.

"An' I di'n't see Farnell Armer turnin' down the money when it was offered."

"He was positively agog to learn how much it was," I said.

"Hmm. So much for him makin' his own way, as the girl said, sir."

"Does anything strike you as odd, Ol' Hal?"

"Odd, sir?"

"Well, if Corlis Glover was trying to remove suspicion from her lover Farnell, why didn't she try to blacken the name of Master Deyning?

"You mean if she planted the belt end?"

"Exactly. She could at least have said, 'one person you

SUSANNA M. NEWSTEAD

need to consider is Deyning.'"

"Oh, sir, don't ask me about the odd ways of women. They'm very strange animals, I think, an' that's why I in't never bin married, see."

I laughed out loud.

"Let us go down to see Master Farnell Armer. It's time we spoke to him about the death of Margery Cook."

Farnell Armer was standing outside his forge in the bright sunshine. He bowed low to a man seated on a roan horse and as he rose from the bow he saw us approach.

"I will deliver it Monday, sir. It shall all be as you request," he was saying.

The man rode away.

"Do we recognise him, Hal?" I said from the corner of my mouth as Farnell planted his feet wide and waited for us.

"Aye. Don't we think it's that Lord of Burderop... oh, I forget his name."

"That's the man. Good day, Master Armer! We hate to come upon you at such a busy time, but we'd like to ask some questions, if we may."

Farnell Armer nodded. "I am finished with my task. Please come in, m'lord."

"That was Sir Robert Courcells of Burderop, wasn't it?"

"Aye, sir, it was. He has commissioned many items from me."

"He yer patron then, Armer?" asked Hal.

Armer did not answer.

We entered the dark of the workroom.

"It's Saturday, sir, so my men are out delivering items. We shall not be disturbed."

"You will have heard by now that there has been another

murder at the house of Aldous Pitchcott?"

"Aye, that I have. The whole town knows it now."

"The cook, Margery. Did you know her Master Armer?"

Armer scoffed. "Why might I know her, sir?"

"She was not the cook when you lived with your guardian?"

"It was not my station in life to spend time with cooks, sir. Then or now."

"Young boys are often good friends with the cooks. I know I was very good friends with the cook at Durley when I was a lad. I was always hungry… and he often had a small something for me, day or night."

Farnell nervously cleared his throat.

"So she was found with her head almost cut from her body in the bed of Master Agnew, who swears that she wasn't there when he left his bed this morning," I added.

"In ol' Agnew's bed? Well, there's a thing!" said Farnell, smirking. "Secretive old Agnew, eh?"

"Where were you at midnight last night, Master Armer?"

"Me? You can't think I had any reason to kill the cook?"

"I do not know why anyone would want to kill her. Answer my question."

Farnell sighed. "I work very hard, my Lord Belvoir. The work I do is tiring. It's very forceful, requiring energy. I need my sleep, so I retire early after supper. I take advantage of the daylight hours. Working at what I do by lamp or candle is nigh impossible. I was asleep in bed at home."

"Alone?"

"Alone. I do not have the energy for… anything but sleep, sir."

"Oh, dear. That doesn't bode well fer yer intended, then does it, lad?" said Hal with a scornful look in his eye. "After yer married, I mean."

"It takes someone with quite a bit of power to cut a

throat, doesn't it, Hal?"

"Oh, aye, it does."

"I didn't kill her. Why would I?"

"We also wonder how the murderer entered the house. We think he could have scaled the wall close to Master Agnew's room."

Farnell's face took on an incredulous expression.

"Scaled the wall...?"

"And passed through the window."

"That's just impossible."

"It is just possible, for the window isn't too far up the wall, and a strong man might heave himself up..."

"Especially if 'e 'ad 'elp, lad," added Hal.

"Help? What help?"

"Mistress Corlis is determined that you and she will be married, Farnell. She told us as much. The two of you could have easily determined to kill Master Pitchcott..."

"Fer 'is money..." continued Hal.

"*My* money," said Farnell immediately stern-faced. "Pitchcott stole what was rightfully mine."

"Well, now you have recovered it."

Farnell Armer did not answer but squirmed as Hal added, "You needed the money which yer uncle refused you whilst he lived. Now 'e's dead, you got it."

"Why did Pitchcott leave you the money, Farnell? It was said that he detested you and you him. Why would it come to you?"

Farnell turned his back on me and fiddled with some things on his bench.

"I have no idea."

"But I think you do, and I think that I will soon know it too."

There was a cry from outside the shed.

"Excuse me, my lord," said Armer, and he pushed

open the door.

Mistress Spynner came hurtling over the courtyard, her head rail awry, her long grey plait worked free from its netting, bouncing on her back, her dress streaming out behind her.

"Master Armer... oh, Master Armer, you must help me."

I held Hal back and we stood in the darkness of the workroom, looking out into the brightness of the day.

"What is it, madam?"

"It's Gerald, he's done it again, Master Armer."

"Mistress Spynner... it's..."

"He'll fall to his death!"

"I told you last time that he wouldn't fall to his death. He got up there. He can get down."

"Nooo!" Her anguish was palpable.

Hal and I looked at each other in perplexity.

"Please, can you get him again? Please!"

Armer walked the Widow Spynner further away from the workshop door and the conversation was lost to us. We watched as they rounded the corner to the back of the house owned by the widow, and, curious, we followed at a distance.

In the space at the back was a large chestnut tree. Strange mewlings and screechings were coming from high in the branches.

"Well, I'll be... it's a cat," said Hal.

"Gerald, I expect," I chuckled.

We watched as Master Armer divested himself of his apron and jerkin and leapt up to the lowest branches of the tree. He lifted himself and hooked his leg over the first layer of foliage.

The muscles on his upper arms flexed as he stretched up and grabbed the next branch. Before long, Armer was two-thirds of the way up the tall tree, it took him no time at all.

Hal and I looked at each other.

"He's done that before, Hal," I said.

"Quite the little squirrel, i'n't 'e?"

The cat came bounding down of his own accord, past Farnell Armer and into the arms of a smiling Mistress Spynner.

Armer swore long and hard.

"Master Armer!" cried the widow in distress. "Please!"

Hal chuckled.

The next morning, the blackbird was loudly throwing out his last effort at song before he became silent until the next spring. We wandered at a slow pace, through the forest towards the town, listening to him and the noise of my riding and walking foresters as they called to each other at their work in the deeper trees.

Hal turned in his saddle.

"So what do we do today, m'lord? Will you 'ave that young Armer in and question 'im?"

"No, Hal, I think today we shall ask about the town and see if anyone else disliked our Master Pitchcott enough to kill him and try to see if the death of Margery the cook has any bearing upon their story at all."

We rode up to the house of the town reeve, Nicholas Barbflet. I thought we'd start with his knowledge.

The maid, Alysoun, let us in, and we were ushered up the passageway to Nick's office, a small room at the back of the building.

"Ah, this saves me a message out to Savernake!" said Nick, rising as we entered the room.

He slapped Hal on the back. "Mornin' Hal."

"Mornin' Nick."

"It's been an eventful night."

"It has?"

"I've slept only three hours this early morning." Nick threw some documents he had been working on into a chest, locked it, then yawned, rubbed his stubbly face, and stretched.

"Come… I'll tell you as we walk."

We travelled out through the back of the house onto which Nick had built a kitchen a couple of years ago.

Out of the kitchen door, we turned up through the alleyway known as Crook's Yard onto the High Street.

"There's been a fire in the town."

"No!"

"None hurt, Heaven be praised," said Nick. "At least none badly hurt."

"Who *was* hurt?"

"Master Armer. The fire was in his forge."

"At the back of The Green Man?"

"Aye. You know he's taken some of the old buildings there to work from, then?"

"Aye, I've been there. Hal and I were there just yesterday," I said, worry colouring my voice.

"We managed to put the fire out. No other buildings were damaged save a small outhouse of Mistress Spynner's."

"Her brewhouse backs onto the shed, does it not?"

"Aye. We were lucky the weather was so still, with no breeze. If the fire had been fanned, we might have found, with the sunrise, half the town gone this morning."

"Indeed."

"'Ow did this fire start then?" asked Hal.

"Well, we can't be sure. Perhaps a stray spark from the forge. Maybe it wasn't smothered properly. Master Armer got out, but he's had a nasty clout on the head - falling beam, I suspect - so he can't say much at the moment, but we'll know more when he comes round again."

"Again?"

"Like I say, he got out, head pouring blood, but swooned as soon as his legs carried him to safety."

"Where is he?"

"With Johannes."

I nodded.

We passed between the wall of the drinking house, The Green Man, and the house of Master Baldwin Caspar, a merchant and walked down the lane towards the outbuildings.

The smell of smoke hit us as we were several yards down the alley.

"The building is a wreck," said Nick. "Armer was lucky to get out."

I frowned.

"Did he speak to you at all?"

"No. I was fetched when the flames were seen, but he'd collapsed before he could say anything to *me*."

"Who raised the alarm?"

"A couple of the lads coming out the back of the drink hall to the privy. They saw the flames."

"What time was this?"

"I was called just before midnight. The priory church bell had just rung as I got to the fire. By rights, the lads should have been home at that hour, but I sent them off with a flea in their ear and a warning to Master Green, the brewer."

"What was Farnell Armer doing in 'is forge at midnight?" asked Hal.

"He told us he retired fairly early as he needed to sleep. His job is a tough one," I said.

"'E doesn't work late and rises early with the light, 'e said," added Hal.

"Well, he was there as I saw him come picking his way across the roof. Oh, he was staggering a deal and we had to help him down, but he nimbly managed to get himself over the burning timbers and tiles."

Hal and I exchanged a glance.

"Then he collapsed into Pearson's arms - *he* lives just there," and he pointed to a small cottage at right angles to the lane.

"We got him up to Johannes and knocked him up."

"Hmm. I shall speak to him later. Can we go into the building?"

"There's little left of it now. It was merely a shell anyway. A few re-used beams, some old tiles, a cladding of half timbers sawn with the bark still on it. If it's cooled down, you can look, though what there'll be to find, I don't know."

"We'll look. Thanks, Nick." My eye searched the immediate area of The Green Man's yard.

"Will you be in your office later? I have some questions for you."

"Aye, I'll be there all morning and then at the mill." With a wave of his hand, he turned and was off about his business.

We picked our way across the ground. A few possessions had been salvaged from the forge.

When we first entered the building, the machine Hal had seen was sitting forlornly in the yard, its timbers charred and one arm of the structure broken.

None of the metal parts had been brought out. I suppose they thought it would not melt or be damaged too badly by the flames and left them where they lay.

One door to the forge was open. Some poor-quality floor

tiles, which had been laid just inside the building, were cracked and blackened. Most beams had fallen in. It was a mess of interlaced sooty timbers and rafters, with slides of tiles here and there. Several upright roughly sawn logs that made up the outside were completely gone. It looked like a smiling mouth where several teeth were missing. Water dripped from here and there.

"'Is workbench is gone," said Hal.

"And the other smaller sawhorses and the like," I said. "It will cost him a pile of pennies to set up again."

"Well, he's got a pile o' pennies now, i'n't 'e?"

I strode into the ashy interior.

"Ouch!"

"Careful!" shouted Hal. "God knows what there'll be underfoot. Caltrops I 'spect."

The sole of my boot had trodden upon something in the ashes, something uncomfortable. I felt it through the leather.

Looking over to the furthest wall where Hal had seen the strange contraption, I said, "There's where the two barrels were... only one is left."

"It's the sand one," said Hal, peering at it. "Well, 'alf of it at any rate."

I looked round the shell of the building and coughed at the stink of burning.

"Can we maybe find where the fire started?"

"Well... 'ere's the fire. This is the furnace where the metal was melted."

"There's still the iron pouring thing... whatever it's called. Like a spoon. They must pour metal into a mould?"

"What for?"

"I don't know, Hal. The metalworker's art is beyond me. Hubert will know." Hubert Alder was my farrier and blacksmith.

"Was the fire not damped down properly, as Nick said? Did it flare up and catch the beams?"

Hal peered into the furnace set away from the back wall. "It's cold."

"Cold? It should still be warm, surely."

"It's Sunday. He won't 'ave bin workin' today. Or yesterday afternoon."

"We must ask him. But I would have thought the heat of the flames would still be in the building."

"There's turves here for dampin' down a fire. They've escaped intact, all right."

I pulled open the second door of the forge. It disintegrated in my hand and the whole planked edifice fell out into the yard setting up a mixture of dust and ash. I coughed again.

Well, at least we had more light now.

"Candle end here," said Hal.

"There's a lamp hanging from that beam, one of those that's still connected to the wall. No flame from there."

Hal was sniffing.

"What's that smell?"

"Burning, Hal," I chuckled.

"No, another smell like... like... ahh."

He picked his way over the debris on the floor.

Scuffing the beaten earth and its covering with his boot sole, he found the remains of the corselet of links we'd seen Armer making a few short days ago.

Links were scattered all over the place.

Hal located the emanating smell.

"It's oil."

"For the lamps?"

"No, they're tallow candle lamps."

Hal prodded with the toe of his boot.

"Oil... like we had in the church at Durley when

the priest's room burnt with all the parchments in the church chest."

I put my hands on my knees and bent double.

"Here… and here."

"And 'ere and 'ere."

I looked up. "And here."

Hal was looking at what was left of the work table. "'Ere too," he called. "It's been sploshed around, I think."

"Well, well, Hal. I think we have ourselves a case of arson," I said.

We exited the building to make our way back to Nick's office. Halfway up the High Street, I stopped.

"What?" said Hal.

"It's a fire… not a murder. Why did Nick think he needed to send for me?"

"You mean he said that he would send a message to Durley?"

"Just that, Hal."

I made an about turn, and we travelled back up the High Street to slip into the cool of the alleyway beside Johannes' house. First, I needed to speak to Armer, if I could.

As we entered the backyard, Little Agnes, Johannes' housekeeper, looked up quickly and a broad smile lifted her apple cheeks. She nodded and bobbed a curtsey, standing the broom she had been using up against the stable wall.

"Agnes, is Johannes in?"

She nodded.

Agnes was a mute dwarf.

She made a rocking motion with her arms.

"Somethin' about a baby?" said Hal.

Agnes assented and then made a mute show of coughing

and spluttering.

"A poorly baby with a cough?"

"Well, we shall wait for him to finish. Agnes, is Master Farnell Armer here?"

She nodded and then grasped hold of her head and grimaced. She pointed into the kitchen.

Hal and I passed through the door.

Armer was sitting on a stool, his head in his hands, his elbows on his knees.

"Don't get up," I said as I saw him try to rise.

He slowly raised his head further.

"My Lord Belvoir."

"I am sorry you are hurt, Master Armer. Perhaps you might tell me what happened?"

Armer's head was bandaged, and I looked at the back of it. Blood was seeping into the cloth from the wound on his crown. I perched on the edge of Johannes' table.

"Oh, it hurts like the devil," Armer said as he grimaced.

"Tsooo," said Hal looking round at the wound. "'As Johannes had to stitch it? You might need it stitchin'."

"I'm not a piece of linen, Master Hal," said Farnell, raising himself. "I'll do fine, thank you."

"So what happened?"

Farnell Armer leaned his back against the kitchen wall and closed his eyes.

"I was asleep in my bed."

"At Mistress Spynner's?"

"I sleep at the front of the house on the ground floor in the main room."

"This was before midnight, I take it?"

"They tell me it was because they heard the priory bell tolling."

"They?"

"The lads who also noticed the fire."

"Ah, yes."

"And one or two others who live close by who came to help. I heard the noise. I sleep quite lightly."

"They were shouting? Raising people to fight the fire?"

"No, I heard the noise of the fire first and the falling beams and tiles."

"Ah, so you were the *first* to get to the shed?"

"Aye, I think I was."

"And then these two lads arrived?"

"They were afraid it would spread to the thatches of the businesses further down the alley and to the houses across, so they raised the alarm."

"The fullers and tanners, yes. Go on."

"I ran into the building just before they arrived."

"Whyever would you do that, lad?" asked Hal incredulously. "Did you *want* to be roasted?"

"I have some... some things in there... had some things which I had been working on, and I couldn't bear to see all my hard work go up in smoke."

"We saw your wooden thing in the courtyard."

"Yes, I managed to get it out, but it wasn't whole." His voice was sad and angry at the same time.

I went back in to see what else I might salvage and - wallop. Something hit me on the head."

He moved his hand to the back of his skull but didn't make contact.

"The next I knew, some lad was trying to drag me out and the whole roof came down."

I looked at Hal. This wasn't the story we'd had from Nick.

"The lad had to get back out of the door, or he'd have been skewered with burning timber. I tried to get out the same way, but it was impossible."

"How *did* you get out?"

"I had a ladder at the side of the forge. I managed to get

it up to a hole in the roof and went up it. Then I crossed the tiles which were left and jumped into the arms of Pearson, the castle man."

"The building continued to burn until they all managed to get it under control," I said.

"It's a mess now. I think you'll be needing somewhere else to work from, lad," said Hal.

"You didn't see anyone in the building?"

Armer looked up at me intently then.

"Anyone…?"

"The first time you went in…anyone? Was there anyone there? Did you feel perhaps you weren't alone?"

"No… no… I…"

"You say something hit you on the back of the head? Where were you standing when this happened?"

"Standing, m'lord?"

"Yes, I am trying to work out what might have hit you."

"One of the beams, I expect."

"If one o' those beams hit yer, lad," said Hal. "There would'a bin no point in draggin' yer out!"

"They're hefty things, Armer."

"A glancing blow then," he replied.

"Or a good thwack from a piece of timber."

"That's a good guess, Aumary," said Johannes, entering through the passage door.

"I found slivers of bark in the wound and caught in his hair."

"Bark?"

"I suspect he's been hit with a log. A log that was laid by to feed the furnace in the forge."

Armer's expression was horrified. He sat on the stool, looking up at the doctor with an open mouth.

Then he said, "Someone hit me?"

"That's right, young man."

"But why?"

"You annoyed anyone recently, Armer?" asked Hal, training his beady eye on the man's face.

"Er... annoyed no... how... what... how might I annoy anyone?"

"Someone's out to get you."

"No. No. That's simply not true."

"We found traces of oil spread about the forge, Armer. We think someone wanted to destroy your work, maybe even destroy you."

"But why?"

"What might you know about the death of Margery Cook?"

"I told you, sir, I don't even know her. She didn't work for Pitchcott when I was young. Besides, I wasn't even in that house when Pitchcott moved here. I had moved out long before."

"You saw nothing... nothing the night of her murder, which might help us?"

"No."

"Johannes, what did you learn at the kitchen in St Martin's?"

"That Pitchcott's dinner was nothing more than some bread, cheese and sallet. The poisonous leaves, no doubt, were in that. Margery denied all knowledge of it. However, it would have been easy to add the leaves at any stage. The kitchen is not always watched, and there's a deal of coming and going."

"Was Margery killed because of her involvement in the poisoning, do you think?"

"I would be very surprised," answered my friend.

"I hear she has been a loyal servant for many years," I added. "Did she see who put the leaves in the dinner and had to be silenced?"

"Who was in the courtyard when you came to, Farnell?" asked Johannes, looking at me.

I nodded. "Yes, who was quick on the scene?"

"The two lads who were in the drinking den. I don't know them well. Then, the ale master…"

"Master Green?"

"Yes, him. Then lots of other people. Mistress Spynner came out in her shift and shawl."

"And other folk?"

"Folk who lived thereabouts. Master Nick came. The farrier from the corner."

"Simon Smith?"

"Aye, him."

Hal looked up quickly. "Might he want to destroy a competitor's business premises?"

"No, not Simon. Besides, he's a farrier, not a blacksmith," I replied. "Certainly not an arms smith."

"A couple of the tanners who sleep near the yard. They came up to help."

"Hmm. Tell me, Farnell, did you see Master Deyning at all?"

"No, sir. Why would he be there? He lives at completely the other end of town."

"Hmmm. I just wondered."

"It's about the money, i'n't it?" said Hal, folding his arms across his chest. "Or the death of Master Pitchcott."

"Did you know anything about the death of Master Pitchcott, Armer?" asked Johannes.

"No, sir, nothing."

"Well, we'll let you recover. Best you get home to rest, I expect, eh, Johannes?" I said.

"Yes, indeed."

"But I can't rest. I have to deliver my hauberk tomorrow and my men will be coming into work too. I have work for them to complete. Somehow I must try to recover what's in the forge and..."

"Not today, you don't," said Johannes. "That's a very nasty wound. Men with less thick skulls have died of wounds less grave than that."

"I can't rest."

"Get your men to help you move stuff out. I'm sure a couple of the young men at Angel Yard will help you, too, if you ask."

"Where do I take it all, sir?" asked Farnell, his voice breaking with the strain.

"Master Pitchcott had a workshop and warehouse up at St Martin's. Your fellow forgeman Simon Smith has a cart. Get them up there. I'm sure your cousin will oblige you by giving you some space until you find a place where you can go."

"Everild?"

"Why not?"

Farnell looked at the floor.

"Aye, sir." He licked his lips. "It's a thought."

"And I have a mind to pay your forge one more visit just for completeness before you move anything, Farnell."

Suddenly there was a whoosh as the kitchen door opened.

Corlis Glover staggered into the room.

"Oh, Farnell!" she cried, out of breath. "Oh, Farnell! I heard... I thought you were dead!"

And she went down quickly before him and cried onto his knees.

Hal and I left the doctor and Corlis Glover ministering to Farnell Armer and returned to the forge on Angel Lane.

I passed into the interior of the building and looked at the floor.

"Where was I walking, Hal, when I cried out that I'd trodden on something, something which made me jump up?"

"There, sir," he moved forward. "Just here."

I bent to scrutinise the ashy debris and reached out to the floor; straightening, I held out my forefinger and thumb.

"This is the culprit, Hal."

Hal peered at my fingers.

"Well, I'll be…"

"Yes…" I said emphatically. There, between my finger and thumb, was a tiny metal ball, the sort of metal ball which had killed Master Aldous Pitchcott.

Chapter Eight

W<small>E SEARCHED AND FOUND</small> hundreds of tiny balls littering the floor, under the ashes and debris.

"What are they?" asked Hal, his fist full of them. He poured them with a clatter into a metal bowl he'd found by the main door.

"I have no idea, but we must ask Master Armer when he comes to tidy up."

Hal started to collect a few others.

"Hal, keep a few in your purse, will you?"

He rolled the balls between his palms to clean them and dropped them into the leather bag on his belt.

"Aw…" he said as he stared at his hands. "They're sooty."

I smiled. Hal was so fastidious about his clothes and his person.

"Now, back to Master Nick's."

We walked back up to the town reeve's house, smiling and nodding to a few people we knew.

"Nick, might you make me a list of the people with whom Aldous Pitchcott was at odds? It wouldn't be right just to consider his family when others may have wanted him dead for one reason or another."

Nick sat back in his chair. "You think one of *them* might be guilty?"

I shrugged. "Who knows? Until I speak to people, I won't know the depth of hatred folk might have had for him."

"As I said, he wasn't popular in town."

"So others may have wished him dead."

"How did you get on with Master Armer?"

"Ah... yes..." I said. "Why did you think to send for me, Nick, if you believed the fire was an accidental one?"

"Because I didn't."

Hal looked up at me suddenly.

"Why not?"

Nick sighed. "Anything to do with that family, and I am suspicious because of what's happened already. It may have been an accident, but when Johannes told me that the head wound sustained by Armer wasn't, in his opinion, accidental, I thought to send for you."

"Hal,... the little pellets?"

Hal took out the six little balls from his purse and held them in his palm.

Nick took hold of one and drew it up to his eye.

"What's this?"

"The same type of little ball which killed Pitchcott."

"Ah yes... but many of them."

"There were 'undreds of them on the floor of the forge," said Hal.

"Hundreds?" said Nick in surprise. "Then Master Armer must be spoken to again."

"Who else do we speak to?"

Nick crossed the room and took a piece of parchment from a chest.

"Here are three folk who crossed swords with Master Aldous Pitchcott that I know of. There may be others. I only know about this because they appealed to the town council to arbitrate." He tapped his pen into the ink and scribbled. He handed the note to me.

"But he was a councillor," said Hal in a tone which said, 'That's hardly fair.'

"It was naturally up to the *rest* of us. We heard the grievance, of course, but for lack of evidence, we could come down on neither one side nor the other."

"So it was left hanging?"

"It was."

I looked down at the parchment.

"It was still hanging in the air when Pitchcott was killed," added Nick.

"I see that Master Green, the ale master, was in dispute with our man Pitchcott."

"Indeed he was."

"Well, that is very interesting, isn't it?" I said. "What was that dispute about?"

"Ah... that was rather odd."

"Everything about this matter is odd, Nick," I said chuckling. "It doesn't surprise me at all."

"According to Master Pitchcott, Green and two of his neighbours had stolen a couple of yards of land on each side to extend their properties."

"But Green's property is a distance away from Pitchcott's," said Hal.

"The alehouse is, but Green has another house."

"Ah... don't tell me... on St Martin's."

"St Martin's, yes."

"In the time of Deyning Senior it was a certain shape and configuration. By the time Pitchcott came to it, it had... shall we say, changed... according to Master Pitchcott."

I frowned.

"Surely there were written deeds?"

"Oh yes, but looking at them, no one could actually

fathom what they meant on the ground; they were so old. Pitchcott claimed that Green, Fulbert Tanner and Eustace Grounder had stolen yards of land from him."

"Tell me, Nick, is it likely?"

Nicholas Barbflet laughed out loud.

"I wouldn't put much beyond Master Green, but the other two… nah… I doubt it. However, there's more. Best you get it from Green himself."

And so we did.

Apparently, the vintner had been trying to get the contract to supply the castle with wine. Evidently, he had large stocks in the port of Bristol and was angling for them to be bought by the castle butler when the king was in residence.

Eventually, after much negotiation, he convinced the royal victuallers to purchase his wine for the castle. However, he wasn't content with that and had tried to knock Master Green from atop the pedestal as 'ale master to the castle'.

Green had been one of the ale suppliers to the castle for years and no other had tried to compete with him or his fellow brewers. Naturally, more ale had to be found than Master Green or the brewers of the town could supply when the king was in residence, for the consumption rose tenfold, but no one tried to monopolise it until Pitchcott. We tackled the ale master.

"'You stick to wine, Master Pitchcott', I said," recounted Green when asked. "'And I'll stick to ale. Then we shall both be happy'. But no, my lord, he wouldn't have it and kept sniping, carping, and meddling."

"And to get back at you when the ale contract didn't come his way?"

"He accused me of land grabbing, sir."

"By which time you and he were sworn enemies,

I suppose?"

Green's eyes narrowed. "No, m'lord. I didn't count myself an enemy, but I'm damned glad he's gone. He was trouble in the town, that's for sure."

"And Eustace and Fulbert? How did they become involved?"

"They stuck up for me, for our lands all border each other as they've done since our grandfathers were mere twinkles in our ancestors' eyes. We know where one strip ends and another begins, and there's never been a cross word about it until Pitchcott was thwarted with his ale plans, sir."

"Hmm. Were you ever heard to threaten him, Green?"

Green swallowed. "Not in public, I don't think so... no."

"In private?"

"I might'a said I'd part his cods from his pizzle, sir, maybe once."

Hal guffawed. "'E sounded as if someone had already done it," he said under his breath.

"On your oath, Green, did you kill him?"

"No, sir. On my oath," and he placed his hand on his heart.

I then showed him the little metal balls we'd found at the forge and watched carefully for a reaction.

He was as surprised and incredulous as everyone else when we affirmed that this had killed the merchant.

"Oh, no, sir. I have never seen anything like that before."

"Your building is gone, Green, I'm sorry to say."

"Ah, well, sir. I didn't use it. I won't say the rent from Master Armer wasn't welcome but... it wasn't much of a place, was it? I expect I'll flatten it now and extend the alehouse."

And that was that.

"Nasty manipulative, vindictive sod... er... soul wa'n't

he, sir?" said Hal. "Old Pitchcott."

"Amongst other things, I think, Hal," I said.

We walked back to my office and to dinner at the castle.

I reached for a piece of parchment and started to scribble some notes with a piece of charcoal as I usually did when faced with information about many different people.

I broke off a piece of bread and chewed.

"I can't for the life of me see the connection beyond the obvious between the cook and Master Pitchcott, Hal."

"I'd 'ave that woman Deyning in 'ere m'lord. That man of 'ers won't crumple under questioning, but she might."

"I understand that Pitchcott must die for Everild to inherit, which would keep her husband happy. But why the cook? What did she do or know?"

"Perhaps she saw them under the window?"

"No, Hal. Pitchcott was dead by then."

"Ah, yeah." He scratched his beard.

"Maybe she knew that they'd killed 'im."

"How, Hal? She'd never been seen at the castle. Never went there and never had a need to go there."

"Heard them plotting, maybe?"

"They are a careful pair. Think how quiet they kept their marriage."

"So 'oo did need to come up 'ere then?"

"Deyning with his furs, perhaps. Armer with his wares. Agnew with Pitchcott as the merchant's secretary."

"And that girl Corlis... just the once we think."

"Ah, again, that was after the event, Hal."

"Hmm."

"Despite what's said, Master Green, who is supplying the castle with ale. 'E comes too." said Hal.

"Hmm. Him too."

"And no doubt, 'is employees."

"What can they possibly have against an ageing vintner?"

Hal shrugged.

"Well, I suppose you're right. Two people we need to speak to again: Mistress Deyning..."

"Without her 'usband."

"Yes, and Master Armer. But we shall leave him till tomorrow."

"I'll go and get her then, shall I?"

"Yes, Hal," I chuckled.

"'T'would be a pleasure, sir," he said with a nasty grin.

Mistress Deyning kept me waiting. It was an hour after the priory chapel had rung for sext before Hal brought her to my office in the castle.

She looked around the room with a haughty expression and sat on a stool in front of my table as I bade her.

"Mistress Deyning, I am sorry to put you to so much trouble." I crossed my fingers behind my back as I said this. It was, of course, a perfect lie. "I need some information from you."

"I can tell you no more, sir. I know no more than I did when I was last questioned."

She smoothed down the skirts of her blue-green bliaut. I noticed that her little blue shoes had been cleaned and that she now also wore pattens to walk the town roads.

"Firstly, what were you doing at the gable end of the house under the window of the man Agnew and the room of your father, which is a little higher up?"

The woman jumped as if I'd kicked her, but quickly recovered her poise.

"When was this, sir? I walk around the house often. I come from the brewhouse or the stables…"

"This was early the morning that Mistress Cook was found dead."

Everild Deyning's eyes quickly moved away from my own.

"I am not sure that I was there at all, my lord, that morning."

"Your footprints were found, and I noticed that your shoes, the same pair you wear today, madam, were muddied. You had been standing in wet soil."

"Perhaps I'd been in the garden plucking vegetables for the day's meals?"

"Mistress Deyning, you are trying to tell us that you do this sort of work yourself? I find that hard to believe. You have a kitchen servant and you had a cook to do those tasks for you, not to mention a steward and men-servants."

Her nostrils flared.

"I don't believe that you do any of those tasks yourself."

Her eyes came up to meet mine and they were hard and full of anger. It was a while before she said, "Oh, all right."

"That's better," said Hal, settling himself against the door to listen.

She turned and looked at him with a glare that said, 'Keep your place, you're nothing but a servant.'

He grinned disarmingly at her.

"I had gone out because I thought that Agnew was up to no good."

"In what way?"

"He was always sneaking about after dark. He often came in late when we'd all retired. He had his own key, but I wanted to know where he'd been. I repeatedly asked my father and he'd tell me that it was none of my business and, with a chuckle, he'd dismiss it as 'Agnew's own business'."

"He'd say he was about his own business."

"Everild's chin jutted, "Yes. When Aldous was... killed... I wanted to know what Agnew was doing, so I began spying on him."

I saw Hal shift his position and look at me.

"I was under the window very early that morning, as you say."

"Doin' what?" asked Hal.

She didn't answer him.

"Were you alone?" I asked.

She gave me a perplexed look, "Alone, my lord?"

"Your husband was not with you? You didn't help him to climb up to the window of Agnew's room and...?"

She stood up suddenly, and Hal stepped forward.

"NO!"

I nodded to Hal. He subsided.

"Your husband didn't climb into the room?"

"He had left for work by then," she answered, breathing quickly.

She seated herself again and continued. "I heard Agnew with a woman and thought it sounded like Margery, the cook."

"Ahhh..." said Hal quietly behind her.

"And could you hear what was being said?"

"Quiet voices only."

"Did this assuage your thirst for knowledge? You wanted, did you not, to ascertain if Agnew and some woman were carrying on an affair under your roof?"

She nodded. "I really didn't think it would be Margery. I thought maybe a woman of the town. I was shocked when I learned it was her."

"So you stood in the flowerbed and listened? What could you hear?"

"Nothing further, so I left. I had what I'd come for."

Hal looked straight at me as if to ask, 'You believe her?'

"Have you any reason to think that Margery knew anything about your father's death, madam?"

She shook her head, a little chastened now and not quite so belligerent.

"No, my lord, I can think of nothing. She was merely a cook. I gave her the day's instruction; she would go out with the kitchen maid, buy food at the market and in the shops, and return to cook. At night after supper, she would bed down in the kitchen... though obviously..."

"She wasn't there all night, every night, for she was also in Master Agnew's bed."

"Yes, so it transpires, the loose hussy," she said. "I cannot understand what possessed her to take that oily little spot for a lover. He's abominable."

"Companionship in a hard and lonely life, perhaps, madam?" I said. "One of drudgery and thanklessness."

Everild sniffed. "She might have chosen better. Agnew is revolting."

"She didn't think so. And he was fond of her."

"Fond? He cannot be fond of anyone."

"'E's fond a' you," said Hal, pushing off the door once more. "He sticks up for you, you know."

"I'm sure I don't know why."

"You haven't shown him any particular favour?"

"Certainly not. The only person to do that was Aldous."

"Did you know, madam, that your father's money would be divided between you and Farnell?"

"I knew, yes. It was discussed. We both knew... we told you..."

"You have no problem with that?"

"Why should I? According to Farnell, and I have no reason to disbelieve him, much of the money is his anyway."

"You believe it is true that Pitchcott stole his nephew's

inheritance?"

"It was like him. Yes. I told you, sir, he was not a pleasant man."

"And your husband, what does he think?"

Her head shot up, and her eyes flared, "Richard has nothing to do with any of this."

"I think I must beg to differ, madam. The house is now his, his old family home. The fortune his father lost is now his, through you. It is very much to do with him."

"'E's got a good reason to want the ol' man dead," said Hal behind her back.

"We did not kill Aldous."

"No? Then someone else managed that."

"And we must be eternally grateful to them, sir," said Everild Deyning, clenching her teeth in a savage stare.

"Of course, there may be another way?"

"Oh?"

"That you paid someone to do it for you."

Once again, she leapt up and shouted, "NO!"

I heard Hal chuckle, almost under his breath.

"It's possible. You are wealthy. Deyning has the money, despite his pleading poverty. You might have engaged the services of a soldier or an assassin."

"NO!" Everild Deyning was red in the face. "That, sir, is a lie."

"Perhaps it will be for a jury to decide."

The woman stood there, breathing hard and staring at me.

"I think I've a mind to arrest you, madam. I think the rest will follow once that has happened."

"You have no right to arrest me. I am innocent."

I stared at her for a while then I stood.

"But I will let you go home, Mistress Deyning. Think carefully on everything I've said. I will call on you again and ask you further about the deaths of your father and Margery Cook…"

"And my answers will be the same. I do not know anything."

"Thank you, Hal. Let her go home."

I turned my back on her and fiddled with some parchments on the pot board behind me.

She stood fuming for a moment, breathing angrily through her nose, and then I heard Hal open the door. There was a rustle of skirts, and they were both gone. However, craning my neck, I watched them from the window.

Hal accompanied her to the end of the castle drawbridge, one hand on her elbow. She indignantly shook him off and stalked down the High Street on her own, the hem of her skirt and her pattens stirring up the dust of the roadway.

"What now, sir?" asked Hal when he returned.

"Back to Agnew. Get him, too, will you, Hal, please?"

Hal sighed. "Right you are, sir."

The door banged as he left. I chuckled.

When he'd gone, I scribbled a little of the conversations I'd had with Farnell and Mistress Deyning on my parchment, locked my room and made the short journey across the gateway to the guard room where my friend Sir Andrew Merriman was polishing his sword.

"No one to do it for you today, Andrew?" I asked.

"Ah, Aumary. No. Young Peter is sick."

"Oh, that's bad."

Peter was one of the young lads who hung around the castle and did various jobs for those who couldn't afford a servant. Recently he had become Andrew's special servant, almost a squire, although he was not from a noble family.

"What can I do for you?"

"What's the gossip about Agnew... Pitchcott's servant? Anything?"

Andrew laid down his sword.

"Gossip? Well, let me see."

He ran his hand over his face.

"Nothing terrible that I know about. He's somewhat disliked because of his association with that objectionable vintner. He was devoted to him, it seems."

"He was seen quite often here at the castle?"

"Yes, when his master got the contract to supply wine, he was here often."

"Hmm. Apparently, he goes out at night. Where does he go?"

"Ah... then you want to know about his extra little jobs?"

"What extra little jobs?"

"You know he plays the flute?"

"I do. He told me so himself," I said.

"He's in demand for parties and feasts, weddings and wakes. That sort of thing. I've heard him play; he's very good."

"Oh, so that's where he goes at night."

"I imagine so."

"I know he teaches when he can."

"Yes, some young folk in the town."

"And Aldous Pitchcott allowed this?"

"Did he know?"

"I think he did."

"Ah, well then... yes, he allowed it. I've never heard anything evil against him."

"Thanks, Andrew."

"And have you heard anything amiss about Richard Deyning?"

"The furrier? No nothing. Why?"

"You know he's married Pitchcott's daughter, Everild?"

"No! I didn't. That bit of gossip hasn't reached me yet. That was quick on the merchant's death."

"Before, actually," I said.

Andrew looked puzzled. "Deyning used to own…"

"Yes, I know."

"Well, that's convenient."

"And do you know ought about Farnell, the other person in this puzzle?"

"Only that he's an armourer. He's been here once or twice. I hear we don't have a use for him at present, but you never know. It would be up to the king's procurer. He would say yay or nay to Armer's work."

"Hmm. Armer knows his way around the castle?"

"Oh yes, parts of it he does."

"Thank you, Andrew."

"What is this about? Are you any nearer finding out who killed the old toad?"

"I have some ideas… but they need… refining."

Andrew laughed. "Writing it all down, are you?"

He always laughed at me and my scribblings, for he could hardly read himself. Being the younger son of an impoverished knight, he had little learning.

I heard Hal returning.

"I'll let you know what I think later."

"Master Agnew, please be seated."

Agnew wrung his hands. "My Lord Belvoir. I am sorry I can't help you further with this…"

"Oh, but I think you can, Robert," I said, being over-friendly and using his given name.

I perched on the edge of my table once more and looked

down at him.

"I have heard something which I can't quite understand."

"Oh? And you think, m'lord, I can help? Well, I doubt I'm in a position to..."

"The morning that Margery Cook was found..."

"A sad, sad and horrible day, sir. I am still shaking from the... reeling with the shock, I am."

"You say that the woman didn't come to your room the night before."

"I think that's what I recall, sir. Yes."

"Then can you explain to me how very early, before dawn, Robert, and so in the semi-dark, you were heard in your bedroom, speaking to Margery? And she was answering you."

There was silence, and Agnew's face changed. Gone was the simpering, mild-mannered man of business. His face momentarily took on a hard and angry look.

"No."

"I'm afraid you were heard. Why did you lie?"

Back was the Agnew of old. "Oh, sir... sir... what would you have thought of me? I was trying to protect Margery from..."

Hal smirked into his grey beard. "She was dead, Agnew. You weren't protecting 'er from anything," he said.

"No, it's true, isn't it? True. It was me I was protecting, wasn't it?"

"You told me that she wasn't with you at all that night," I said.

"Yes, sir, I did."

"What happened?"

"I was out, sir. Out all night."

"At your flute playing."

"You know about that?"

"I do."

"Then I can tell you I was out at one of my paid engagements. You know then that I play about the town and environs, and am sought after for..."

"Marriages and wakes, yes, I've heard," I said.

"I played, and then because there was such good food and wine, I stayed and... I'm afraid I had too much, and I slept on the floor of the hall till just before dawn when I came home to find Margery in my bed asleep."

"What happened then?"

"I told her to go back to the kitchen and went to the office."

"Then?" asked Hal.

"She didn't appear, and so I went up again to my room. I thought to chivvy her along for someone might realise she'd been there. I thought she'd fallen asleep again. Only she wasn't asleep. She was dead."

"Why was she in your room that night?"

"I can only think she'd been waiting for me. I must have forgotten to tell her I would be out till late," said Agnew. He began to wring his hands again and lick his lips.

"I was walking about the hall wondering what to do when you arrived, sir."

"You found her dead?"

"Just after dawn, m'lord." He looked up with tears in his eyes. "I am so sorry I lied to you, sir. I didn't know what to do or think. I was so frightened and upset."

"There was no one about?"

"No, sir. Then the Mistress Deyning..."

"Yes. She came in."

I lifted off from my desk and went to the window.

"You have been missing from the house a few evenings, haven't you?"

"I have. I play many times for people for their celebrations," said Agnew.

"Are you alone, or do you have more musicians with you?"

"Mostly alone, yes," he answered. "Sir, who was it who heard me that morning?"

I turned back to him and was almost not going to tell him.

Then, "Mistress Deyning. She was under your window," I said.

"Oh, oh, no! Oh, how horrid! No! That's awful! Oh no, not Everild!"

"She has been wondering where you go for some time, I think, for, of course, she has been slipping out herself to meet with Deyning at night. Before they were married, and her father was killed."

"Oh no, sir. She wouldn't do that; she is a good woman. A woman of morals."

"I wouldn't stake your flute on it, Master Agnew."

Agnew looked crestfallen.

"In fact, I'm really surprised that you haven't come across each other at night wandering up and down."

Agnew shook his head. "Oh no, no, no."

"So let's have it. Where was this place where the food was so plentiful, the wine so good, and the hospitality so excellent that you didn't come home till dawn?"

"It was Master Chapman's, sir. The mercer at the end of the High."

"Ah... what was it?"

"Celebration of the birth of his son."

"Anthony and his wife, Hilda? You realise I will check?"

"Oh yes, sir, of course you will. I'm sure."

"So let's go back to the night your master was killed, Master Agnew. Where were you then?"

"I cannot..."

"You told me you were in your bed."

"Ah yes… I was playing at the Hall of Master Chasier."

"Margaret's father?"

"Yes. She was handfasted to…"

"Xavier Fuller."

"Yes, sir. I see you know them."

"I do, and again I'll check, Agnew."

His head fell. "Yessir. I'm sorry I lied, sir. It was a foolish thing to do. I should have known you would see through me. I am a foolish man, and you, sir, are a clever and observant one."

"You are still convinced that Deyning is the culprit?"

"Who else, m'lord?"

"If it's Deyning, then it's also your mistress, for I do not think that Deyning would act alone."

"Oh no, sir… it's not Everild. She is a sweet woman. No, no. It isn't her."

Hal shifted his feet. I could see that Agnew's obsequiousness made him uncomfortable.

"You are very fond of Everild, aren't you, Robert?"

The man looked up, his eyes guarded.

"It's not what you think."

"Oh, what might I think?"

"I love her, yes, but as a father might a daughter. That's all."

"I see. You have known her all her life, haven't you?"

"I see you have been asking around, sir. Yes, I have. I was but twenty-one when I entered the house of Master Pitchcottt, and little Everild was a tiny baby then."

"Did you know her mother?"

His eyes flickered again.

"For a short while only. Then she died."

"Did you also know Farnell's mother? The other sister?"

"No, sir. I did not. She lived away from the Pitchcott household."

"So Everild Pitchcott becomes Mistress Deyning. How do you feel about that, Robert?"

"I would not have chosen the man for her if I had been her father and her father did not approve of the man, as you know. But it's done now."

"I must say that I do not think that Deyning nor Everild will keep you on much longer, Robert. Once you have outlived your usefulness, I think they will dispense with…"

"Give you a boot up the backside and lock the doors on you," said Hal with typical gruffness.

"Oh no, sir. I can't see them doing that."

"I think they will."

"No, no, I am far too useful."

"If I were you, Agnew, I'd practice tootling on yer flootle even 'arder," said Hal. "You're gonna need a new job, or I'm a Welshman!"

Chapter Nine

*W*E LET MASTER AGNEW GO. He turned his back on us, red-faced and angry and marched out of the castle gate like a man going to war.

Hal stood in the gateway with his arms crossed over his chest and watched him, chuckling.

"Where to now, sir?"

"Now? Now I think we are for home, Hal."

"You don't want to get Master Armer in here and give him a proddin' then?"

"We shall, Hal, but I think that will be tomorrow's task."

"Is 'e our boilin' fowl of the day then?" he grinned.

"I think he is. Sometimes it pays to let people think about things. I know I have said it before, but they often get jittery when nothing happens. They start to imagine all sorts, and before you know it, they have betrayed themselves with an action."

Little did I know what form that action would take.

The following day proved to be the hottest yet and, after a misty start, began with a sky as blue as Hal's cotte.

We jogged along the chalk road to Marlborough, already throwing up the heat from previous days of sunshine. Today there was no breeze. The trees on either side of us were still and limp. The grass was browning and beginning to lie flat.

We sweltered in our gambesons and vowed that we'd doff them for cooler garb as soon as we reached the castle.

"Right, Hal. Let's have our master armourer up here and see what he says about these little balls. I imagine he'll be at the old forge or Pitchcott's house."

Farnell Armer came into the office complaining that he hadn't the time to spend messing about speaking to us.

"My Lord Belvoir," he bowed. "I really must protest. I have told you all I know, and I have so much to do if I am not to fall so far behind..."

"Sit, Armer," I said as if the man was a misbehaving dog.

He was so surprised and, being used to obeying the orders of his betters, he sat down on the stool without another word.

His face, though, was red, his expression angry and wary. He wiped his sweating forehead.

"I apologise for bringing you away from your work, but I must ask you some further questions. For instance, what do you make of these?"

I took his hand and put the six small metal balls into his palm.

He grimaced and rolled his head sideways in a gesture of annoyance, his eyes rising to the rafters.

"I've told you before, I have no..."

I walked behind him, leaned into his shoulder, and whispered into his ear.

"It won't do, Armer. It won't do."

Farnell Armer looked down at his palm.

Calmly he put the small balls on the table, contained them so they wouldn't roll and sighed.

"That's better. Now, we *know* you made them."

"I didn't..."

"You made them and hundreds like them. They were scattered on the floor of your armoury when we looked yesterday after the fire."

He sighed loudly in exasperation. "Yes, I made them."

"Why did you lie?"

"At first, because I didn't want anyone to know what I was doing, and then when you told me that Pitchcott had been killed with one, I didn't want you to think I'd killed him."

"But your lying makes me think that more strongly, Armer."

"I did not use these to kill him. I didn't kill him."

I walked back round to my desk and, as was my habit, perched on the edge.

"What did you make them for?"

Armer shook his head.

"I can have you confined in the castle cells until you decide to tell me."

Armer sighed again.

"They are one of my new ideas. The wooden contraption..."

"The one we saw in the courtyard after the fire?" asked Hal, who was in his usual place leaning on the door.

"Yes. That is a small trebuchet. I made it to test my idea."

"And your idea is?"

Farnell looked up at me with wide eyes.

"The usual huge trebuchet fires rocks many feet into the air..."

"Over walls mostly," said Hal.

"That's right. They're designed to break down walls,

and if you're lucky, you might get a few of the enemy folk with the splintering rock. Or maybe the rock itself."

I picked up the balls and rolled them around in my hand. I could now see where this was going.

"I wondered if small metal balls might be loosed in the same way, but at people directly?"

"Not if they were wearing maille," said Hal. "Maille'd stop these."

"It depends. They are small enough to hit where maille doesn't cover. Or they'd stop those who have no maille."

"They won't work like a trebuchet. For castles and such."

"No, but I wondered if they'd work out in open battle, like a hail of arrows. They might stop a spear line. Many soldiers are not maille clad, the poorer sort. Oh, maybe they won't kill, but they'd stop, sir, and bruise nastily," said Farnell. "I also wondered if they'd be useful to toss over the castle wall at an enemy besieging."

"Well, they *have* killed."

"It was as much a surprise to me as it was to you, sir, when you said that one of my balls… just one… had killed Master Pitchcott. I was, well, I don't mind saying, staggered and amazed."

"Unlucky, I'd say," said Hal.

Armer turned to look at him with a puzzled expression.

"That the ball 'it 'im where it did. Right where the doctor says a man is most vulnerable. On the side of 'is 'ead."

"My small torsion-throwing machine throws them some distance and they are quite speedy, but there's no control over *where* they hit, sir," said Farnell.

"No, I can see that," I said, sitting behind my table again.

"So somehow one of these balls was loosed at Pitchcott, and it hit him with such force that it penetrated his skull."

"How that might happen, I don't know," said Armer, staring at the wall. He took his lip in his teeth.

"My trebuchet wasn't used, that I can tell you. No one would know how to use it…"

"Aw, c'mon, Master Armer," said Hal chuckling. "It's not difficult to fathom."

Armer turned to look at Hal again. "No, it's a scaled-down machine, I know. I expect you understood, knew what it was when you first saw it."

"I've seen the bigguns. It wasn't 'ard to work it out."

"You simply couldn't fire it at someone and, in such a small space as this, succeed in killing them. They'd just run, or turn and fight you. And how would you get it in here? Unlike a slingshot, it's too big to carry around with you."

"No, I agree with you," I said. "It could not have been used in here."

Farnell Armer touched the back of his head. It obviously still pained him.

"Then how, sir?"

"I don't know. Yet," I said. I leaned back and thought.

"Who knew about this machine of yours?"

"Knew I'd made it and what it might do?"

"Yes. Did your men know?"

"No, sir. I did it when they weren't around. They saw the machine but had no idea what it was for. And the balls were kept in that barrel. They didn't see those. I wanted to…"

"Keep it secret, yes, I see."

"Anyone else know about it, Armer, especially the little balls?" asked Hal.

Armer shook his head.

"I can't think… no. No one I know."

"Mistress Corlis?"

Armer's face turned red again. "No! How would Corlis know? How could she know what to do?"

Hal shrugged. "She's a bright girl. She met you, I'm sure, more than once in your forge of an evening. Are you sure she didn't see anything?"

"She's a woman. What would she know about an armourer's trade?"

"Don't you underestimate a woman, young man," said Hal with a snigger. "Theym'z not all soft and daft."

I smiled, remembering my last enemy, my last extremely deadly enemy.

"It might be the last thing you do one day."

Armer's eyes opened wide.

"No. She's never been interested in any of it. She's never even asked questions."

"Hmmm."

"Armer, who has? Anyone?" I asked.

Armer took his head between two hands and pressed the heels into his eyes.

"I don't know. No, no one I can think of. Like I say, I was keeping it quiet."

"Well, someone got hold of a ball."

"Yes, sir, they could get a ball, maybe steal it, but how could they launch it?"

"I wondered if a catapult might do it?"

"Yes, it might... but the same applies," said Armer. "Who in his right mind is going to let a man aim and fire a catapult at him in a small space like this?"

"A slingshot is to be discounted for the same reason," I added.

"He'd duck and move about and fight back. Even Master Pitchcott would, if he was threatened."

It was then I heard my name being called from the space outside the door.

"Sir Aumary, are you there?"

It was Johannes' voice.

"Here, Johannes!" I shouted. Hal opened the door.

"Ah, I have some news."

"Oh?"

Johannes entered the room and immediately spotted the little balls on the table where Armer had dropped them.

"Ah…"

He then nodded to Farnell.

"How is the head, Master Armer?"

"Better thank you, doctor," said the young man with a smile.

"Sir Aumary, I…"

"It's all right, Johannes. You can speak out. Master Armer here has just admitted to making those little balls."

"Ah, has he?"

"I am sorry that I've tugged you all awry. I was so worried you'd think me the murderer."

"You're not free of suspicion yet, Armer," said Hal flintily.

Johannes nodded. "You may have made them, young man, but did you poison them?"

Armer's jaw dropped. "No, I most certainly didn't, sir."

"I was puzzled, Aumary, as to how Pitchcott died," said Johannes. "Yes, the ball had penetrated his skull and it might be enough to kill him after a while. He'd be stunned by the blow of it and unconscious. The blood would seep into his brain. But was it certain that he'd die of it before he could tell anyone who aimed it?"

Suddenly I was transported back to a night four years ago when a murderous attempt on my life had resulted in a knife wound which had turned out to have been poisoned. Oh no, not me, it was my brother Robert who sustained the wound.

You remember that, don't you, Paul? We recounted that tale when we spoke about the time when I was at first Lord of Durley and warden of the forest.

"However the ball was introduced into the body, it hadn't gone far into the brain. I started to wonder if poison was used."

"And...?"

"Yes. Aconitum, I think. Coating the pellet."

"Jesus..." said Hal. "We all handled the bloody thing."

"It was a fail-safe, I suppose. I don't think it was truly needed, but it was well thought out."

"So we now know that Pitchcott died of the poison and the pressure of the little ball on his brain, but we are still searching for a way that it got into him," I said.

We were all silent.

None of us had any idea.

"Diabolical it is, like Master Agnew thinks," said Hal.

"Diabolical indeed, Hal," I sighed.

The sun beat down on us as we crossed the castle bridge and made for the town a while later. I had a mind to visit the house of Master Pitchcott one more time and look at the room where the cook died.

The steward Thomas Parfitt took us to the room. It was unlocked, as Master Agnew had said.

"What are we looking for?"

"I'm unsure, Hal."

"Parfitt, might you stay and answer some questions?"

"Yes, my lord."

"Where were you when the cook was lying dead in this room?"

"I have a room at the other end of the hall, sir. I was there, asleep." He shrugged, "I was there when the alarm was raised, for not only is it my sleeping place but my working room too."

"We saw you arrive, I believe. The other staff?"

"The kitchen girl you met, sir. She sleeps with the cook in the kitchen. The maid comes in from the town, the grooms - one sleeps in the hall, and one in the stable, one manservant sleeps here in the hall, and the other lives out."

"And that is the sum total of people who live or work here?"

"Yes, sir."

"The kitchen girl must have realised that the cook did not sleep there every night?"

"I imagine so, m'lord, though cook ruled her with a rod, and she was, I expect, sworn not to say anything. She would have been beaten else."

I saw Hal grimace.

I was not as sorry for the cook as I'd previously been.

"Thank you, Parfitt. I'll let you know when we leave."

The room had been scrubbed and cleaned. A new mattress had been procured and clean linen had been laid on the bed. The place was tidy.

I walked over to the window and looked out.

"It is still possible that the murderer climbed to the window, Hal."

He joined me in looking out.

"But if the man is the same as killed ol' Pitchcott, then the first attempts were made from inside the 'ouse, weren't they?"

"All doors locked. All shutters bolted."

"Yes. No one that wasn't let in could get in."

"Or out without being seen."

I walked around the bed, which was almost in the centre of the room.

"What was the woman doing here? Agnew says he was out at a wedding or something. Hal, can you just go down to the Chasiers' and ask if Agnew was there playing for them when Pitchcott was killed?"

"Right you are, sir. I won't be long. It's no long step from here to Herd Street."

"We shall both go to the Chapmans' to ask about the night the cook died on our way back to the castle."

Hal clomped down the stairs.

I stood looking at the bed for a while, trying to imagine what had happened.

I sat at the head.

When the woman had been found, her head had been to the top of the bed, slightly askew; her body was angled across. The sheets were tangled and disordered; Agnew's shirt lay under her.

Would she, I wondered, have lain upon Agnew's shirt waiting for him to return? If someone had come upon her in the night, would she not have screamed? If it was someone she didn't know, would she have let them get behind her?

If she was asleep, why was the bed so disordered?

It was still quite dark, so did she not see the person approaching her?

No, Mistress Deyning had heard the cook speaking with Agnew just before dawn. She was alive then.

I stood at the head and mimed the action of cutting a throat. Grab the hair, or grab the chin, pull back, swipe the knife across the throat, and stand away quickly. The murderer must have been sprayed with blood, but perhaps not greatly if he had been behind her.

I went back to the window. There was no blood on the sill or the frame.

I searched Master Agnew's coffer. There were clothes here but nothing to suggest any had been bloodied.

I came across a small linen bag.

Carefully I drew it out and pulled the strings. Out tumbled a flute about a foot in length. I looked it over. Nothing but an ordinary flute.

I replaced it.

I moved to the small pot board, which stood in the corner.

Here were some business parchments and another bag.

I opened this one, too—another flute. This flute was lighter in colour and slightly smaller in length. However, it was slightly fatter than the last one.

I turned it over. It had no holes.

"My Lord…?"

I looked up quickly.

"Ah, Agnew."

"My Lord, what are you doing?"

I ran my hands through my curly black hair.

"I am trying to picture in my head, Agnew, what happened here the morning that Margery was killed."

I put the small flute back on the pot board.

Agnew picked it up quickly and replaced it in the linen bag.

I smiled. "That must be one you are making, eh, Agnew?"

"What, sir?"

"The flute. You'll not play it; it has no holes."

The man looked quizzically at me. "Ah no… I mean, yes… it is one I am fashioning. I have yet to make the holes."

"Tell me, do you make all your flutes? I noticed another in your chest."

"You have been going through my things, m'lord?"

"Yes. It's necessary, I'm afraid. I'm sorry."

"I make all my flutes, and I can also make other instruments."

"Where did you learn to do that?" I asked.

Agnew stepped to the chest and put the second flute into it.

"My father was a musician, sir, in Buckinghamshire. He belonged to a troop of tumblers and players of music who worked for the lord. I learned at his knee."

"How did you come from there to work for Master Pitchcott? You are literate, Robert. I doubt your father was."

His eyes narrowed. "That is very clever of you, my lord. I was a bright lad, they tell me. The Lord of Buckingham, Sir William Giffard, saw my potential and had me sent into education with his own lad. Then I came of age and went off to Master Pitchcott."

"You owe your advancement then to the Lord Giffard?"

"I do. I am ever in his debt."

"Why did you not stay with him? To pay him back?"

"I am a free man, m'lord. I travelled for a while. I ended up at Pitchcott."

"Your master valued you highly. He left you a goodly sum in his will."

"He did, sir. We had a good relationship. He could be curmudgeonly when he wanted, but all in all, sir, he was a good master. To me."

"I'll leave you to it, Agnew," I said, making for the stairs. "God keep you."

"And you, sir."

I stood out on St Martin's. The sky was black over St Peter's. Large rain drops began to fall all around me.

Damn. I had no cloak.

I made off quickly in the direction of the Green and Herd Street, where I thought Hal would be waiting. I couldn't see him anywhere.

Ah well, he'd catch up with me. I began to walk along Silver Street. The rain was falling in earnest now; huge fat drops.

Folk were hurrying before me and quickly disappearing into houses and other buildings.

I quickened my pace, made the end by Kingsbury Hill, and turned the corner through a deluge of huge drops. I remember thinking I might shelter in the alley that ran beside Johannes' house. Suddenly the place was deserted, the street completely empty.

The sky was inky black now, and I heard a rumble of thunder in the distance. I caught the tail end of the flash of lightning for the next rumble from the corner of my eye, along the edge of the forest at Granham Hill. A few more paces and I'd be out of the rain.

Suddenly the Heavens opened. The roadway disappeared in a veil of semi-transparent drops falling in a complete sheet. The noise of the drops striking the hard ground was deafening. It was like the hissing of a hundred geese.

The thunder boomed above me; I could see no man; I could see nothing.

Rain dripped from the end of my nose, and in moments, my hair was a flattened, sodden mat of droplets which dribbled down my neck. My cotte over my gambeson was soaked through.

I shivered. Best to go to Johannes' house. I could just make out the High Cross which lay almost in front of his parlour window. It was a dark grey shape in the silver curtain of rain.

I slipped on the mud of the roadway and righted myself by putting out an arm to the house wall on my left-hand side.

That movement saved me.

Out of the mist of rain came an object which, as it passed me, whined in my ear like a flying insect.

I looked back to the corner of Silver Street.

I could see nothing. No one.

The next moment, I was in the alleyway and the rain ceased to drum in my ears.

I caught my breath and looked back again.

Nothing.

I took a deep breath, shook myself and turned to go up the dark alley to the back gate of Johannes' yard.

Back out into the rain momentarily, the drumming and hissing began again and I turned to open the gate with the rain and thunder beating above me.

The whining sound came once more and I quickly began to turn my head to the dark alley.

There was a dull thwack as a searing pain shot up my temple.

I staggered against the open gate and fell senseless into the yard.

Chapter Ten

I CAME TO with several people staring at me from above. Or it seemed like several. I realised later, it was in truth, only two.

Little Agnes' face loomed above me and her features, though I could tell it was her, seemed skewed and enlarged.

I tried to rise, but a heavy hand pushed me down again, and Johannes' voice, distant but recognisable, told me to lie still.

I felt light-headed, and there was a terrible pain in my head. I knew I was going to vomit.

Suddenly a coldness was on my forehead, and the nausea passed. The pain in my head intensified and I thought I heard myself groan.

Then came the pain of my knees and wrists, followed by a soreness in my palms and the realisation that my forehead and nose were scratched and bruised.

Someone gently took my hands and a warmness enveloped them.

They were patted with something, and then they began to sting. The same happened to my forehead.

Johannes, for it must have been him, turned my head

slowly and gently brushed the damp hair from my temple.

"Gods, Aumary! If it hadn't been raining... I think, well, I think you'd be dead now."

"What?" I heard myself say.

"Your wet hair plastered to your head saved you the worst damage. You are lucky you have thick curly hair."

"What damage?" My voice sounded far away and slightly slurred.

"You were hit with something small. We haven't recovered it from the alleyway. But I suspect it's the same weapon as hit Pitchcott. God Almighty in his Heaven was looking after you this afternoon, Aumary Belvoir!" chuckled Johannes.

"Knees hurt, wrists hurt."

"You fell on them. You put your hands out to save yourself and fell on your forehead. No real damage, just a jarring."

"How did you...?"

"We heard the gate bang open and hit the wall with a slap. It echoes here in the kitchen, even above the noise of the rain."

The thunder cracked above us again, and it made us all jump.

"Agnes heard it and looked out of the window."

Little Agnes had finished her work with my forehead and hands, and now stood over me. She mimed me removing my wet clothes.

Slowly, oh so slowly, I sat at the edge of the kitchen bench on which they had laid me and waited for the dizziness to pass.

Agnes helped me out of my sodden cotte and gambeson.

The shirt was sticking to me, and Agnes helped me peel it off, then she ran upstairs to find me some clothes belonging to Johannes.

Slowly we managed to get all the wet clothes off me and Johannes wrapped me in two large towels to preserve my modesty and to dry me off.

Agnes returned and busied herself at the fireplace, her back to us as Johannes eased clothes over my head and around me.

Eventually, I sat back, exhausted, and a beaker of warmed wine was put into my hands.

Johannes went to the front of the house where his workroom lay and returned with a couple of pots of salve, which he spread liberally on my palms and forehead. He assured me that my knees and wrists would mend themselves in time.

Once more, he looked at the blue mark on my temple and tutted.

"This should take out the bruising and it will heal well. You're lucky. Pitchcott was not so fortunate. He was bald and took the full brunt of the ball."

"Why, Johannes? Why?"

"Why did the murderer try to kill you? I suspect you are too close for his comfort."

Suddenly I remembered Hal.

"Hal will be wondering where I am. I was meant to meet up with him on Herd Street."

"He's the least of your worries. He can take care of himself. Sit still and rest."

"But…"

"He'll find out where you are, I'm sure."

There was a deafening clap of thunder right above us and the plates on the pot board rattled.

"If he has any sense, he's sheltering too."

At last, the doctor sat down in front of me.

"SO, tell me… what did you see?"

"Nothing. Absolutely nothing."

"No people about?"

"They had all gone scurrying for cover when the rain started. It was dark and the rain was so dense. No one could see anything."

"But your assailant could see you."

I looked over to my cream woollen supertunic drying before the fire.

"I really must wear darker colours. This is the second time I have been visible in bad light conditions."

Two of my villeins had been able to see me in the darkening forest a while ago because of my cream linsey-woolsey cotte. Good job they had, for I would have been dead and buried under a holly tree, and no one would have been any the wiser.

"You had no idea that the man was following you? Stalking you?"

"None at all until I got to the alleyway and heard the first ball go past me."

"He missed with the first one?"

"He did."

The rain outside began to slacken. The hissing ceased.

There was another peal of thunder and it growled in the distance as it rolled away.

Johannes leaned his elbows on his knees.

"Whatever it is, this weapon, it's easily carried and disguised."

"Not a crossbow, then."

"No. If there was no one about, then we'll have no witnesses. I must admit, as I dragged you in and laid you down, it was going through my mind that someone must have seen what had happened, but..."

"It's unlikely."

"Think back, Aumary. What have you learned today or recently that this person may consider a threat?"

"We say him, but we mustn't lose sight of the fact there are two women in this puzzle."

"Ah, yes."

"Yesterday, I spoke to Mistress Everild Deyning. I had words with Agnew twice and spoke to Armer, which you know about."

"And before this?"

"I spoke to Master Green, and Nick told me about a few other folk who hated Pitchcott."

"Of course, there may be others."

"I've no doubt."

"But…" said my friend with a sombre look, "It's the recent information which I feel has pushed this person into a panicked deed of attempted murder."

"I can't think straight. I'm so tired. I'll think better if I have a rest."

"Go and sleep on the palliasse in the workroom. I'll see if I can send the neighbour's lad down to the castle to leave a message for Hal."

"Thank you." My eyelids were closing.

"It will all look better in a while."

"Come, let me help you." Agnes opened the passageway door and smiled.

"Thank you, Agnes. There's no doubt your quickness saved me."

She smiled back at me, her pink apple face happy.

"Who knows what they might have done if they'd had you at their mercy," said Johannes. "A swift knife in the ribs after felling you to make sure, and away up the alleyway?"

I laughed tiredly. "Your alley is not a good place for me, Johannes."

This was the third time the alleyway had been a danger to me.

"I think I'll come in the front door from now on."

I slept for two hours. Johannes said that sleep was good and restorative but that the sleep of concussion could be dangerous.

When I awoke, I was pained and stiff.

Hal was waiting for me in the kitchen, and he rose when I entered and helped me to a seat.

"I leave you for the time it takes to 'ave a pee, an' what 'appens?"

I ran my hands through my hair, forgetting the soreness of my palms, forehead and temple.

"Johannes has told you what happened?"

"Aye, 'e 'as."

"What did you learn at the cheese men, the Chasiers?"

"Agnew was there, as he said. Played his flute till late, then went home."

"Hmm."

"We bin talkin'. Johannes seems to think it's something you learned recently that made the killer act..."

"Yes, I know.

"So what 'ave we learned?"

I sat back and rested my head on the wall.

"That Farnell had the opportunity and the brains to manufacture something which might kill Pitchcott."

"Not 'is trebuchet!"

"No, but perhaps something else. He is a clever man. There's maybe something else he's made that we haven't yet learned about."

"Aye, I suppose that's possible."

"We've learned that Everild is a sneaky woman and was often out and about late at night. So was her husband. They could have acted together. She had a motive to want her father dead and there was no love between them. She was close enough to Farnell that she might have obtained one or two of the little balls from him."

"I suppose so."

"Agnew was also out and about at night. His motive would be harder to fathom except for money…"

"But he's better off under Pitchcott," said Johannes. "He has a job, a roof over his head and a role in the house. With Pitchcott gone, he's rootless, unpopular with the mistress, and soon to be out of a job."

"Hmm."

"Corlis… well, she might act with Farnell."

"Master Green?" said Hal. "And his cronies?"

I shrugged, and the action hurt me.

"With the death of Pitchcott, they all ceased to fight with him about the land they are accused of stealing. Legal business like that is costly."

"Who in the town was in dispute with Pitchcott then?" asked Johannes.

"Green the ale man, Fulbert Tanner and another neighbour called Grounder all have land which abuts the Pitchcott house and land."

"Tanner is a town councillor, for goodness sake, and I know Eustace. He's a very upright man. Not wealthy. He would capitulate rather than fight in court. I can't see him being a murderer either."

"Green would, though," said Hal. "He's the fightin' type."

I smiled. "So I cannot really see what we've learned that would make someone so jittery that they would try to kill me for what they think I know."

Hal scratched his cheek with a rasping sound.

"I reckon it's something you've been told or 'ave seen that you don't know you've been told or 'ave seen…"

We both looked at him in perplexity.

"If you see what I mean?" he added, grinning. "You need to do your writing it all down, don't you, sir," he finished.

"You know, Hal, you're right."

I stood shakily.

"Come! Back to the castle. I want to think about this for a few days. I want to go home. Home to Durley."

I stood on the top step of the manor stairs. A charm of goldfinches went tinkling overhead.

I looked out over the trees of Savernake.

Four days I had been home, enveloped in the bosom of my family; my three children, my lovely wife and my manor workers. I felt refreshed.

The weather was still warm, but wasn't as oppressive as it had been. One more thunderstorm had chased away the heat and now the once thirsty ground had more of a green tinge; the plants and trees had recovered a little. We were all more comfortable.

Hal came out of his room on the south wall, stretched and yawned, his arms above his head, looked at the sky and disappeared inside again.

I lifted a hand to wave at John Brenthall, my chief wood warden, as he came in the gate with his son Peter, followed by his dog Maxime. Peter's mother came out from the undercroft beneath me and met them in the yard. There was laughter and happiness, and I smiled as I watched them.

I smiled, too, as I saw Master Gervase Mason enter through the gate and look around. He had dismounted from his pony outside the walls and was leading the animal by its reins.

"Ho, Gervase!"

He looked up.

"My Lord," he said as he nodded a bow.

"Welcome to Durley!"

I yelled over my shoulder into the screens passage where I knew Henry, my steward, was filling the wine and ale jugs for the day.

"Henry, ale for Master Mason!"

Gervase was a small but powerfully stocky man with strong arms and a barrel chest. Today he was dressed in green and wore no coif, as was usual.

He threw back the flap of the pannier strapped to his pony and took out a large leather pouch. Cedric came out from the stable to take the beast, and Gervase trotted up the manor steps.

"God smiles on you today, sir, I hope," said Gervase, flicking back his grey hair. "Last I heard, you had taken some sort of blow to the head and were laid low."

"You heard correctly, Gervase. An assassin, who perhaps decided I was too close to unmasking him, needed to be rid of me. He struck me on the head. It's all healed now."

He shook his grey locks.

"Lord above, I wouldn't have your job for all the stone in the world. If I am to be injured, it won't be by an assassin."

"When I took on this role, Gervase, I didn't think my life would ever be in danger. However, it's not the first time I have been the target of a murderous villain."

"Aye, I remember when you were poisoned, sir. We really didn't expect you to survive."

I shrugged. "I would not have done so had it not been for Doctor Johannes and Master Gallipot, the apothecary."

I slapped him on the back. "And my good and vigilant friends who cared about me."

I looked up as the goldfinches returned to the elder tree growing by the steps.

"Ale, Master Mason?"

He shook his head. "No, thank you, m'lord. I drink no ale but with food."

"Shall we look at the church, and then we can discuss what we might do over some wine?"

The man's eyes sparkled.

I called into the hall.

"Henry, can you find Crispin and ask him to meet us by the church?" I heard him answer from the depths of the hall. "Oh, and can you ask Bevis and Alf to join us in front of the church?" These two were my main village carpenters.

As we walked from the walled manor, we talked about the town and the castle.

"Of course, you know that the serious work there began in the fourth year of our Lord John's reign?"

"1203, yes. It was the year I became the underconstable. I had very little to do with the castle before this."

"There has been a steady stream of improvements since then. The king has spent a great deal of money and effort on making this fortress the most modern and secure of castles."

"And yet someone got into the castle, through locked and barred doors, Gervase, and killed Master Pitchcott."

"Aye, that *is* a puzzle, sir."

"No doubt when we find out what happened, and rest assured we shall, it will be the simplest of answers."

"It's no easy task to design and build a castle of such complexity and impregnability, sir."

I smiled.

"Your task here will be much less difficult, Gervase. Perhaps a two-storey addition to the south face and a new doorway. Our priest Crispin will explain what he needs, I expect."

"You trust him to do as you wish, my lord?"

"It's not what I wish, Gervase, it's what he needs, and

Crispin is a fair man. He will not spend my money will-I-nil-I on unnecessary additions."

Gervase chuckled, "Then he will be the first priest with whom I have worked who does not want everything for nothing, m'lord."

"Crispin and I are boyhood friends. He is a good man."

"But it must also be to the glory of God, sir? That we must agree upon."

"This is a plain little church, Gervase. We have nothing here which is fanciful or overly decorative. Maybe one day when I am in my dotage... well, maybe we shall rebuild and enlarge the building, but for now, a porch will suffice."

What, Paul? Did I ever rebuild the church,
you ask? No, lad, I never did. I expect I shall
leave that job now to my son Simon.

"I am sure we can make something worthy of you all and God," said Gervase smiling.

"Ah, and here comes that good man, Master Mason."

Crispin came jogging around the corner of the manor wall as we entered the lych gate. Then all was talk of timber for roof beams and floors, stone for the walls, and tiles for the roof.

My carpenters came running up the slight slope.

I left them talking to Master Mason about the scaffolding, roof beams and floorboards. We had many timbers laid by in our wood barn, for that winter and others in previous years had been unkind to the forest, and many of the very old trees had fallen. We had logged them, ferried them by cart to our barn and laid them by for future use. We would have plenty of good oak for our building works. And we had permission from our lord the king.

The men would begin the dismantling the next day.

I stood in front of the south wall of the church at Durley two days later and watched as my men helped dismantle the wall to a certain level and width.

Timbers had been ferried to the building, and the carpenters began to take their adzes to the larger pieces to fashion the beams required for the scaffolding.

I'd seen this process before, of course.

Holes were dug in the ground around the church and everything was measured with strings and plumb lines. Upright posts were hammered into the ground. I watched Bevis handle the timbers as if they were mere blades of grass, his muscles straining as he lifted them to rope them to the uprights.

The sun shone. I came and went as the day progressed.

The shadows of the posts grew up the side of the church wall, now laid bare and soon a criss-cross of posts and rails grew out of the surface, like a tracery of rigid branches. Bevis, aided by his apprentice and a couple of the other lads from the village, nimbly scaled the ladders placed at the side of the wall and fixed the timbers in place.

Now the scaffolding was secure.

I had work to do, but I watched transfixed as the first pieces of timber were driven into the stone of the existing wall.

I turned to Alfred Woodsmith, who was at an outdoor trestle fashioning smaller pieces of wood with an adze.

"Alf, how do the masons ensure the scaffolding is safe when they are further up the wall? It seems to me that a structure like this is unsafe when stones…"

"Ah, m'lord."

Alfred put down his adze and wiped his hands on his front, leaving sawdust prints on the breast of his dark green tunic.

"See those holes." He pointed

"Aye, I see them."

"That is where the stones of the original church wall will be chiselled out, and the new wall will be keyed into it."

"Yes, but…"

"If you look there…" He pointed again. "When the masons begin to lay the stones, they will leave little gaps here and there at regular intervals. This is where the horizontal timbers will poke out."

"So timbers are inserted into the very building stones? The existing ones."

"Yessir."

"Why? So that a platform may be built upon which to stand?"

"That's right, sir."

"So you carpenters build as the masons go up."

"We go up with them, my lord - yes."

"They build a bit of wall…"

"And we go up and add our beams and uprights, above them, then build a platform. We take the platform apart as we go and build it further up."

"Then how do you stand?"

"Ladders, sir."

"Hmm. If you were building a castle wall, would the process be the same, Alf?"

"I've never built a castle, but I can't imagine it would be very much different, my lord."

"Hmm." I scratched my bearded chin.

"Of course, building a castle, you'd need big machinery to get the stone blocks up the wall. We haven't got that here. We are at most fifteen feet from the ground. Eighteen perhaps at the apex of the roof of the nave."

"Machinery?"

"Winches which are driven by powered wheels."

"Ah, yes, I have seen those at Marlborough castle."

"A man drives them by walking inside the structure. The torsioned ropes lift the blocks and lower them again. Sometimes animals are used."

I nodded.

"So we shall not need those here, Alf, as you say. Our building isn't high enough."

"No, sir. It's much easier to build what we are building, though keying in the stones is a master mason's job."

"When you take the scaffolding down, Alfred, what happens?"

"Happens, sir?"

"When it's all done and the building is finished. You will take all your poles away?"

Alf looked puzzled, not sure where I was leading him.

"Yes, sir, we'll have no further need of them."

"Do you remove the horizontal poles sticking in the walls?"

Alfred Woodsmith laughed. "Do you think, sir, that the whole thing will fall down if we take the poles away?"

I chuckled with him.

"No, Alf. But I wonder what happens to the holes which are left behind?"

"Ah. That depends on the masons, sir. I have known some workers leave the wood in place and saw it off close to the wall. Well-seasoned oak won't rot, sir. It will be there in years to come, as good as new. As good as the blocks the masons build with. Others remove the wood altogether, pull out the putlogs and block up the holes with mortar."

"The what, Alf?"

"Putlogs, sir." He chuckled again. "Aye, daft, I know. That's what they're called."

"Because they're logs which have been put there?" I said, smiling widely.

"That's right, sir." He picked up his adze again.

"A-course, some really lazy so-and-sos don't cut them off flush to the wall."

"They don't?"

"No, they leave a bit sticking out. Don't suppose it really matters but, well, I wouldn't do that, m'lord." He shook his brown curls. "It isn't tidy."

"No, Alf. I know how very tidy you are. How meticulous. Your work is exceptional, I'll say that."

Alfred Woodsmith, who was normally responsible for the finer stuff, like furniture and decorative items, puffed out his chest.

"Nice of you to say so, m'lord Belvoir."

I slapped his shoulder and turned to walk down the slight slope.

The sun was casting long shadows now. Soon everyone would down tools and go home to supper. The swifts were screaming at their evening feasting of high-flying midges.

I'd reached the lych gate before realising exactly what Alf had said.

I retraced my steps.

"Alf?"

"M'lord?"

"You said the putlogs sometimes stay in place?"

"Yessir."

"If a carpenter doesn't cut them off at the wall. How long might he leave them?"

Alf put down his adze again and looked up at the westering sun.

"That depends on the lazy sod who does the work. Why, I've seen logs as long as six inches poking out the wall." He tutted and shook his head. "Sheer laziness. Now they *will* rot in time because…"

"Thank you, Alf… you have just solved a riddle for me."

"I have?"

"You have."

Alf rubbed his clean-shaven chin. "Well, I'll be..."

"Time for supper," I said. "Down tools and to the hall with you."

Alfred Woodsmith grinned at me.

Chapter Eleven

*B*EFORE SUPPER, I went into my office and scribbled a few notes onto parchment.

I needed to get back to the castle the next day and look at the eastern wall, where my room lay. It had been built, in part, into that wall and lay under the wall walk.

If it was as I thought, then I knew how the murderer had got into the room; or rather how he had had access to Master Pitchcott.

What I still couldn't fathom was how the ball had become embedded into the merchant's head. The shutters had been bolted over the window spaces from the inside.

The next morning, I had Hal leaning out of the window of my office whilst I slithered down the side of the castle bridge and stood on the small patch of ground between the castle wall and the moat.

Here, the ground was just three feet wide. I looked up and called to Hal. His head poked out of the window as far as he was able to lean.

"What can you see?"

"I can just about see you," he called. "There's not much room to squeeze out."

SUSANNA M. NEWSTEAD

"I'm looking up, and the holes begin not quite two feet above my head."

"These putty logs you told me about?"

"Yes. The first one is sawn quite close. The next is about two feet higher and sticks out quite a way."

"There are two just under the window," yelled Hal. "They'm quite long too. Sawn off."

"Right, Hal. We need a mason with a ladder."

I scrambled back up the side of the bridge, missing my step once or twice, for the grass was slick with the rain and overnight dew.

I brushed my blue cotte free of detritus from the wall and made my way back up the few steps to my room.

Hal was still looking out of the window when I re-entered, and he turned as I came back into the room, brushing my hands of dirt.

"You think the man came this way? 'E'd 'ave to be daft!"

"Or daring."

"A sane man wouldn't climb a castle wall in the dark without..."

"The dark was what would protect him, Hal. No one would see."

"No one would be passin' at that time of night anyway."

"The watch might be up in the High Street, but, no, they don't come down as far as the castle."

"And the castle wall guards were only patrolling every so often. They wouldn't be looking straight down anyway. Certainly not to the edge of the moat. Not in peacetime."

I scratched my chin.

"Was there a moon, do you remember?"

"Aye, a sliver of one."

"Hmmm."

"Even if someone did manage to get up 'ere and let's face it, if 'e did 'ed 'ave to be one o' them little creatures that

Old Lady Mortemer 'as…"

"A monkey, I think they're called, Hal."

"Yeah, one 'o them. Even if 'e got up there like a monkey, 'ow's 'e goin' to kill Master Pitchcott?"

"I have an idea, Hal. That's why I need a mason."

Hal shook his head.

"'E can't get in the window."

"Maybe he didn't need to."

Hal looked at me and brushed his fingers through his beard.

"You know what?" he chuckled. "I think that blow on your 'ead did more damage than we thought."

I showed my teeth to him with a severe stare in which there was no real malice.

"Now, now, ol' Hal. That's no way to speak to your paymaster!"

Hal grinned back.

"I suppose you want me to go and find a willing mason with a ladder?"

"One who won't mind a dunking in the moat if we fail in this."

Hal tutted. "Tsk. I shan't tell 'im that, mind."

The door closed behind him, and I made for the window and closed the first shutter, leaving the other open. I looked over at the place where Master Pitchcott had fallen. There, in that space, had lain his pallet, now removed. His body had been angled. The window was here. My polished plate lay there.

Stepping over to the pot board, I placed my plate exactly where I usually had it when looking into it to tidy my beard. I noticed the dent in it again.

I strode about the room, pacing it out, looking at angles and eventually, Hal returned.

"This is Treddlan. 'E says fer a penny 'e'll do what

you want."

"Thank you, Hal. Treddlan, I want you to go out onto the face of the eastern wall right by this window. Take your ladder and place it just here." I gestured to the wall from the inside. "Climb the ladder. Hopefully, it will be long enough for you to reach the shutters."

The man grinned. "That's all I have to do, m'lord?"

"We'll then give you further instructions."

The mason walked to the window and opened the shutter.

"Begging your pardon, m'lord." He looked down. "No, I've no single ladder long enough. However, I can rope two together."

"Do it, Treddlan."

He tugged his forelock and was gone, and as he left, I shouted after him

"Make sure you take a long knife with you."

He turned on the step, his face wearing a rather suspicious grimace. "A knife?"

"A long-bladed one. Or one of those long metal flat things I've seen you masons using."

"A cement spatula, you mean, sir?"

"The very same."

"Aye, sir. We all have one of those."

Hal tucked his thumbs into his belt.

"So, what now?"

"We wait and we close the shutter again."

It wasn't long before we heard a shout at the base of our wall.

"I'm coming up, m'lord. I got Little Willy with me to steady the ladder at the bottom. Don't want to end up in the drink."

"We hear you. Climb, Treddlan!" I shouted.

"They 'int daft these masons, are they?" asked Hal.

"They are ever conscious of the dangers of their job, Hal. We'd be the same."

"A gaggle of wild and naked maidens ready for the ravishin' wouldn't get me up that bloody ladder," he added.

After a few heartbeats, we heard the grating of the wooden ladder as it hit the stonework.

Up came Treddlan.

"You all right down there, young Willy?"

"Aye, Da, I'm holdin' it."

"You just keep yer feet on the bottom rung."

"Yes, Da."

"Right, m'lord, I'm by yer window."

"Can you hear me, Treddlan?"

"Perfectly, my lord."

"Can you insert your knife into the gap between the shutters and push up? Lift the latch?"

"It's metal, sir."

"I know, but I want to know if it's possible."

We watched as a sliver of dull and scarred metal came through the small gap between the shutters. It was just long enough to show on our side.

"Lift, Treddlan."

"I'm lifting."

"Now push the shutter."

"Which one?"

"It doesn't matter."

The black iron latched bolt lifted out of its socket.

Treddlan pushed and the shutter eased open.

"Well done, man!" I cried.

His face appeared in the space of the window.

"Now, with a free hand…"

"Wait a minute, m'lord." Treddlan put the cement spatula in his teeth, making it difficult to speak.

"Wite!"

"Can you throw this small ball so that it hits that piece of metal there?" I gestured to my polished plate.

His forehead wrinkled in puzzlement, "Irl 'av a go, zir," he muttered through his lips.

"You all right, Da?" said a worried voice at the bottom of the ladder.

"Ferfectry, rad," said Treddlan looking down.

I folded the little ball into his hand and he aimed and threw. He missed.

Hal retrieved the ball.

"Another go, Treddlan."

This time his aim was better and he hit the metal roundel with a resounding 'dong.'

The plate fell to the ground just where it had been discovered the morning after Master Pitchcott's murder.

"Thank you, Treddlan," I said. "Please come up for your reward."

There was a squeaking of wood against stone and a grating sound. Treddlan disappeared.

Then, after a moment, there was an almighty splash.

I looked down into the moat.

"Treddlan?" shouted Hal.

I laughed, "No, Little Willy. I think he forgot how narrow the grass is there. I think he stepped back."

"Ack! He all right?"

"Yes, his da is fishing him out," I answered, laughing loudly.

"So now we know how the man got up the wall."

"The putlogs."

"Yes."

"And the man might 'ave lifted the latch so?" Hal took

his knife and lifted the black metal latch from the inside.

"Or... let's play out something else. We don't need a mason and a ladder for this."

I moved away from my window and stood by my table.

"Close the shutter, Hal."

My man-at-arms dropped the latch into place again.

"Now, you are Pitchcott. You are lying in your bed. You're woozy with sleep. What do you hear?"

"The man climbin'..."

"I doubt it, Hal. It would have been quieter than our ladder climber. The ladder creaked and rattled. No, you hear this..."

I rapped on the wood of my table with my knuckles.

Hal looked surprised.

I rapped again.

"That wakes you."

I rapped again.

Hal moved to the window.

"I 'ears the rappin'; I wonder what on earth it is. I open the shutter... and..."

"What do you see?"

"A man suspended in the air," Hal said, breathlessly.

"Just so, Hal. You step back in horror. How can this be? It's not possible."

"The man throws the ball at me..."

"Or however he did it..."

"And misses, 'itting the metal plate you 'ave there."

"Quickly, Master Pitchcott turns and tries to move out of the way. He's on his way to the door... maybe to call for help or to bang on it... who knows?" I said. "He has to go around my table. The side of his head is to the window."

"And then... the man throws another ball and wallop, down goes Pitchcott."

Hal looked up at me suddenly. "Christ's bones, that's

fiendish."

I shrugged.

"But I think that's how it was done. I just don't know what with."

Hal sat down with a bump on my stool.

"But... but to get up there and do all that, you'd 'ave to be a monkey!"

"Who do we know who can climb like... well, you said a squirrel, didn't you?"

Hal grinned.

"Armer, it must be Armer."

"Maybe," I said as I picked up my metal plate.

"Two dents now, Hal."

"Argh. A blacksmith'll get them out for you!"

I took my metal plate down, tucked it under my arm, and Hal and I walked into town.

"Shall we see what Master Armer has managed to do about his goods and chattels, Hal?"

"You goin' ta arrest him?"

"Not quite yet. I have a few more questions I need answering. One of them entails a trip to Master Chapman's."

"Anthony?"

"On St Peter's Street, yes. We never did get to ask the household if Robert Agnew was there the night of the celebration for the birth of their child, did we?"

"Well, it was rather overtaken with you 'avin' that knock on the 'ead."

"Hmm." I touched my temple. It was still sore, despite Johannes' salve.

We came to the house of Nicholas Barbflet on the High Street and were just about to pass when we heard a terrible screeching coming from the open window of the front room on the ground floor.

"Well, it's a start," said a voice. "At least you have a sound from it. What about you, Adelina? Have you been practising as I asked you?"

The answer was another terrible squeaking squeal.

"I think you are both blowing far too hard. Shall we try it - *softly*?"

I laughed. "Master Agnew at his lessons with the girls."

"Ah yes, 'is flute."

Out of the door, at a rapid pace, bowled Nicholas. He was jamming his coif on his head and it seemed he couldn't get out of the house fast enough. The door banged behind him.

"Ah, Sir Aumary!"

"Good Morning, Nick."

"Is it?"

I looked at Hal. "The sun is shining, the air is warm but not too hot, and there have been no further murders or fires."

"Ah..."

"Music lessons not quite going to plan, are they?" asked a grinning Hal.

"It's like the screaming of a dozen tormented mice. I am going down to the mill for some peace," said Nick, clasping his hands to his ears. "It's wonderful when Master Agnew plays. When the girls play, it's like a thousand demons shrieking in your ears!"

We laughed and listened again.

"No, this is how it's done," we heard Master Agnew say.

A beautifully soft and woody note came dancing out of the window. The note lasted a long time.

"This is what you are both doing."

There was a shrill and piercing tone which made our ears crackle.

"Can you hear the difference?"

"He's very good with them," said Nick. "But God's teeth, I'm not sure I can stand another week of this."

Then a beautiful trill of notes wafted out of the window.

"If you practise hard and do as I say, then this is the sort of thing you'll be able to play," said Master Agnew behind the wall.

He began to play a mournful and beautiful tune which suddenly grew into a rapid trill of a dance tune I had heard played on our village green by one of the young lads on his rebec.

"Never, never in my lifetime," said Nick grimacing. "Can I see our Adel ever being able to play like that."

"'Es very good in't 'e?" said Hal tapping his foot in time with the tune.

Nick scoffed, then groaned. "*Years* of practice, I suppose."

Nick suddenly realised that he hadn't asked after my health.

"How's the head? We were all worried about you. I heard from Johannes that the killer had targeted you too."

From the window came a better attempt at blowing by the girls.

"Thank you, yes. It's better, Nick."

"We need to make sure that all the holes are covered by the fingers, like this," said Master Agnew in a soft voice.

Another note on two instruments came out of the window.

"Ay," said Hal, "They're getting better."

"Doesn't last, Hal," said Nick. "They're fine when he's here and forget it all when he's gone."

"Lift a finger, the bottom one," said Master Agnew.

"Mind you, he's a wonderful minder of children." Nick laughed. "Does tricks and keeps them well amused. They love it when he comes to the house."

"Oh!" asked Hal. "What does he do?"

"Oh, you know. The sorts of things that amuse young girls. Finding walnuts from behind their ears and hiding an egg in a cup and making it disappear, that sort of thing."

"The sort of thing you see at fairs and such," said Hal. "Performed by jugglers and the like."

"That sort of thing, yes."

"A much better sound, girls. Much better," said Agnew. "Now shall we attempt, do you think, to lift one finger after another and blow on each lift?"

Hal chuckled. "They're marching on."

Nick shook his head. "I tell you. They will have forgotten it all by supper time."

We all laughed.

"Well, I can't stand here all day. I, too, must march on. God keep you both," and he turned into the alley at the side of his house, tying the strings of his coif loosely under his chin.

We carried on walking, and the noise of the flutes faded into the noise and bustle of the town's High Street.

Master Armer was in one of the unused stable rooms at the back of the Pitchcott house.

He had recovered the mail shirt he'd been making at his forge and was rubbing it with oil to clean it and make it free of soot, checking the links as he went.

We watched him for a moment until he realised we were there.

He stood up and bowed. "My Lord."

"You found yourself somewhere to work, Armer?"

"Yes, sir, thank you. It's not ideal, but it's a start."

"I was wondering if you might do me a favour, Armer. I have a polished steel plate that I use to look into for trimming my beard when I'm staying at the castle. It's been damaged. I wonder if you might beat the dents out for me and re-polish it?"

I watched his face as he took it from me. There seemed to be no recognition. I felt sure if he'd been the person to throw that ball at Master Pitchcott in my room in the castle wall, he would have realised that the dents were made by his own work and I would have seen something in his face.

There was nothing. He simply scrutinised the surface, tilting it this way and that.

"I can do that, sir. It will be some time though because I must finish this hauberk for Sir Robert Courcells. It's late already."

"When you can, Armer."

I wandered around the small workshop.

"Might you be able to tell me, Armer, where you were six days ago during the terrible thunderstorm we had at, ooooh, I think it was just after midday, wasn't it, Hal?"

Armer put down his rag as Hal nodded.

"Aye, sir, I can. I had just managed to get Simon Smith's cart up the hill to St Martin's. I was unloading my gear when the rain came down. My men and I managed to wheel the cart in here just in time."

"Where are they now?"

"Martin and John are out delivering, sir. They'll be back shortly. Simon, the farrier, came with his cart shortly before the rain and stayed till it stopped."

I nodded.

"Why do you want to know?"

"Someone attacked the Lord Belvoir, Armer," said Hal.

"Attacked you, sir? Who? How did you fight them off?"

"It's unimportant now, Armer," I said. "Take care of yourself. Like me, you might find yourself the victim of another attempt on your life. I think the man is getting rather desperate."

Armer's face drained of colour.

"The doctor thought the fire in the forge was an attempt to kill me. You think so too, sir? But I can't think of anyone who might want to kill me. I really can't."

"Just be careful, that's all. And oh, Armer,"

"Yessir?"

"We noticed that you are an excellent climber. Are there any other tricks you can perform? We saw you climbing the tree for Mistress Spynner's cat."

Armer laughed. "No, I don't do that sort of thing for fun, sir, only for that damned cat. He's up and down that tree ten times a week. Mistress Spynner is always worried, but he never fails to get down. Why, sir?"

"No matter, Armer. Good day to you."

"God go with you, sir. I'll send a message to the castle when this is done," and he touched my steel plate with mucky fingers.

"You don't think it's 'im, do you?" said Hal as we walked around the corner.

"He could be lying. We shall need to talk to his men to verify his tale. They mustn't be allowed to confer. We might find that his men will be loyal to him, Hal, and say what he wishes them to say."

"Want me to ask Simon Smith? He won't lie, not to us, m'lord."

"Yes. Go down to his forge now, Hal, and see what he has to say. I am off to question Mistress Deyning again."

"Fer goodness sake, don't you go getting yerself in any dark alleys. Stay out where folks can see you."

I laughed. "I'll meet you at the High Cross."

The manservant let me in with a scraping bow.

"M'lord. The master and mistress are in the hall."

"Good. I shall speak to them both."

Husband and wife rose as I entered from the screens passage. The remains of dinner were laid on the tabletop. I thought Mistress Deyning looked taut and stiff and I wondered if they had been arguing in the moments before I'd arrived.

In my mind, I had a picture of the man who had scaled the wall by standing on the putlogs and heaving himself up, but I realised that a woman in man's clothes could do it just as well. If they were unafraid, dainty but strong, they could indeed do the job as well as any man.

Do not underestimate a woman, Hal had said. I had cause to know that indeed.

Everild Deyning, although petite and slight, might be strong for all I knew.

There was no point in running around the subject, so I came straight to the questions I had gone there to ask.

Mistress Deyning looked peeved that there was no polite preamble.

"Master Deyning, Madam, I need to know where both of you were when we had the terrible thunderstorm six days ago. I believe it was just after midday. I left this house after speaking to Master Agnew and walked down to town. I didn't see either of you here. Where were you?"

They looked at each other, and then resignedly, Deyning wafted his hand at his wife.

"I was in my chamber with a headache," said Everild. "It's often the case in such sultry weather."

"Alone?"

"I sent my girl to Master Gallipot for a remedy. She came back drenched some time later."

"And you, Deyning?"

"Alone at my place of work. I am afraid I have no one to vouch for me."

"Again, Master Deyning?"

"I spend a good deal of my day alone, sir. Alone in my office. My workers are in their own work shed at the back of the building."

I wandered around the hall.

"They tell me, Master Deyning, that you are a Marlborough lad."

Deyning's eyes narrowed.

"That's right, sir. My father and his father before him - all Marlborough men. Born and bred in this house."

"So, no doubt, as a child, if you were anything like me, you played at the nearest edge of the forest. Out all day in the sunshine, active, growing as brown as a filbert?" I smiled.

All the while I was speaking to him, I was sizing him up. Could he have scaled the wall of the castle? Might he have been adept at placing his feet just so on those small projections of wood called putlogs? Could he have heaved himself up by the power of the muscles of his upper arms?

"No doubt you climbed the trees of the forest, in search of eggs as I did."

Deyning folded his arms over his chest.

"My Lord Belvoir, you know as well as I that taking eggs from the king's royal forest is an offence."

"Aw, I am not going to arrest you for a crime you might have committed as a boy of eight, Deyning," I chuckled. "It was a crime for me too, but I still did it."

Deyning scoffed gently.

"And I scrumped apples from the priory trees further down the hill and guzzled on the cherries of their orchard," I admitted.

Deyning moved to a pot board and offered me a drink.

I accepted.

"All boys climb trees, m'lord. I was no exception."

"Tell me, do you think you could still do it?" I sipped; a good Pitchcott wine, I thought.

Deyning chuckled, "I doubt it, m'lord. I am definitely not as nimble as I used to be over twenty years ago."

"Aye, lack of practice…"

"You practise with sword and buckler, sir, I'm sure," he said quickly. "I hear you are to be found of a morning in the castle bailey with your men at arms. You will not have lost muscle and your ability to climb. You are a knight."

"Oh, how did you hear that I keep myself fit at the castle?"

"My cousin by marriage, Farnell. He is sometimes to be found at the castle. I believe he's seen you."

"Farnell naturally has an interest in all things military, sir," said Everild sitting at the furthest end of the long table.

"Might I ask your interest in my physical abilities, m'lord? It's a strange subject to…"

"Oh, I'm just wondering how the man got into the castle, Deyning."

"Ah, that again. Climbing through windows," said Everild. Both Richard and Everild laughed, their eyes rising to Heaven in disbelief.

My face, however, was perfectly straight. "No, madam, not *through* windows."

I watched the man's face. I waited for some betrayal. I did not see his Adam's apple swallow in fear. There was no outbreak of sweat on his forehead, neither did his eyes flicker with guilt.

"Not through windows… but I thought you said…?" interrupted Everild.

"I believe that our murderer climbed the face of the castle wall by using the small projections of wood left by the builders and gained access to the shuttered window from the outside."

There was a hushed silence.

"And you think that Richard could do this, my Lord Belvoir?" asked Everild, wide-eyed and white-faced.

I shrugged. "It isn't as impossible as it seems for the right man."

Deyning frantically shook his head. "Then, m'lord, I must tell you, I am not the right man, for I could not do it. On my oath, I could not. My head for heights is not good."

I stared at the man.

No, somehow, I didn't think he could. Besides, his feet were quite large.

"I would end up in the moat, and I must say, sir, I cannot swim either," he said with slight embarrassment.

Everild Deyning's voice was shocked and quiet.

"You think, m'lord, this is how my father was killed?"

"I do, madam."

She crossed herself.

"Then it was the devil himself. He took him. No man could do that, sir, but only one possessed of the devil!"

I ground my teeth in frustration as I walked through The Green, past St Mary's, through Church Alley and out past Johannes' house to the High Cross.

Hal was there lounging on the steps talking to a matron of the town.

He saw me and jumped up. The matron coyly swished her hem and was gone.

"What did you learn, Hal?"

"That Farnell is telling the truth. The cart *was* in the workshop out of the rain, and Smith came up the 'ill to retrieve it. All the men were there at midday, just as the rain came down. Simon 'ad to wait till it stopped to wheel 'is cart back to the forge down there." Hal pointed across the road to the building on the corner of The Marsh.

"So Farnell was amongst folk when I was being hit."

He nodded. "The Deynings?"

"They were both alone, but I can't see either of them scaling the castle wall."

Hal fingered his ear. "Ah, no."

"Must we look for further enemies of Pitchcott's, Hal, in the town?"

I must admit to feeling a little dull and disappointed as we made our way down the High Street to speak to Master Chapman.

My suspects were dwindling. All seemed to be accounted for when Pitchcott, the cook and myself were being attacked.

We were about to call through the door when Master Anthony Chapman came striding up behind us.

"I have followed you, m'lord, down the High Street. I had no idea you were coming to us." He smiled and bowed.

"Master Chapman, good day. I believe congratulations must be offered, for you have a son, I've heard."

"We do. Hilda presented me with a son but a short two months ago."

"Might we have a word about the celebration you threw for the birth of this son, Anthony?"

I had met Anthony before. He had been a suspect in a death in the town a year or so ago. He was a tall, haughty lad of about twenty-six with light brown wavy hair. His shoulders were broad and his waist and hips small - a good manly figure. He had been an excellent catch for the plainest but one of the richest girls in the town, Hilda Caspar. I knew it was a marriage of money and business, but then, so many were.

Anthony looked strangely at me and then at Hal, and then he opened the house door.

"Please, sirs, follow me in."

I had been in this lime-washed room before when questioning both Anthony and his father. This was a splinter new house of only two years, built at the further - and still developing - end of town, by St Peter's church and opposite the castle. The house was narrow but deep, fading into darkness down a hallway.

A servant came from that darkness, but Anthony Chapman waved him away.

I heard Hal say, "Welcoming as ever," under his breath, and I remembered this was a family of skinflints and misers.

We would be offered no wine nor ale, no place to sit.

"I'll come to the point, Anthony. You had a celebration for the birth of your son…"

"Peter, sir."

"A good name."

"In the third week of his life. We dared not celebrate before this, for you know how thin is the line of life, sir, which attaches babies to their families."

"I have cause to know, yes, Anthony. This celebration, what form did it take?"

Anthony wandered away from me and stood at a table at the edge of the room. I saw Hal stiffen in the hope perhaps of ale being poured for us both, but no.

"Form, sir? Why, we had a feast as is right and proper. After the child was named."

"You could have no official baptism, for the church is closed, is it not?"

"Yes, the priest came and baptised our lad soon after his birth, but we celebrated his birth here on the day we gathered together our family, friends and neighbours."

"Did you have music?"

Anthony smiled.

"We did," he nodded. "Two of the servants play pipe and tabor, and one has nakkers. We cleared the largest hall and had dancing for a while."

"Who did you engage to play for you?"

"Oh, I see," said the young man. "Apart from those of the family or servants who can play something or sing, sir, we had Master Robert Agnew, Pitchcott's man - the man who was murdered..."

Anthony broke off as he suddenly realised what this might be about.

"You were saying, Anthony?"

He licked his lips.

"The man who was killed in the castle, sir, his secretary. It's his pleasure to go about the town and play for weddings and the like."

"For which you paid him in..."

"Some money and food and drink, as much as he could consume, sir. He plays the flute, you see, m'lord, and he is very good."

"We've 'eard 'im, lad," said Hal, staring hard at Chapman.

"What time did he leave?"

"Leave? Oh, I don't rightly know. We were all deep in our cups by about..."

"Surprised your cups were deep enough," whispered Hal under his breath, looking away innocently.

"About an hour before vigils."

"It was a good party?"

Chapman laughed. "It was, sir."

"Did anyone see Master Agnew at that time?"

"Oh I don't know, sir. I do know that he was well away with drink just before the vigils hour for I saw him myself, slumped in the corner with an empty cup."

"He tells me he drank and ate too much, for the food was plentiful and the drink good. He didn't go home but spent the night on your floor."

"That is very likely true, sir. Chambers might know more than me. He will have seen to the tidying of everything the next morning, if not on that night."

The man was fetched from the depths of the house.

Chambers, the servant we had seen dismissed through the back door, screwed up his rather protuberant eyes.

"Yes, my lord, he was here. He was rather the worse for drink, and slept propped up in the corner. He went back to his home before first light."

"So he played for you all?"

"As we ate, sir," said Chapman

"And then for the dancing?"

"Yes, sir."

"And then ate his fill, drank too much and passed out in the corner of the hall?"

"Yes, my lord. He was still there in the morning," said Chambers with evident disgust. "He hadn't stirred at all, not moved a muscle."

"Though he's perfectly capable of it..." laughed Chapman.

"I beg your pardon, Anthony?"

"Oh, I'm sorry, my lord; I refer to his ability to entertain, sir. He is most amusing."

"Amusin'?" asked Hal. "On the flute?"

"He is a clever entertainer, sir. We didn't engage him simply for his musical ability."

"Got yer money's worth then?" said Hal quietly. "Typically."

"He is very versatile."

"Oh, what does 'e do then?" asked Hal. "Besides tootle."

"Master Agnew is a man of many talents, sir. He can do conjuring tricks. Most adept with sleight of hand is the man," said Chapman.

"He can make things appear and disappear, my lord," said Chambers, smiling. "He's able, and I don't know how, to tell you what you might be thinking."

"It's a trick, it must be," said Hal.

"Undoubtedly, but very clever," said Anthony Chapman. "I don't know how he does it, and I have puzzled over it."

"So Master Agnew entertained you with tricks and illusions at some point in the evening?"

"He did, sir, royally. He was well worth his food and drink."

"And he was here all night, insensible in the corner?"

"He was," said Chambers.

"Well, thank you for your help," I said, turning to leave.

"Oh, by the way," I turned back.

"When was your party?"

"It was the night of the day before we had the terrible storm, sir."

"The night Master Pitchcott was killed?"

"I believe so, sir."

"Hmmm."

"My Lord Belvoir, is Master Agnew under suspicion that you ask such questions about him?"

"We must leave no stone unturned, Anthony, though I must say that Master Agnew has no motive for the murder of his master."

Chapman shook his head. "He is such a genial man. I cannot believe him guilty of such perfidy. He gave us much more than we paid for, that's for sure. Why, he even had us laughing at ourselves and our attempts to walk on a line as he had done earlier, didn't he Chambers? How we laughed!"

The manservant grinned inanely.

"Walk on a line?" said Hal. "What was 'e doin' then?"

"Why, he tied a rope to a beam there and another to a

sturdy piece of furniture upon which all us men sat to weigh it down, and he walked above the floor, sir, a good four feet above the earth, and never fell off. Naturally, when we all tried it, we fell off. It was a huge joke, sir. We laughed for hours!"

Hal turned to me, his face wide-eyed and incredulous.

Well, I'll be bugg… buried in Burbage," he said. "'Es a bloody monkey!"

Chapter Twelve

"**N**OW, HAL, we mustn't jump to conclusions," I said as we walked the short distance back to the castle. "Master Agnew was in the Chapman house all night."

"Did they lock him in?"

"I expect so."

"But 'e's such a clever beggar as 'e could get in and out without anyone knowin' 'e'd gone."

"It's possible, Hal, but what on earth could his motive be? He was happy in the household of Master Pitchcott. By all accounts, he could make extra money even when working for his master. Pitchcott didn't seem to care."

"Now, I understand what Mistress Deyning meant when she said that the merchant told 'er that it was none of her business and said it was 'Agnew's own business'. It was true... 'e's running another business," said Hal. "An entertaining business."

"Agnew was well-placed. As Johannes said, why get rid of Pitchcott to his own detriment? It makes no sense."

"But 'e's the only one, as I can see, as can get up the castle wall."

"We don't really know that, Hal."

"Humph!"

"However, there's something else which puzzles me. The night Pitchcott died, Agnew told me he was at the Chasier's playing for their party, but that was the wrong night. He was at the Chapmans' party."

"Mixing up his parties?"

"The Chapmans are very close to the castle, Hal."

"But he was drunk!"

"We must speak to him, see what he says. Men sometimes betray themselves. Their guilt shows in their face."

"Not that one; he's as shifty as a shite shoveller."

"You think it would be impossible to rattle him?"

"I reckon 'e makes out 'e's a bit short in the top larder, sir, but in reality, he's sharper than a serpent's tooth."

"We must try to poke him, see if the snake will spit and see what happens."

The following day, it rained.

It rained hard, as it turned out, all day. The High Street became a soup of pulverised mud, dung and offal, for, yet again, it was market day.

Hal and I trotted from the castle up the street on horseback, for we had no inclination to dirty ourselves to such an extent so early in the day, and arrived relatively clean shod at the Deyning house.

The place was in uproar.

The steward, hopping from foot to foot frenziedly, suddenly opened the door and bowed us in quickly, muttering something about blood and water. He left us puzzled on the doorstep and raced out of the house and through the gate.

The grooms were absent and our horses had to

remain in the yard as we went into the hall through the screens passage.

"What has happened here?" I asked, scanning the large room, which was in some disarray. One of the grooms stood open-mouthed, his hands hanging at his side. The kitchen girl was just disappearing through the door, screeching.

"Oh my lord!"

Everild Deyning, a cloak thrown over her shift and her hair hanging free, approached us. It seemed she had been attempting to marshal the staff into some sort of order.

She wiped her hand over her forehead.

"I simply do not know what is happening in this house."

"Sit down, madam, and explain to me what *has* happened."

"Farnell has been attacked, sir."

"He's been living here?"

"Now he no longer has premises off the High Street and we have the room, he has been staying here whilst he sorts his business. It seemed foolish for him to continue living in the alley with Mistress Spynner and working from the back of our buildings, climbing the hill every day."

"Yes, indeed. I see that," I said. "You say he has been attacked but not killed."

Everild Deyning crossed herself.

"No, sir. He lives. The knife grazed a rib."

"A knife wound?"

I could see that her hands were bloodied, and her shift was splattered with blood.

"You found him?"

"No, sir, Agnew found him. I came up a blink later."

"Have you sent for the doctor?"

"We have, and Richard went out to work early before we discovered the calamity, so I have dispatched Thomas to fetch him back."

She touched her forehead again, and I noticed her hand was trembling.

"Why would anyone wish to hurt Farnell, sir?" I saw she was on the edge of tears.

I didn't answer her, for a theory was forming in my brain, but needed more thought.

"What the devil 'appened then?" asked Hal, impatient for the details.

Mistress Deyning did not ignore Hal as had been customary for her, but this time answered him quite civilly.

"I heard a shouting and a noise, much as I did last time we…" She stopped and swallowed. "I rushed down the steps to see Agnew standing on the stairs at the other end of the hall, coming out from his room. He was nearer and leapt into Aldous' room where Farnell was staying."

"When was this?"

"At dawn. It was not yet fully light. And it's turned into such a dull morning."

We had risen before dawn and rode up the street as the sun, what we saw of it, was lighting the world.

"Someone had tried to kill Farnell in his bed as he slept. Agnew was the first into the room and I followed him. Farnell was writhing around drenched in blood and I… oooh."

The young woman sat down stiffly on the hall bench and put her face into her hands.

"It was horrible."

At that moment, Deyning burst in through the hall door, followed very closely by the steward, Thomas, and Doctor Johannes. The little maid Aebbe followed him a moment later.

The manservant went to the mistress and tried to get her to drink some ale. She refused it, pushing away the cup.

"Everild?"

Richard Deyning rushed up to his wife, but there was no embrace, no soft words of comfort.

"What's happened?"

Then the tale was repeated.

Johannes strode up the stairs with his medical pack in his hand. He nodded to me as he passed.

"Sir Aumary."

"We'll speak later, Johannes."

"Were all the doors locked?" I turned to the steward.

"I had unlocked them a moment earlier."

"Anyone might have come in unseen and gone up the stairs," said Agnew. "We were all rising and about our own business in our rooms."

I noticed the man was wearing a long shirt but no hose. His legs were bare, but he had soft slippers on his feet.

His shirt was a little bloodied.

"You answered his call for help, Agnew?"

"Aye, m'lord, I did."

"You were in your room underneath?"

"Yes, sir. I heard a thumping of feet on the floorboards above me, as if a man was running, and I heard Master Farnell cry out piteously."

"Then what did you do?"

Agnew shook a little as he explained that he'd searched quickly for his knife.

"Though what I thought I could do, sir... I am a timid man, a man of business, and I don't know if I could stick a knife in anyone... even to save my own life, but I took it with me."

"And then?" asked Hal.

"I came out and ran up the stairs. The mistress followed almost on my heels, and then we found Master Farnell bleeding on the bed."

"He said that a man had attacked him in the pre-dawn

light as he lay in his bed," said Everild.

"The shutters of the room were closed?"

"Aye, sir, they were. It was quite dark in the room. It faces west, and the day isn't bright today," answered Agnew.

"Who was next to come into the room?"

"John, sir. John the groom."

"I told him to stay with Farnell and staunch the wound whilst I came down to send someone to fetch Richard and the doctor," said Everild. "He's still there."

I nodded. "Please, will you all stay here."

I ran up the stairs followed closely by Hal.

Johannes was working quickly on Farnell, who was lying on a blood-soaked bed, grimacing as the doctor cleansed and stitched the wound to his side.

"You are very lucky, young man," I heard Johannes say. "This, I think, was meant for your heart, but your ribs deflected the blade. You're a fit man with fine muscles, and these protected you."

Farnell took in a sharp breath.

"Jesus, aid me. For the life of me, I have no idea what I have done to deserve such treatment from this man, whoever he is."

"You have no recollection of who it might be?"

"No, my lord. None. The first I knew was the sharp pain in my side as I lay in my bed. It was that which woke me."

"The room was dark, but you saw no shape or shadow."

"A shape, yes, hovering above me. A man of small stature with long hair, that's all."

He winced again.

"I cried out loudly and the man fled."

"Where did he go?"

"I had managed to raise myself a little and there was a ray of light from the open doorway to the stairs. He went that way."

"But he can't 'ave done," said Hal. "'E would 'ave bin seen by those in the hall."

"That is the way he went."

"Not through the window?"

"No, no, m'lord. He wouldn't have had the time to open the shutters and I would have seen his face as the light hit him. As it was…" Farnell Armer clenched his teeth once more, lapsing into a pained silence.

"Hal, can you check the room for escape routes? We have not considered that there may be a door or a hidden stair somewhere here."

Hal turned to the eastern corner of the room and began to pace, looking up and down and banging the walls here and there with his clenched fist.

I remembered well a house in another place where several hiding places had been secreted in the building. Did we have something similar here?

"We'll speak further later," I said to the armourer. "Take your ease for a while and recover a little."

Hal turned to me. "Nothin'. As empty as a nun's cradle."

I nodded.

"Johannes, we shall see you downstairs."

Once back in the hall, I looked over the people there. No one had moved. The groom had gone to stand by the outer door, but that was all.

"My lady, gentlemen, tell me again where you all were when Master Armer cried out."

"I was in my room up there." Everild Deyning pointed to the stairs at the eastern end of the hall.

"Anyone with you?"

She shook her head. "Richard had left me not a few moments before."

"I was also in my room, m'lord, alone. I was dressing when I heard the cry," said Agnew.

"As Everild has said, I had gone from the house moments before this happened, I suppose. When Thomas found me, I was halfway down Herd Street on my way to the warehouse," said Richard Deyning.

"He was, sir," said Thomas Parfitt. "I called to him and he turned back to me. He was walking by the junction of the Marsh and the Oxford Road. He turned around and we hurried up the hill together."

I turned to the groom called John.

He stammered. "I... I... was just coming from the kitchen, sir, with ale for breaking our fast."

"Why did you come through the house?"

"I wouldn't normally, but it was raining, m'lord."

"I saw him, sir," said young Aebbe. "See, he left the ale pots and bread plate on the table when the rumpus started."

"And where were you, Aebbe?"

"Coming from the front door. I had just come in the house, m'lord, from home."

"Thank you, all of you."

"Might I go and put on some clothes, sir? I feel a little chilly and vulnerable in just my shirt," asked Agnew.

"Certainly." I noticed once more that the man's shirt was a little bloodied.

"You'll need to hand it to the laundress, Agnew. There is blood on it."

"Oh no, no, no, that's the second shirt in a few days. It must have become bloodied as I leaned over the poor Master Farnell."

"We found another of your shirts under the body of the cook Margery, Agnew."

"Yes, sir." The man's face took on a sad expression. "I tossed it on the bed, meaning to put it for the laundry the morning before she..." He looked down at his shirt. "Terrible, terrible."

"Mistress Deyning, you too are bloodied," I said.

"I, too, leaned over my cousin, my Lord Belvoir. It is his blood."

"Of course, if I were thinking that you were the would-be murderer, madam, I might think that the blood spurted there when you took the knife ineffectually to his heart."

The woman's eyes opened wide.

"Why would I do that?"

"He is all that stands between you and a considerable fortune. Oh yes, you are a wealthy woman with the money your father left you, but think how much wealthier you'd be if you could have it all."

"That is a lie!" shouted Richard Deyning standing up quickly. "Everild has always known the fortune would be divided between the two of them. She has been content with that arrangement for a long time."

"And she might have planned to kill Farnell many moons ago, Richard," I answered.

"Aye, money is a powerful motivator," said Hal, shaking his head ruefully.

"I did not try to kill my cousin." Everild put both her hands to her cheeks.

"There, there, mistress," Agnew laid his hand on Everild's shoulder and stood close to her. "He lives, he's all right."

"No, he lives and is all right, but it's such a terrible shock to find someone wanted to kill him in this very house. Poor Farnell!"

Agnew simpered. "I had no idea you were so terribly fond of your cousin."

Everild shook his hand from her shoulder and moved away slightly. "I have said it often enough. He's like a brother to me."

"People have been known to kill their kin. Their beloved

brothers," I said.

"Cain and Abel," said Hal quietly.

Agnew drew himself up to his full height and stood, bristling.

"That is preposterous. Why should she do such a thing? She is a well-bred lady, sweet-natured and kind. She could never kill anyone."

Everild looked towards Agnew with a puzzled expression on her face. It was as if she couldn't understand why Agnew was so vehemently taking her part.

"I *didn't* try to kill Farnell!"

"No, you didn't," said a voice from the stair.

We all looked up.

Farnell stood shakily at the top of the steps with Johannes behind him. I could just make out the groom John behind them.

"It was a man, of that I am sure."

Farnell struggled down the stairs and came to sit on the bench by the central fire. His body was cross-bandaged and he wore a cloak loosely thrown across his shoulders over nothing but his braies.

He was pale and his face seemed drooping as if his expression was sliding from his skin.

"It wasn't Everild."

"But no one left the stairs," said Hal scratching his head. "Nor went out of the door. At that time, you would have seen them, Agnew, as you stood on the stairs, and you, Deyning, on the street."

"Perhaps not if they continued down to the ford, or dodged into one of the other houses," said Deyning.

Farnell lifted a tired head. "I am not at odds with anyone on this road. As far as I know, I have no enemies in this town. Why would a neighbour want to kill me? For that matter, why would Everild want to kill me?"

"That is what I say, young man," said Agnew jutting his chin. "It's ludicrous."

I stepped into the middle of the group.

"Please, everyone, go and dress and we shall all come back here to the hall, for I think I might see just a way forward in this dark business. I will tell you all what I think when we reconvene."

Johannes looked up quickly. "You know who the murderer is?"

"I have an idea, yes."

"Well..." said Hal. "If that person is 'ere, you don't think it risky that they'll bolt when you let 'im go from the room?"

"No, Hal, I don't."

"You sure they're in this room now?"

"Yes. I think the murderer is with us now, Hal."

"Well, I'll be buried in Burbage!"

I called in the other groom from the stable and the girl from the kitchen and they lounged by the walls in silence.

Everild Deyning, now dressed in dark brown and cream, with a wimple and veil of fine cream linen held in place by a metal circlet, came to sit at the long table. Agnew, in his pale green short cotte, stood at her back but not too close, for she turned to look at him and growled. He took a step back.

Deyning was seated at the head of the table as was his right, his hands steepled before him.

Thomas Parfitt stood behind him.

Farnell Armer sat on a cushioned bench some distance away and Johannes hovered over him.

The other servants clustered to the back wall and tried to make themselves invisible.

"I will take you all back to the day Master Aldous Pitchcott came to see me at Durley Manor. He told me that you, sir," I nodded to Richard Deyning. "Had defrauded him of some money."

Deyning scoffed and, folding his arms, looked away.

"Pitchcott also told me that his life was in danger, for there had been two attempts to kill him recently. I didn't believe him. However, when I discovered that he had enemies within his own household, I thought it might be a good thing, at least, to talk to those involved. And I met you, Deyning." I nodded to the furrier. "And you, sir," a nod to the armourer. "You, Mistress Deyning, and you, Agnew."

"No one in his household would kill him. It's ridiculous to think of it," said Everild.

"On the contrary, madam, they did."

Flustered, the woman subsided into mutterings.

I walked around the table.

"I was distracted from the truth by the fact that Master Pitchcott also had enemies in the town. Many more, I think, than I have been able to discover." I chuckled under my breath. "I had a feeling that half the town might have been glad to see the back of him."

"That's the truth," said Hal, perched on a stool by the stairs.

A few backsides shifted uncomfortably on seats.

"But we kept coming back to the money which was divided between you, Mistress Deyning, and you, Master Armer, and so I set myself to discovering who might have been able to kill Master Pitchcott in his impregnable prison at the castle."

Everild Deyning stood up, anger distorting her pretty features.

"I will not listen to this. It is nonsense. Farnell and I are perfectly happy with the promised money and property.

There is no ill will and neither of us would kill the other for a greater share."

Her nostrils flared prettily, and she breathed quickly, making her small bosom heave under her brown dress.

"Well said, coz," said Farnell, moving carefully on his seat.

"No, madam, but I think there was one other who minded the arrangement very much. Please sit."

Everild's face grew pink and she sat down, a puzzled expression on her face framed in its pale linen.

"Let us go back to the days when you and Farnell were youngsters."

I saw the look which passed between the two cousins.— total bewilderment.

"It is said that Master Pitchcott adopted you, madam, when you were but two years of age because you were the child of his beloved sister and a man with whom she had become involved outside marriage, a man of whom we know nothing."

Everild jutted her delicate chin.

"And that he also took on you, Farnell, a little while later, for you too were born to a sister out of wedlock. It seems we know nothing of her beloved at all, either. He, too, is a mystery. We do not know if you were born in wedlock, or out of it."

I looked Farnell Armer in the eye.

"However, I think we *do* know, don't we, Master Armer, a little about the man who sired you? I think we now know he was a married man without children. That he was later widowed, and, feeling that he was unlikely ever to have children, he took a bastard child into his family, and although it was said this was merely a wardship, the child was treated as a son."

Armer's eyes flickered in recognition.

"Am I right, Armer?"

Reluctantly, "Yes, sir," he whispered.

"All went well for a while—boy and girl, cousins, and as happy as brother and sister. And then the young man, for now he was fourteen and could do as he wished, decided that he would not go into the family business and he broke away and apprenticed himself to a blacksmith in the county of Buckinghamshire. His uncle was not happy at all. All his life, he had wished for the boy to follow him into the wine trade. He had built up a good business. He had no one to follow him. Farnell *must* follow him in the business. Must follow him, for Farnell was his natural son."

There were a few sharp intakes of breath.

"I would not, sir."

"No. He had, too, for many years, hoped that you would marry Everild, indeed, he had planned it. For you *were* his natural son, were you not, and born to a mistress, I suppose, without the knowledge of his wife? When his wife died, he could acknowledge you and bring you into the house."

"You are correct, sir."

Everild went pale. "Farnell, is this true?"

"I'm sorry, yes it is."

"That you are his son?"

"He told me a little while ago. He'd cut me out of the will, he said, if I breathed a word, though we now know it wasn't true."

"Oh."

"I didn't want anything to do with him or his money. The property which had belonged to my mother, part of her dower, should have been mine, but he took it as his own. I was furious. Eventually, of course, in the end, he couldn't bring himself to disinherit me truly, and so all the money and the remaining property now comes back to me."

"I think you'll find, Armer," I said, "that he took it to

invest, and you will be grateful to him, for he has more than doubled the value of it…"I shifted my gaze.

"This is correct, isn't it, Master Agnew?"

Agnew breathed in deeply through his nose and spat angrily, "Yes, my master used it wisely, and it's now worth considerably more than when he took it into his keeping."

I nodded. "Thank you.

"Then poor Master Pitchcott was to reel from yet another blow. His beloved adopted daughter, his niece, the child of his sister, had married without his consent or knowledge. Her bridegroom was none other than the man with whom he had a business dispute. He had so hoped that she would marry Farnell, as we said…"

"But they couldn't marry for they're cousins," said Johannes with a furrowed brow. "One Pitchcott's offspring and the other his sister's, we've learned."

"No doubt our master vintner would have somehow circumvented that small obstacle. If that arrangement was good enough for our king, then why not for Pitchcott?"

Many years ago, King John had married his cousin Isabella of Gloucester. It had ended in divorce, for it seemed that the marriage was doomed and not considered seemly by God, who had willed them childless for years. A divorce was obtained and John married his present Isabella. This second marriage had produced a child, Henry.

That's right, Paul, who is now our king.

"Besides," I said. "Pitchcott was able perhaps to make up a wholly false story about the children not being related. It is, I'm sure, the sort of thing he might have done. Now Everild could never marry her cousin, for she was already married to his enemy. In a fit of anger, Master Pitchcott makes a new will. He leaves everything to Farnell, in the hope, perhaps, that he will see sense and carry on the wine business, perhaps in addition to his armoury. We shall never know."

Farnell slowly shook his head.

Deyning stared open-mouthed. "But… but… the foolish man. If he had simply waited."

"He was a man of action. He did not wait. He would not wait."

"But, m'lord," said the steward. "Why kill him?"

"Because if he had signed the new will, it would have utterly disinherited Everild, and that could not happen."

Thomas looked straight at Deyning.

"You, sir, have profited from this. This house and all the monies and the business."

Deyning put up his hands. "I'll not deny that the money is welcome. Neither will I deny that having the key to my childhood home again is gratifying. But I didn't kill him for it."

Everild was staring at her husband as if he was some beast with horns.

"It wasn't me, I tell you."

"Did you plan all along to marry me and kill Aldous? Was our marriage truly nothing more than a business transaction?"

"Of course not," said Deyning unconvincingly. "I didn't kill him just to get you and his money."

"No?" Everild Deyning stood and fumed. "All the time sweet words were being poured into my ear, you were plotting…" Everild grimaced. "Oh, my God! Sweet God, he warned me… Aldous told me…"

"NO! Everild, you must believe me…" Richard rose quickly.

"Sit down, please."

They both looked at me and slowly obeyed the tone of my sharp and hard voice.

I carried on. "So, Aldous Pitchcott is killed before he can sign the new will."

"Not me, I didn't kill him," said Everild quickly. "I didn't even know about it."

"The new will was never signed. Everild and Farnell share the monies and properties as was planned originally. Everyone is happy. All except one person."

Hal looked at me from his scrutiny of Deyning's face.

"'Oo's that then?"

"All in good time, Hal," I smiled.

"Now, let us examine the day Master Pitchcott is attacked."

"First poison and then strangling," said Johannes.

"No, sir," said Thomas Parfitt. "Firstly, the master was almost hit by a rock. Then a short while later, there was a fire in his store shed."

"He escaped both of these. Why?" I asked.

"Someone was very determined that 'e should die," said Hal. "They tried often enough."

"But they were, don't you think, rather inept. These attempts were, forgive me, half-hearted, bungling efforts, not the well thought out and clever action of the final deed which, against all odds, eventually succeeded and puzzled us."

"You mean that it's as if the murderer had meant us to see those bungling attempts and all the time was driving towards something more fiendish?" asked Johannes.

"Exactly that, my friend." I grinned. "The murderer wanted us to think that he could not possibly be the killer because he could in no way be involved, for he had no motive and was on Pitchcott's side to the end. He appeared worried about the attempts on Pitchcott's life and was there for his master."

Hal had now worked out what I was actually saying.

"'E made sure we thought well of 'im. We'd never think of him as the culprit. 'E fed us with what 'e wanted us to 'ear."

"He did, Hal."

I walked a little further around the table and stood by the middle of the board.

"The person who killed Master Pitchcott also disposed of poor Margery Cook, for only she could tell me the truth. Since I was determined to speak to her, she had to die before I could do so."

I saw the little kitchen maid, Otille, flinch, and wondered what she was thinking.

"Otille, the cook was not kind to you, I know."

The girl looked at her feet. "No, sir."

"The morning she was killed, what did you think had happened?"

The girl blanched and stuttered.

"She is no longer around to beat you. Tell us where you thought she was."

"I thought... I thought she was in Master Agnew's bed like normal, sir."

"You had been sworn never to tell, hadn't you?"

"Yessir."

"Now tell me truthfully. That night, the night she died, the cook was missing from her bed in the kitchen, wasn't she?"

The girl's watery eyes left my face, travelled over Everild Pitchcott's and came to rest on Master Agnew's face.

"Yes, sir. She was with Master Agnew."

"She might have been in my room, girl, but she was most certainly not with me. I was out playing at a party."

"She went up real late," blurted the girl loudly.

Agnew looked confused. "Ah, yes, the night she was killed, she came late to my bed. I came back very late from my party and we..."

"Now we shall never know, for she lies dead and cannot speak," I said. "The night the master died, was she with Master Agnew, Otille?"

"She wasn't in the kitchen."

"I wasn't in my bed either. I was lying on the Chapmans' floor and only got back here after dawn."

"You tell me you saw her and talked with her then," I said.

"Yes, sir. I wanted her gone, for I didn't want anyone to find out."

"I heard them," said Everild. "From the window. Talking."

"I think you heard her moments before she was killed, madam," I said.

Everild took in a small breath and stared at Agnew.

"So now we know the cook was killed to keep her from speaking to me. What might she have told me?"

Hal sniffed "That when she was supposed to have been with Agnew, when 'e says she was with 'im... she wasn't?"

"Do we think so?"

Everyone was silent.

"Or was it that she knew how the poison had reached the plate of Master Pitchcott?" said the doctor.

Hal shrugged. "Either way, she wasn't allowed to speak to you."

"Now we come to the attempts on the life of Master Armer."

"The fire in the forge?" said Armer, sitting up a little straighter and grimacing at the movement.

"The blow to the back of your head. This was meant to incapacitate you so that you become a casualty of a tragic accident. Fires in forges happen all the time."

"But I was saved."

"So another attempt had to be made."

"This murderer is rather a bungler, isn't he?" said Johannes. "He can't seem to do it first time."

"Our murderer is now getting desperate. He wants Everild to have *all* the money. He doesn't want Armer to have his half. He isn't thinking; he's panicking."

"Why?" asked Deyning.

"Perhaps Master Armer has said that he will move out soon and get his own house and workshop. If he does, the money will go with him and he'll spend it. He has to die before he can do this."

"I did say as such; I told Everild and Richard that I would move out as soon as I got myself on my feet, that it wouldn't be long," said Armer.

"Hmm. You were overheard, I think."

"But why," asked Johannes. "Is the murderer so set on the path of Mistress Deyning having *all* the money?"

Little Aebbe pushed off from her wall.

"It's him." She pointed to Master Deyning. "He wants it all."

"You think that's right, Aebbe?"

"Me ma used to work here before they left... that lot, the Deynings. She says they were all grasping bastards."

"Aebbe!" shouted Mistress Deyning.

Little Aebbe looked at her feet. "I'm only saying what she told me."

I smiled.

"This person doesn't want the money for themselves, Aebbe," I said. "They aren't really interested in money. They couldn't care less about this house or its contents. Neither do they have much of a care for the business beyond the ordinary."

"Then what do they care for?" said Thomas, his red mouth open in perplexity, showing his discoloured teeth.

"My lord," he added.

"They only care about Everild Pitchcott, as was."

Several people called out then, "What?" and "Why?" and "Who?"

Everild was silent but watchful.

"Why? Because they love her dearly. And who? Because they are her father."

I tilted my head to look over the table.

"That is correct, isn't it, Master Agnew?"

At first, Robert Agnew's face was expressionless. Then he smiled.

"How did you know, sir?"

"It was the way you stuck by her through all her rebuffs. She would bait and insult you, but never once did you retaliate. You never grimaced or groaned. You took it. You told us she was a good woman, a wonderful mistress. It was all too amiable, Agnew. All too perfect. There had to be a reason."

I smiled, "You told me yourself, not quite willing to keep the whole secret that her father was likely a clerk, though you had to add that he was probably in holy orders to deflect us from the truth. You could not quite keep it to yourself."

Agnew smiled ruefully and dipped his head.

"She is my daughter by Master Pitchcott's sister, sir. By Matilda Pitchcott."

There was complete silence in the room, and then Everild Deyning rose slowly with a shriek which jolted us all.

"Nooo!"

She put her hands on the tabletop to steady herself. "You *foul* creature. *You* cannot be my father."

"I am sorry, Everild, but it's true. Robert Agnew *is*

your father."

I walked around the end of the table.

"And he is also a murderer."

Chapter Thirteen

*E*VERYONE STARTED TALKING at once; all except Everild, who sat down abruptly, large-eyed and pale under her cream head cloth.

I took charge again.

"Master Agnew managed to get himself a job here in the household where his daughter was to grow up," I shouted. All fell silent.

Into that silence, Robert Agnew sighed. "I was a penniless scribe, a lowly scribbler who made music and did tricks for extra money. How could I marry my love and give her a decent home?"

"I suppose her family whisked her away when it was known she was with child?"

"They did, sir. I tried to keep her in sight. I moved around to be close but never saw her alive again, my Mattie. When Everild was born, I knew I had to stay with her, so gradually, I got into a position where I could become indispensable to Master Pitchcott. After a while, I was appointed his secretary. Then I could see my little girl every day."

I saw Everild shiver.

"Then came the time that she wanted to be married to Deyning?" I said.

"They thought they'd been so secret about it, but I heard them plotting the marriage. I told my master, though sadly, he was too late to prevent it."

"You didn't think he would take the action he did, though, did you?" I asked.

"I didn't think he would try to ruin her life, to disinherit her... no."

"And so he had to die before he signed the second will?"

"I had to stop him. He was going to ruin my little girl's life." He looked up. "He was a beast of a man, sir. He wasn't honest. He wasn't kind. Oh, he was a good businessman and a fair master to me, but he wasn't a good man."

"You found the second will in the man's office, I suppose?"

"He had no idea that Everild was my daughter, so nothing was kept secret from me."

"Why did you try to kill Master Armer?"

"He was taking what was rightfully my girl's. I couldn't have that."

I shook my head. "He had what was rightfully his as Master Pitchcott's son."

"No, sir. He's a bastard."

"And Everild is not?" shouted Armer in anger. He would have gone for Agnew's throat if he had been whole and uninjured. As it was, he doubled up in pain, and Johannes was quickly there with a potion to give him relief.

"Tonight, Agnew, you went into Master Armer's room with your knife. You tried to kill him but failed. You had to flee quickly."

Agnew grimaced. "I fled the room, yes. I... I... I'm not good with a knife. Not close at hand."

"You managed to cut the cook's throat well enough,

Agnew." I said as Hal added, "But you were seen 'alf way up the stairs a moment later?"

"Yes, sir."

"Ah, I have it. I suppose you slid down the wooden rail very quickly... not difficult for a man of your agile skills. Then you'd be there as if coming out of your own room to go up the stairs again if anyone saw you," I said.

"You are quite correct, sir."

"And the blood on your shirt was that of Farnell."

"It was easy to conceal it in the half-light."

"Tell me, the night you killed the cook, what happened? There was a shirt...?"

"Margery was going to tell you that I had not been with her the night I needed her alibi. She wouldn't lie for me. So I had to rely on my being at the Chapmans' all night."

"Ah, I see."

"So I made love to the woman, and afterwards, when she was sleepy, I pulled back her head and killed her. I was very bloody, but that was no problem. I squeezed out of my bloodied shirt and left it under her. Then I washed myself and poured the water out of the window."

I saw Everild with her mouth open and her eyes huge. She simply could not take in the coolness and viciousness of this man, who, it transpired, was her natural father.

Agnew stood up tall. "How did you know, sir?"

"Know what, Agnew?"

"That I had murdered my master?" he said.

"Your tricks... the family connection to tumblers and jugglers. You admitted as much to me and the rest of the information was supplied by the customers you played for and entertained, especially the rope walking."

Agnew smiled smugly. "But you don't know how I did it, sir? You don't know that."

I walked around his back. "Oh, but I do, Agnew."

I looked to my man-at-arms, who was captivated by the scene before him.

"Hal, the bag?"

He cleared his throat.

"Ah, yes. It's 'ere."

My man-at-arms fished in the front of his gambeson and came out with a small bag I had asked him to fetch from Agnew's room earlier.

"This, I believe, is the murder weapon."

I saw Johannes lean forward to look more closely.

Agnew groaned as I opened the bag. Everild sighed, and Deyning said, "What - did he play him to death?"

I had taken out the small light-coloured wooden flute, which had no holes—the one I had found in Agnew's room earlier.

"This little thing is lethal in the right hands."

Farnell was blinking at it. "That thing?"

"Perhaps you remember Master Agnew coming into your forge, Farnell?"

"To the forge? No, I don't think... wait! Yes."

Farnell swivelled to face me, grimacing at the pain of it.

"He came with a message from Pitchcott. One last plea to abandon my work and come into the business."

"And on that day, at that time, you were, I suppose, making those little metal balls of yours?"

Farnell was going to deny it, but I could see his mind replaying the scene in his head.

"Aye, I had a few on the bench." He quickly looked up at Agnew.

"You bastard, you stole them."

Agnew smiled sweetly at him.

"It was an easy matter to palm some of them. I knew they would be really useful. One day."

"And you could throw suspicion onto me... you snake..."

Agnew bowed as if he had just completed a performance.

I scanned the table for a small item I might use in my demonstration and found a pottery plate.

"May I?" I asked Mistress Deyning.

She nodded absently.

"Hal, set this up there on the pot board."

Hal took the little yellow pottery plate and placed it in the middle of the top shelf. I took one of the small balls I had kept in my purse, loaded it by rolling it into the end of the flute and put it to my lips.

"Watch. No one must move."

I took a huge breath and released it all at once, forcefully and quickly into the mouthpiece of the pipe.

The ball went flying but missed the plate by half an inch. Again I loaded the pipe and blew hard.

There was a shattering of pottery. Otille jumped. I imagine she had heard this sound a few times in the kitchen and had had her knuckles rapped and her wages docked.

Again we had silence.

"You climbed the outside wall of the castle, Agnew, by holding onto the putlogs and heaving yourself up. Your small and perfect feet trod easily on the large wooden pegs left by the builders. It was no real feat for a man of your dexterity and athleticism."

Agnew beamed as if I had complimented him.

"Now, I must admit I don't know what happened then, but I am guessing that you either rapped upon the shutters or you lifted the bolt from the outside with a knife."

"You are quite correct, my lord. I rapped on the boards. You should have seen Aldous' face when he saw me fifteen feet up in the air with no ladder to suspend me," he laughed.

"You shot your ball but missed and hit my polished plate."

"I did. But the master was panicking then and I had time to reload and aim. It would not have mattered where on the head I'd hit him. He would have fallen unconscious, and the poison... you realised I used poison, didn't you, sir?"

"*I* did, Agnew," said Johannes quietly.

"Ah, yes. You, too, are a clever man. The poison would do its work after a while. I didn't think anyone would work out what had killed him."

"When you visited my office to collect your papers, you retrieved the little ball, the one with which you missed, didn't you?"

"Yes, sir, and at the same time, planted Master Deyning's belt end, which I'd earlier cut from his belt."

"In this way, you tried to incriminate both Deyning and Armer."

Agnew nodded. "And then, after I'd killed my master, I went back down the castle wall, returned to the Chapman house and entered through the window."

I chuckled. "Your drunken stupor was feigned, wasn't it?"

"Yes, indeed. I never drink too much, my lord, never. I only ever drink with food and then never to excess."

"So there you were, still in the same place when the steward saw you the next morning. Seemingly much the worse for wear."

"I was sober when I returned home, sir," he smiled sheepishly.

"That is the most fiendish story I have ever heard," said Farnell.

"And you tried to get the Lord Belvoir with yer little pipe with no 'oles when 'e was getting a bit too close, eh?" said Hal.

"I thought he was a little too clever for me, yes," Agnew bowed to me. "I salute your intelligence, sir. You are a *very* clever man."

"Were you not a murderer, Agnew, I would salute you

too. Your ingenuity knows no bounds."

I handed the flute to Hal, who put it back in its bag and returned it to his jerkin once more.

I saw Agnew look longingly at it as it vanished.

"I must attach you, Robert Agnew, for the murder of your master, Aldous Pitchcott, for the murder of the woman known as Margery Cook, and for the attempted murder of myself and Master Farnell Armer."

"I am sorry about that, sir, really I am. I did not really wish to harm you, m'lord. Perhaps that's why my aim was not true that day."

I touched the spot on my temple, now a fading green-brown bruise.

"Can we find some rope, Thomas?" I asked.

"Oh, sir, there will be no need. I will come to the castle with you. You need not bind me," said Agnew.

"Oh no, Agnew. I'm afraid it's a long step from here to the castle, and I must ensure I deliver you to the gaol master."

I saw Thomas exit through the door to the back of the house in search of rope.

The maid Aebbe came forward to gather the cups and wooden trenchers from the table and take them to the kitchen.

Hal pushed back his stool and was about to come round the table to take hold of the prisoner when Agnew, with no preamble whatsoever, gathered his muscles and sprang for the tabletop. The things placed there rattled and fell. Aebbe squeaked. Otille screamed.

In a trice, he'd knelt, taken and turned Aebbe in his arm. His elbow tightened around her neck, and a knife appeared in his hand. I noted that it was already stained with Armer's blood.

Hal fell back in shock. Everyone jumped. I stepped forward but could do nothing.

"Let her go, Agnew."

"I will kill her… if I have to… have no doubt of that."

Agnew pulled tighter, and Aebbe made a curtailed scream. She began to go pink in the face.

"Let her breathe, man!" I shouted. "What has she ever done to you?"

"Nothing," said Agnew without emotion. "But she is a nothing, a servant, a girl of no importance."

"She is someone's daughter, as Everild is yours, sir," I said quickly. "Beloved of her mother and father and of God."

His eyes flickered then as my shot hit home. He loosened his grip a little.

"I am going out of the main door. No one will stop me. I will let the girl go when I am safely away. No one will follow, or she will be killed. Do you understand me?"

Deyning rose to his feet. "Agnew, I will give you money. Let the girl go."

Agnew howled with laughter, derision in every peal.

"Money? I have money, Master Deyning—more money than I have ever had in my life. My wants are few. I have seen my daughter grow. I have seen her inherit her fortune. I have seen her make a disastrous marriage."

"You will not see your grandchildren."

"I will not anyway. They will hang me."

"Let Aebbe go."

"No, she will come with me."

The man leapt from the table like a springing cat, landing on soft feet on the floor, never letting slip his hold on the girl's throat nor overtoppling. His balance was amazing.

"Come, Aebbe, walk with me."

"No, sir, no…" mouthed Aebbe, struggling.

"Struggle, girl, and I'll cut your throat like I cut Margery's!"

Aebbe's frightened eyes were huge and filled with tears.

"Go with him, Aebbe," I said gently. "He will let you go when he is past the gate."

I searched the man's face and looked at him intently, "Will you promise to let the girl go when you reach the gate, Agnew?"

"If it's safe to do so, yes."

I felt I could trust him in this, at least, this murderer of two people.

"Follow me, remember, and she will die."

He backed towards the main door and through to the screens passage.

Everild stood.

"Agnew…"

Robert Agnew turned a sad face to his daughter.

"I wish you joy, daughter. You have brought your troubles upon yourself, for I do not think Deyning will prove a good husband. I will listen for news of you. Perhaps one day, when I am much changed, I will visit, and you shall not know me…"

"I will *never* be your daughter," said Everild haughtily, her head held high. "Do not bother revisiting. I hope they catch you and hang you. Painfully."

The hurt which flooded through the man's face then was unmistakable.

"I will be there to laugh as they string you up!"

What, Paul? Was she there? …My, my, you will have to wait and see. Maybe we didn't catch him, eh?"

Deyning inched round the table to his wife's side. Agnew saw him and squeezed his captive.

"Stay put, master furrier. You do not want this girl's blood on your hands."

Deyning ignored him and took Everild by the shoulder. She angrily shook him off.

Johannes rose slowly from the table, looking at me.

"Agnew, we can give you a head start. Leave the girl." I heard the appeal in his voice. I nodded in acquiescence.

Agnew placed his lower leg over the girl's blue skirt, pinning her own leg to his and leaned back to unlatch the front door. Aebbe was bent backwards at an alarming angle.

She groaned and whimpered.

"Please, Agnew, do not hurt her. You are not a cruel man; I know this for a fact," said Johannes.

"I will have no need to hurt her if you all play your part and stay put until I'm gone."

Aebbe was straightened up and Agnew sidled out of the front door dragging her with him.

I watched as his hand came through the lessening gap. It lifted the bar of the door, and at the last moment, he withdrew his hand, and the door slammed, the locking bar riding down abruptly into its metal casing.

He's done that before, I thought.

All was silence for a heartbeat and then Deyning made for the door.

"NO!" I cried. "We do as he says."

"But sir, we must follow. He will get away."

I turned for the back door.

"Hal, with me. *No one* follows to the front; that's an order."

We hurried across the room and opened the back door, running out into the courtyard by the kitchen. The groom came with us.

I yelled through the open door. "Johannes, in a short while, go out and see to Aebbe. Please, God, she is all right and by the front gate, as Agnew promised."

I heard him answer me.

"Stay here and guard the door in case the man doubles back," I told the groom.

We ran around the kitchen, the outbuildings, and the stores. I vaulted the wall at the back and slid down the bank, for the place was built on the northernmost hill going up out of the town.

We ran through the plot of some matron whose house lay on the Green. She screeched at us and shook her fist as we leapt over her onion patch.

Down again, through another garden, this one a piggery. The animals squealed, snorted and scattered as we ran through. We slipped and fell a couple of times. This time no one came to look.

At last, we found a way through and exited onto the green space by Herd Street, which was bisected by the road to London.

Hal looked up and down the hill.

"Sir, what if 'e's gone east?"

I shook my head.

"He needs to be away fast, Hal. To the east, there are few houses and then the ford of the River Og, as you know. No habitation. He needs a horse and he can only get one of those at the livery stable by Master Roper's yard. He'll not go up to the one at the other end of the town."

"Ah, yes," said Hal. "That is the nearest. Master 'Orsman's."

The rain was coming down steadily, and the ground was slick and slimy. Mud from the piggery and the gardens clung to our boots and splashed our leggings.

Hal looked down at his feet. "Aw, so much for us staying clean!" he yelled. "What a mess!"

I laughed at him. Here was his fastidiousness about his clothes and his person.

We leapt across the road, which was a torrent of tumbling clods and uprooted plants, bits of dung and little stones, and made the side, which was marginally cleaner.

Hal and I ran down the alleyway between two houses on Oxford Street and came out on the Marsh. The place was soggy underfoot, lying as it did by the river. We picked our way through the puddles until we came to the wide London Road, slightly higher.

It could be a busy road, but there was little traffic now. It would have been bustling with folk that morning, a market day, folk coming from the forest and further afield to the town to buy and sell their wares. Now, most travel was finished, and folk had made their way there, churning the roadway with cartwheels and horse hooves.

We looked down the road. There was Agnew, alone, loping along at a fast pace and jumping the puddles with an easy spring. He did not look back until he reached the entrance to the Rope Yards. We ducked behind a tanner's cart just in time and were not spotted. He had abandoned Aebbe, it seemed.

Hal poked his head around the wooden body of the cart. "Gone in."

"Good! We follow. He has only one way out."

"Or the river, sir."

"Aye, or over the river."

I loosened my knife and slid it from its scabbard. Hal followed suit; we would not be taken by surprise again.

"He's a slippery sod, isn't 'e?" said Hal. "Making out he was so soft and scaredy when all the time he's as hard as a 'untsman's 'atchet."

"I think his heart was soft for one thing and one thing only, Hal - Everild Pitchcott. Pity she could not reciprocate."

"Nah, she's as 'ard as 'e is."

"It's in the blood, I suppose, and let's face it, Pitchcott was no gentleman. She didn't really stand a chance, did she?"

I put my finger to my lips and we carefully peered around the corner.

"I want a horse now. I can pay you what you ask." We saw Master Agnew arguing with the liveryman, Master Horsman himself.

"I haven't got one you can take and not bring back, Master Agnew."

"Oh, for Christ's sake, I'll bring him back."

"You said you were going to Salisbury. You didn't say you were coming back."

"I will come back," reiterated Agnew. "Just get me the damnable horse now."

"Master Agnew, what's the hurry?" asked Edwin Horsman, lifting his arms genially. "You don't normally..."

"This is an exceptional case." Agnew looked back, and we just managed to duck out of sight.

Master Horsman sighed. "Wait here then."

Agnew, agitated, paced up and down. His knife, I noticed, was back on his belt. I hoped against hope that it was not also stained with the blood of poor Aebbe.

I stepped out into the yard and advanced. Hal followed closely on my tail.

Agnew saw us out of the corner of his eye and swivelled to meet us.

"I'll say it again, my Lord Belvoir, you are an exceptional man."

I bowed. "Coming from you, Agnew, that is something."

"How did you know I'd be here?"

"Something called logic, Agnew. It's a thing I have learned over the years. A thing the Greeks of old discovered. I'm surprised a man of your knowledge doesn't know about it."

"Oh, I do, sir. I, too, have read many of the classics."

"My logic tells me you'll need a horse to escape quickly. You need to be out of town by the nearest route, and that, Agnew, is south, and the only place to get a horse is here."

"Some'ow, Agnew, I didn't think you'd be a ridin' man," said Hal grinning through his beard.

Agnew nodded. "You have no idea how well, Master Hal."

"Tell me that the girl Aebbe lives, Agnew."

"She does, my lord. I keep my promises."

The man shuffled his feet. "So what now, my Lord Belvoir?"

"I have no wish to hurt you, Agnew, but I must take you to the castle. How I do it is up to you."

"In bits or 'ole and 'earty," said Hal. "That's what."

The man's gaze pierced mine with a stare as sharp as one of my wife's sewing needles.

He shook his head. "No, sir; you will not take me there."

Unaware of the danger, Edwin Horsman came out from the stable leading a mare by the reins.

"There you are, Master Agnew," he said jovially. "Mabel will cost you…"

He saw us, and a grin split his face.

"Why, my Lord Belvoir. It's good to see you. And Master Hal too."

Distracted by us, the liveryman took his eyes from his horse and Master Robert Agnew.

Springing from a standing start, Agnew leapt onto the horse's back like a flea to a dog and kicked the poor liveryman in the head in one movement.

Down went Edwin Horsman with a grunt. Forward went Hal to bar the horse's passage.

Up came Agnew's foot, and Hal just managed to avoid the fierce kick it would have delivered to his face.

I ran backwards as the rider gained momentum and made for the gate. He pulled the reins to turn the horse for the London Road, and I leapt for his stirrup, kicked his foot hard and placed my own foot there in an instant.

Up I went and grappled with the man.

The horse reared, not used to two riders, and both of them fighting. Agnew and I slithered to the muddy ground. My foe recovered his wind and his knife.

I scrambled up and drew mine. I made a feint for his chest.

Without a breath's notice, the man flipped over and backwards, out of my way, and my knife-thrust danced in thin air.

Hal came up behind him, his sword in his hand.

Agnew felt his presence and swivelled to try a blow to Hal's middle. Hal sucked in his belly and danced away. I saw Agnew quickly looking for a way out.

The livery stables lay at the top of Master Roper's yard where he had stores of wood and other equipment.

Here too the stables had stacks of straw ready to be used that evening. These were loaded up against the wall of the nearest building. Agnew turned and ran and jumped as high as I have ever seen a man jump, bounced from the topmost stook and landed on all fours on the shingle roof of the stables.

"Hal, the rope shed!" I cried, for I thought I knew where Agnew would end up.

Without as much as a wobble, the man ran up the slope of the stable roof and disappeared to the other side, where lay the roof of Master Tim Roper's main shed.

We heard the tiles grate as Agnew landed on them and a pattering as he slipped on the wet lichen and moss which coated the roof. The footsteps receded.

We ran around the end of the yard, through the

forecourt of the rope yards and past the end of the first rope shed.

These sheds were very long, and we passed alongside cautiously, lest Agnew jump down on us from above.

"There!" cried Hal. "Slimy bugger's making for the main street again."

Indeed he was. The end of the shed stopped about twelve feet short of the London Road and with customary elegance, Agnew launched himself from the rooftop onto a cart standing at the end of the building.

He landed with an 'oomph', rolled head over heels to the floor, and was up and running in a trice.

We followed on the ground.

Quite a few people were trying to cross the bridge. It was not the wide stone bridge it is today; it was a rather small wooden edifice that only allowed one cart to pass at a time. There was some argument as to which cart had entered the bridge first, and we heard raised voices as we thundered up the road towards the obstruction.

"Make way for the constable!" I yelled.

Folk turned as they saw us pursuing Agnew up the street.

"Felon! Harrow, harrow!" yelled Hal at the top of his lungs. This was the cry one was supposed to utter when needing help to waylay a malefactor. Those that heard it were supposed to give you aid.

Three women screamed as Agnew ploughed into them, elbows jutting, scattering them and their geese as he fled. One man with a pack on his shoulders stepped back and overbalanced, plunging over the bridge rail into the water. Luckily, it was not too deep and the man sploshed upright, swearing and cursing.

Two young boys desperately tried to trip Agnew up with sticks, but he waved his knife at them, and they thought better of it.

I heard the clatter of feet on the wooden boards of the bridge.

The cart at the nearest end was empty. Agnew vaulted it as if it had been made of parchment. He jumped, landed on the side, circled his arms to regain balance, stepped into the cart bed, set his foot onto the other raised side and was off, all in one fluid movement. The ox which drew it looked back in astonishment.

"God's ditties!" yelled Hal. "He's got bloody wings 'e 'as!"

"Just certain feet," I said breathily. "And power... oh yes... power."

Agnew came up to the second cart. This one was full of wooden palings.

Again he sprang up to the cart. This time, he took the side rail with his hands, lifted himself on his arms so that he was almost standing on his head, hovered there momentarily and flipped over to land on the wood. He slithered about then, losing his footing on the cart contents, but again put his foot to the edge of the cart and leapt off with a forward roll to break his fall.

More people were crowding onto the bridge on foot. We yelled as we passed and darted around the carts. It took us longer to pass them than it had Agnew to vault them.

Two more carts drawn by two oxen apiece were lazily going up the London Road side by side, the drivers chatting and laughing together.

Agnew met them at their tail. He jumped up to the empty bed of one of them, tiptoed across, stepped onto the driving seat and stood a second to look back at the bridge and us.

"Oi, you, geroff! I ain't givin' you a lift!" shouted the carter.

Agnew smiled and made his way fearlessly onto the

backside of the oxen. With one foot on each beast, he stepped up the animals' backs as light as a breath of wind. I swear the beasts did not feel him.

"Bugger off!" screamed the carter.

Our man launched himself from their nose ends, tucked himself into a ball, straightened at the last moment and landed on his feet. He wavered but a little and then was off at a pace up the hill, the carters gesticulating and shouting obscenities at him.

"We'll never catch him," puffed Hal as we came up level with the two carts.

Had they been drawn by ponies, I might have commandeered them, but they were dull and plodding oxen and were not fast enough.

We struggled up the hill as quickly as we could go.

Agnew looked back.

I could see the frustration on his face as he saw us still pursuing. The gap, however, had lengthened. We could not gain on him. He was too lithe and rapid.

We rounded the bend as the road left the town environs and wound its way into the forest.

This was my home territory; I knew every inch of it.

I willed him to make a mistake and go into the trees.

"Oh, please, Agnew," I said to myself. "Go into my forest. She will have you."

The gods must have heard me, for the man took it into his head to disappear into the trees at the side of the road at Forest Hill.

"Now, sir," I said aloud. "I have you!"

Chapter Fourteen

"WHERE DOES 'E THINK 'E'S GOING, EH?" asked Hal. "Does 'e know 'is way around in there?"

I chuckled. "I doubt it, Hal. Not as we do."

We followed the man into the trees.

Many think - and I know I've said this before, but it bears saying again - that a forest is a place thick with trees as far as the eye can see. This is not so. The forest covered some one hundred and fifty square miles and extended from Marlborough's southern boundary in the north to Collingbourne in the south. It covered the distance from East Kennet in the west to Hungerford in the east. However, it was not all trees. This area contained large tracts of common, bushy scrub, leas, bog, river meadows and downland. Areas of trees punctuated these parts, some of them dense. Coppices of managed trees were dotted about. It was easy to become lost in them if you did not know the place well. None but the most knowledgeable could navigate by the sun in Savernake.

The foolish man had taken the track we know as Brown's, a narrow defile between tall oak trees leading eventually to White Road, merely named for the whiteness of its chalk surface. This was a straight track which marched its way to an earthworks and the junction with another track which led deep into trees at the edge of Forest Hill.

Agnew could move north and end up at the scarp of the hill overlooking the town and the River Kennet, or go into the forest further and head southeast into the trees.

"Let's see which way he goes, Hal."

He turned southeast; we could see his green tunic, pale in the flashes of watery light between the trees. He'd slowed down through tiredness and with the exertion of travelling on a less certain surface.

The recent rain had made the going sticky. However, the rain was slackening now and we were wetted more by the drips from the overhead branches than from the rain from the Heavens.

Our legs were fouled with soil, pig muck and chalk mud and wet with brushing through the ferns and grasses at the edge of the path, which grew over and obscured our way.

White Road was wider, and we all made a better pace along it.

Finally, we made the road to Braydon. Here were stretches of open land where forest dwellers kept their sheep and cattle.

Agnew looked back once and saw us emerge from the trees.

Raised and cheery voices reached us from the large clearing. Laughter rang out over the meadow.

Agnew saw the folk there and made for them.

His intention must have been spotted, for five men turned and stared at him malevolently. He faltered. We gained on him.

"Hold that man!" I shouted. "In the name of the warden."

Agnew turned abruptly and ran at a fast clip to the young trees at the side of the meadow, realising that he could not intimidate five grown men who held knives, forks, sticks and other items of working gear and who would do my bidding without question.

We followed.

"Fan out and pursue!" I yelled to my forest men. "We go this way."

I took hold of my sword pommel in its scabbard and jogged to where Agnew had disappeared.

A few hundred yards into the trees, the coppice became denser. I stopped and put out a hand to halt Hal, who was puffing beside me.

There was complete silence. No birds chattered. No animal stirred. Just the drip, drip, drip of the leaves onto the undergrowth and our breath ragged and gasping.

"Something isn't right," I whispered.

Then - and I would not have seen it but for a slant of light from the emerging sun, a sun which at that moment broke away from a cloud and poured down liquid gold onto the forest in broken lines - I saw as if in a slowed dream, like an insect captured in amber, a stone come flying through the undergrowth, straight for us.

"Hal! Duck!"

"Oomph!" My man-at-arms threw back his head and fell rearwards into the sodden undergrowth.

"Belvoir to me, to me!" I cried, leaping across him and looking him over for injury.

This cry was the phrase used when any Belvoir man was in need of help. It was also the battle cry uttered when plunging into the enemy in a fight.

"Hal! Hal!"

"Wha... wha...?" said Hal woozily.

"A stone hit you. He's above us somewhere in a tree." I scanned the place; on the floor like this, we were fairly well hidden by the fully grown ferns and bracken.

Hal shook his head. I saw a trickle of blood emerge from his beard.

I chuckled. "Your thick beard saved you."

I looked around as one of my men from the Braydon meadows thrashed through the undergrowth and ducked down.

"Stay here with him. I'll try to draw our felon off. Recover, Ol' Hal, and then go home."

"Like Hell, I will," said Hal, trying to rise.

I looked at the forest man, past his yellow hose to his brown tunic and cheery red face.

"Adam, isn't it?"

"Aye, m'lord."

"Look after Master Hal."

"You can't go after him on yer own," said Hal, with a worried look. Removing his leather glove, he rubbed his jaw with his hand.

"Christ, them pipe things deliver some punch, don't they? I reckon it's broken." He moved his jaw about with his fingers.

I chuckled. "Stay here."

The forest trees were in full leaf, dense and thick. I looked up as I wound my way further in.

Brambles snagged me, ferns whipped my legs, and tree roots tripped me.

"Agnew!" I called. "This is my forest. I know her well. You cannot escape."

All was silent.

I knew he was somewhere close, for there was no movement, and the range to blow his pipe was not great.

I narrowed my eyes and scanned the trees in their middle branches.

There!

No!

It was merely a clump of mistletoe, a darker green in the new pale green of an oak.

I turned as a sound issued from behind me.

No!

A rabbit went scuttling away, its white tail bobbing, its feet thumping the ground.

I looked above me. A squirrel's drey could be mistaken for a crouching man.

A few more steps took me to a clearer space with no brush. Nothing but old, brown oak leaves, ivy and twigs covered the ground.

Agnew came down on top of me and punched hard. I heard my scabbard slap on the tumbled and drenched leaves. I turned under him and reached for his throat.

He was too quick and was up and running again, this time heading back to the Salisbury Road, which he'd just left.

I have never seen a man leap as well as Agnew. You would swear his mother or father was a deer. He covered the ground at an enormous pace, seemed to hover in the air, and barely touched the ground before he was off again.

Once or twice I saw him stumble, for the ground was not even, and no matter how well he trod, he could not guess what was under his feet at this speed.

I kept pace with him and rarely lost him, leaving my forest workers and Hal far behind.

The trees were quite dense as we came up to Cadley. I saw the little cotts of Osmund, my forester, and Alfred Safernoc, the son of my old reeve, on this side of the road. The tower of the new church came into view.

Again, I heard voices. Women chatting, children playing, dogs barking, and goats bleating.

Agnew looked back. I had gained on him. He was uncertain. He didn't want to go amongst my people who would obey me without question and lay hands on him.

He zigzagged across the open space before the church and came out onto the main road he'd left not a long while before.

I saw him turn. From his hip, he took his knife.

Was he going to fight?

I slowed and walked towards him, taking in gulps of air.

With one eye closed, Agnew threw the knife, holding its sharp, pointed end in his hand. Before that one had landed, he had another in his hand ready to throw.

'Ah,' I thought, 'this is one of his tricks. Throwing knives and narrowly missing his target.' Though this time, he came very, very close to hitting it.

I ducked and sprawled on the ground, rolling over and over to present a moving target.

Three knives came for me before I ceased to roll and rose to hide behind a friendly holly bush.

The man had seen where I had gone but had either run out of knives (I did not remember him having so many when we had been in the house on St Martin's) or would not waste his ammunition on a futile action.

He turned and made off up the road.

A woman on a beautiful mare was riding before a cart driven by a man I recognised. Her hood was up against the drips of the trees and the mizzle of rain.

My sight was a little blurred from my roll in the grass.

There were no other people on the road. I scrubbed my eyes with my dirty hand.

Suddenly, I noticed Agnew had sweetly approached the woman. She leaned in the saddle to speak to him.

He grabbed her from her horse, set her down and forced

her away, attempting to set his foot in the stirrup.

The horse sidled. Agnew swore. The woman recovered and made to push the man away from the beast.

He turned and flashed his knife at her.

I stood and ran towards them, freeing my sword.

The man driving the cart was leaping from the driver's seat when Robert Agnew launched himself feet first at him, and suddenly, the driver sprawled on the ground, winded. Agnew, turning in the air, landed beautifully on two feet again and made once more for the horse.

The woman had hold of the reins and was backing her away.

"You shan't have her," said her confident voice.

Two men were rapidly coming up behind. They had been only a few yards away, nonchalantly swaying in their saddles at a slow pace, laughing and joking until they saw what was happening to their mistress.

I staggered up to the group, out of breath and groggy.

The man set his foot once more into the stirrup and hopped. The mare sidled again.

All at once, the woman dropped the reins, leaned into the back of the cart and came out with a large pot. Standing behind the felon, she lifted the pot high above her head and brought it down hard on the head of Robert Agnew.

The two men dismounted from their beasts and ran up.

I was now close and steady enough to see Agnew's eyes roll up in his head. He wavered a moment and then gracefully - yes, even in unconsciousness, the man was elegant - slipped to the ground.

I grabbed the woman and held her close.

"Oh, well done, well done, Lydia, my sweetheart! Well, done indeed!"

Hal's words came into my head. "Never ever underestimate a woman!"

"You two should be ashamed of yourselves!" I yelled.

Peter Devizes and Stephen Dunn, my two men-at-arms from the castle, looked at their feet.

"We're very sorry, sir."

"I should think so."

"Aumary, don't be such a grump!" cried Lydia. "They weren't to know."

"Their job is to protect you, not leave you out in the open with a murderer."

"Only you knew he was a murderer, Aumary; we just thought he was a traveller who had lost his way, at first."

John Brenthall was sitting, rubbing his chest and regaining his breath in the middle of the muddy road.

"You all right, John?"

"Aye, sir, thank you. God's teeth, I've never seen anyone do that before."

"The man is a tumbler and conjurer. He has many tricks up his sleeve."

I gave John a hand to stand and pulled him upright. He grimaced with the pain in his chest.

"We have no rope to bind him, sir," said Peter, dragging the insensible Agnew to a sitting position against a cartwheel.

"Here, " Lydia fiddled under her cloak and removed her belt. "Bind him with this."

"Take his arms from his tunic, Peter, and clamp them around his body, then bind him with the belt. I don't trust him not to get out of it."

Peter and Stephen manhandled Agnew out of his tunic and shirt and then slipped them backwards onto him again. They tied the sleeves around his back. Now his arms were pinned to his body. They wound Lydia's long belt around him twice.

"When he comes round, we shall walk him back to the

castle," I said.

Lydia looked around. "Where's Hal?"

"In the forest with one of my cattlemen."

"Oh?"

"Agnew, this man, hit him with a stone loosed from... wait, I need to get the weapon from him."

"Is Hal all right?"

I was fishing in the man's shirt and pulled out another small flute-like instrument with no holes.

"This is the thing which spat the stone."

Lydia chuckled.

"Oh, Aumary," she said. "I think the rain has got into your head."

"Watch then."

I stooped and picked up a small flint which abounded in the forest. I dropped it into the end of the pipe and blew.

It hit a birch tree and knocked off a small amount of bark.

Everyone stood with an open mouth.

"Is Hal all right?" asked a shocked Lydia breathily again.

"His thick beard stopped the stone. He's just nicked and was a little disorientated, knocked about. That's why I left him with Adam."

"Where is he, sir? Shall I go and fetch him?" asked Stephen.

"Just past the Braydon meadow. If they have walked, it will be this way or back to the cattle barns."

"I'll find him, sir." He mounted and rode off into the brush.

"Where have you been?" I asked Lydia.

"To town buying pots at the market. Tom Potter and the other potters are there today, and we thought to look around and see what's for sale," said Lydia. "We thought to call in to see you, but Andrew Merriman said he didn't know where you'd gone."

"Ah, yes. We'd been at the Deyning house."

"I take it this man is your murderer?"

I put my arms around my wife's shoulder.

"Yes, my brave wife, he is our murderer."

"Then you had better get him to the castle. Put him in the cart, and we shall turn around. I'll come back with you."

I laughed.

"I cannot wait to hear the tale of it all," she said

Lydia mounted her mare Penelope again.

"And to know how it is you became so filthy, Aumary."

She looked me up and down.

"I don't know! You look like you have been dragged through a piggery backwards."

I laughed louder.

"But, my love," I said. "I have!"

So there we are, Paul. We had our murderer. We took him back to the castle, and he was thrown into the cells at the bottom of the keep.

After a while, the justices came, tried the man and took the evidence, which I had written down in my customary fashion. He pleaded guilty. He went to Winchester to be tried by a higher court and was convicted and sentenced to hang.

Yes, Paul, he was hanged and now he's facing the highest court in creation. I hope God forgives him, for, grudgingly, I have to say, I liked the man.

No, I don't know if his daughter made the journey to Winchester to see him hang. If she did, I hope, Paul, that he did not know that she was there. It would have been the final slap in the face - everything he did, he did for her.

I remembered Master Pitchcott's words… one

cannot rely, sir, on worldly things. They forever disappoint. Two disappointed men: Robert Agnew and Aldous Pitchcott. I hoped I would never be disappointed in my children. Nor I disappoint them.

My daughter Hawise saw me from her perch at the top of the stairs as I wearily returned home and mounted the steps to the manor.

I held my arms open hoping she would come to me and hug me, but she was now nine and beginning to be a proper little lady. She looked at me with a critical eye.

"Oh, Father, what have you been doing with yourself?"

'Oh,' I thought. 'I am now 'Father' and no longer 'Dada'. I remembered the pleasure of hearing her say the word when she was small - 'Dada'. Ha! As the poem ran, 'Worldly bliss lasts but a short time.'

"It's been raining, in case you haven't noticed, and I have been chasing a felon all over the forest."

"And falling in the mud."

"Yes, that too."

She approached me gingerly.

"Are you all right?"

I sighed. "Yes, I'm just rather tired. Hal has been injured, and I..."

Hawise's face went white. She took in a quick, shocked breath. "Oh no! What has happened to Hal?"

"He's all right, he..."

Her eyes swivelled to the block on the southern range of the courtyard where Hal had his room. My daughter adored my man-at-arms, and the feeling was mutual.

I leaned down to kiss her forehead.

"He's all right."

"Phew, Father, what is that smell?"

"Pigs," I said.

She pushed past me and ran down the steps, saying,

"I should make sure that Hal is all right."

"I should warn you."

Her agonised face turned up to me. "Oh no, what... what?"

"He smells of pigs too!"

GLOSSARY OF MEDIEVAL TERMS

Aconite - a plant every part of which is poisonous. Monkshood. Aconitum uncinatum

Apoplexy - sudden unconsciousness as can be seen with a heart attack or stroke.

Baxter - a baker often female

Bliaut - a woman's dress or kirtle.

Brazier - a metal box sometimes on wheels which contains charcoals, used as a portable fire.

Cellarer - the man responsible for the provisions at a castle or monastery.

Cist - chest

Congestion - overfilling of the blood vessels, or lungs. (Archaic)

Cordwainer - shoemaker.

Corselet - an all in one suit of maille, short or to the mid calves.

Cotte - long sleeved shift or tunic. A coat.

Gambeson - a padded and quilted jacket usually worn under maille.

Farrier - man who shoes and sees to the health of horses.

Furrier - a man who deals in furs.

Handfasting - engagement and/or promise to marry.

Hauberk - sometimes a leather corselet or another name for a metal chain one.

Hue and Cry - public outcry to search for and apprehend a felon.

Iberia - Spain

Murrey - a deep red dye and the fabric named after it.

Pallet - simple straw stuffed mattress.

Palliasse - similar to a mattress.

Scabbard - cover for a sword.

Screens passage - a wooden screen placed in front of the doors that led to the kitchen or buttery so as to block them from view. Also to screen the front door from draughts.

Slucies - planks put into the river or moat to restrict water flow or to guide water to a certain spot.

Solar - Generally on an upper storey, a room designed as the family's private living and sleeping quarters. The room was usually situated so that sunlight would be caught for the maximum amount of time in the day

Supertunic - a long sleeveless tunic which covered the bliaut or cotte

Vespers - evening prayers.

Vigils - night time church office.

Vintner - a wine merchant

Wicket - small personnel gate in a larger one.

Wolfshead - An outlaw whose head could be produced for money as could a wolf's.

Author's Note

I have long wanted to write this plot. A mysterious murder, almost impossibly executed under the noses of the authorities by a clever felon who is an agile gymnast - which is what we'd call him today.

Worldes Blis is an early song possibly from the reign of John himself and is all about disappointment. This was a common theme in the Middle Ages, often written about: You can work hard and do everything you're meant to do and still you will not achieve what you'd wished for.

Pitchcott learns he cannot always have his way and that even after death his legacy will be destroyed. One wonders how his daughter and son-in-law will fare too. Cracks are appearing in their relationship even before the end of the story. Master Agnew too, dies a disappointed man, for his daughter rejects him.

Merchants were beginning to be a more wealthy class as the thirteenth century wore on. In towns they owned property, servants and work premises not to mention other buildings which they rented out. They invested, speculated and grew rich. Some were more wealthy than others by virtue of the products they traded; wine and furs are two examples. Even kings borrowed money from them.

Wine for royal castles was usually centrally bought but when the King was in residence, local brewers and merchants were recruited to fulfil a need which couldn't be met by the usual channels.

Putlogs are just as I describe in the book and Mediaeval scaffolding can be seen in many manuscript illustrations. I draw the reader's attention to the building of a 'modern' Mediaeval castle in France - Guedelon (*www.guedelon.fr*) - where scaffolding is constructed and used in the same way as it is in my book.

The holes where putlogs were used can still be seen on some buildings today. On the side of the White Horse Bookshop in Marlborough, Wilts, in Chandlers Yard are some fine extant examples.

Susanna M. Newstead

If you have enjoyed
WORLDES BLIS
(book 14 in the Savernake
series)...

read on for a snippet
of **ALYSOUN**, the hotly
anticipated next book in
the series.

ALYSOUN

Bitweene Merch and Averil,
When spray biginneth to springe,
The litel fowl hath hire wil
On hire leod to singe.
Ich libbe in love-longinge
For semlokest of alle thinge.
Heo may me blisse bringe:
Ich am in hire baundoun.
An hendy hap ich habbe yhent,
Ichoot from hevene it is me sent:
From alle wommen my love is lent,
And light on Alysoun.
On hew hire heer is fair ynough,
Hire browe browne, hire yën blake;
With lossum cheere heo on me lough;
With middel smal and wel ymake.
But heo me wolle to hire take
For to been hire owen make,
Longe to liven ichulle forsake,
And feye fallen adown.
An hendy hap ich habbe yhent,
Ichoot from hevene it is me sent:
From alle wommen my love is lent,

And light on Alysoun.
Nightes when I wende and wake,
Forthy mine wonges waxeth wan:
Levedy, al for thine sake
Longinge is ylent me on.
In world nis noon so witer man
That al hire bountee telle can;
Hire swire is whittere than the swan,
And fairest may in town.
An hendy hap ich habbe yhent,
Ichoot from hevene it is me sent:
From alle wommen my love is lent,
And light on Alysoun.
Ich am for wowing al forwake,
Wery so water in wore.
Lest any reve me my make
Ich habbe y-yerned yore.
Bettere is tholien while sore
Than mournen evermore.
Geinest under gore,
Herkne to my roun:
An hendy hap ich habbe yhent,
Ichoot from hevene it is me sent:
From alle wommen my love is lent,
And light on Alysoun.

Between March and April
When the blossom begins to appear,
The small birds take pleasure,
in singing in their own language.
I live in love-longing,
For the fairest of all things,
She brings me such bliss,
I am totally in her power.
Such luck I have received,
I know it is sent to me from Heaven
From all other women my love is removed
And alights on Alison.
Her hair is wonderfully fair,
Her eyebrows are brown, her eyes are black,
With a pleasant expression she smiled at me.
She has a slender and well-formed waist
Unless she wishes to take me to herself,
As her own mate,
I will give up living a long time,
And fall down dead.
Such luck I have received,
I know it is sent to me from Heaven
From all other women my love is removed

And alights on Alison.
At night I toss and turn, awake,
As a result my cheeks turn pale.
Lady, it's all for your sake.
Desire has come upon me.
In all the world there isn't so clever a man,
That is able to recount all her excellence,
Her neck is whiter than the swan's,
And she is the fairest maid in town.
Such luck I have received,
I know it is sent to me from Heaven
From all other women my love is removed
And alights on Alison.
I am completely worn out from staying awake,
Weary as water in a weir,
Lest anyone takes away from me my beloved,
For whom I have yearned for a long time.
It is better to suffer sorely for a time
Than to mourn for ever after.
Fairest under a skirt,
Listen to my song.
Such luck I have received,
I know it is sent to me from Heaven.
From all other women my love is removed,
And alights on Alison.

13ᵗʰ century English song

1208
Chapter One

"My Lord Belvoir, it's good to see you."

I threw my leg over my horse Fitzroy's ears and jumped down.

"Matthew Steward, how are you? I hear you are a father for the first time?"

Matthew bowed low.

"Aye, sir. A son. John after the king. Six months now. Congratulations to you, too, my lord, for you also have another son."

"I do, and Heavens, how the time flies."

We walked my bay stallion across the yard of the manor of Bedwyn. Hal of Potterne, my man-at-arms, followed me slowly with his favourite grey, Grafton, and a groom came to take them both from us.

Looking up at the sky, I said, "Another fine day, Matt."

"Yes, my lord. My wife tells me it's set fair for the whole month of September."

"Is it now? She knows these things, does she?" I said with a smile.

"She's very good at weather, sir. Her own bones tell her, she says," he chuckled.

I laughed out loud.

"So how is Bedwyn faring, Matt? It must miss its old master and mistress terribly?"

"Aye, sir, so it does. God keep them in his bosom." Matt crossed himself. "He was a fine man, and she was a wonderful lady."

I followed suit. "Yes, they were."

We were speaking about my father-in-law, Toruld Congyre, the father of my first wife Cecily, who had been murdered in 1200. He had owned Bedwyn until his death last year from a prolonged disease. My mother-in-law had died of lung congestion shortly after.

I had inherited the village and demesne and Matthew Steward had run it with the help of the manor's able staff for quite a time. I was well pleased with how he managed it. Bedwyn village had always had an independent status in the forest of Savernake and it was still so.

"I've come to look at the birds, Matt? Shall we go round?"

We took the path around the great barn and made for a smaller building tacked onto the end.

Here were the mews for my father-in-law's prized falcons.

I had no birds at Durley, the village where I lived, for the most part, just three miles to the southwest. For many years, if I had wanted to hunt with birds, I had come here to my father-in-law's home and hunted with him and his hawks. It was his passion, and he had the money to devote to it, for it was an expensive pastime.

Now they were mine and I was determined that I would visit them more often.

This, however, was only my fifth visit since he'd died. My work had kept me from the pleasure and I'd not been to the mews for a while.

"Where's Roger, Matt? He's usually here to meet us."

"Oh, he'll be somewhere about the village, my lord. He never leaves the birds for long."

Matt opened the door of the mews.

There was a fluttering of wings as the birds, standing on their perches, anticipated company. I saw one bird was hooded.

We peered into the gloom of the building. Small windows high up in the wooden wall threw a beam of sunlight down to the floor and dust motes danced in the disturbed air.

The smell from the birds also escaped the door; not a too unpleasant smell, I thought, though there was an added tang I couldn't immediately identify.

I made for the corner where the falcon I favoured most was sitting hooded with her head cocked.

"Ah, my proud Gilda," I said. "How are we today?"

I took a glove from a peg and slipped my hand into it. As I did so, my eye caught a dark patch of something on the floor in the corner.

I ducked under the bird slowly so as not to startle her and eased myself around her bow perch.

"Matthew!"

"Aye, sir?"

Matt came scuttling into the building and screwed up his eyes in the gloom.

"Come here for a moment."

He too ducked under the perch.

"What's this?"

Matthew bent and put out his hand to the sand scattered on the floor.

"Blood, sir."

"Not from the birds' food?"

"I can't say, sir."

We returned to the light from the door.

"Find Roger, will you," I said, "He should know..."

As I spoke, I turned to the space behind the open door where various items for the birds were stored and hung on pegs: the jesses, braces and cadges.

A humped figure lay against the base of the wall.

I threw off the glove. Matt caught it and his eye travelled swiftly to where I'd looked.

"Jesus, it's Roger," he said.

I was now on my knees in the sand before the sprawled man. He was slumped against the end wall of the building, his head on his chest.

I lifted the slight body to the light.

It *was* Roger Hawkes.

Blood coated his bald head, face, neck and upper body. He wore a thin shirt, braies and hose and his shirt had been torn to shreds. Blood had soaked into it.

"Is he alive, sir?" asked Matt breathlessly.

I sat back on my haunches.

"No, Matt. I'm afraid he's dead."

There we are, Paul, my scribe. We begin another tale. A tale which I shall relate to you, and you shall write down for me, for I can no longer write with my ancient and misshapen fingers.

Yes, you are right. It does seem odd. But as you may imagine and will have learned from all those stories you transcribed for me before, this scene was not as it first seemed.

Do you know, the details of that picture are scratched into my brain as cleanly as a stylus scratches into a waxed tablet? The morning sunlight, the smell of the mews, the shadows, all as clear as crystal to me, even forty years later. Yes, you're right, boy, I do have a good memory, particularly for a man of seventy-three.

That might be one of the reasons why King John required me to look into the crimes in my area; the felonies in the Forest of Savernake and elsewhere in north Wiltshire, in the lands of which I was lord, still am lord, though I allow my sons to run the whole thing now.

I had an inquiring mind and a good memory then and I can recall the details of each mystery I solved.

Let's carry on writing, shall we, until the light fades?

Hal, my man-at-arms, came into the shed quickly and bent over my shoulder.

"Looks like 'is birds 'ave 'ad 'im!" he said.

"That is indeed what it looks like, but..." I caught my lip with my teeth and looked around.

"They are all as placid as the perches on which they sit and aren't flying free, angry or upset."

"Would a bird *do* that, sir...I mean...go for a man they know well and attack 'im, to kill 'im?"

"If the birds had young and were protecting them, they might. However, we have no such thing here, Hal," I answered. "These aren't wild birds. These are birds used to people. And kill him? I really doubt it."

I looked over at the four perches where the falcons and hawks sat; my favourite Gilda, a saker and the only one hooded; Parsifal, a sparrowhawk; a lanner, whose name was Flitch; and a female goshawk known simply as Brownun. There was a strict hierarchy of which bird might be flown by whom. A knight might own and fly a saker or a lanner; a lesser man, a goshawk. There were no birds for the higher order of noblemen in my father-in-law's mews.

I scoured the ground under the perches. There were the usual droppings and a few feathers, nothing unusual.

I picked up the falconer's hand.

"See here, Hal, if Roger had tried to defend himself against the birds, he would have been scored about the arm and hand."

"'E isn't."

"No."

"Just the 'ead and chest."

"When you are taking wild birds from the nest, Hal, to rear for yourself, the parents dive at you and attack you about the head. They don't, as a rule, score you on the front of your chest. If you have any sense, you turn your back or defend yourself with, let's say, a buckler held above you."

"Or if you've even more sense, you go when the parents are out."

"Just so."

"You mean, my lord, that someone wants us to blame the birds for Roger's death?" asked Matt with a face as grey as putty.

"I think that's what we are being led to believe, Matt," I said.

I stood up. "Master Steward, can you send someone for the coroner? Hal, might you go back to Durley and fetch Johannes from his room? He needs to see this."

Johannes was the doctor of Marlborough, the largest town in the area. He had been staying with us for a few days, for he was uncle to my second wife and godfather to my three children. He, Hal and I had had much experience looking at corpses.

Hal straightened up and stroked the twin peaks of his long grey beard, worn long in imitation of his Viking ancestors.

"Why would anyone want to kill ol' Roger? He was as quiet as a settin' 'en."

I shook my head. "I don't know, Hal, but I don't think it was the birds."

Matt screwed up his face. "Are you quite sure, sir, about that? I mean, really sure? The scratches and gouges—they look like the birds' talons."

"No, I'm not completely sure, but my thumbs are pricking and when my thumbs prick..."

"Ah," said Hal. "Take it from me, when 'is thumbs prick, then you jolly well know that it's goin'ta be a murder, Matt. No doubt about it."

"What do you think, Johannes?" I asked a while later when the doctor had bent over the body. There was more light in the little shed now, for we had opened wide all the windows—mere wooden flaps over openings in the walls—and the sun had crept around the right side of the building.

Johannes clicked his tongue.

"I know nothing about birds, Aumary, but I can tell a knife wound when I see one."

"Where? Show me?"

"Here, in the neck. It was meant to be covered by the scratches but failed to be hidden well enough to fool me."

I leaned over the body of Roger Hawkes.

"Yes, there...I see it. Where the neck meets the shoulder."

"A major bloodline runs up there."

"So he bled to death?"

"Until I get him somewhere where I can really examine him, well, I can't say exactly, but, yes, I think so."

"When the coroner comes, we shall take him into the

large barn and put him on a trestle."

"Aye, a good idea."

"I have looked around the bird shed. There's nothing. No knife." I looked around again.

"We'll need someone to look to the birds. I must go and ask Ralph."

Luckily, Roger's son Ralph was all prepared to step into his father's boots. This was often the case, for the position of falconer was handed down from father to son.

The young man ran his sleeve over his eyes and nose and stood as I entered his house.

He knew that his father was dead. It was all over the village, but I told him more of the unfortunate circumstances surrounding his father's death, since it was I who had found him.

"I am so sorry, Ralph. I will do my best to investigate and bring the perpetrator to justice."

"Aye, sir. I know you will."

"Meanwhile, do you think you might carry on looking after the birds?"

"Aye, sir. It's what I've been trained for."

"Good man."

"Do you want to take one of them out today, m'lord?"

"No...er, no...not today, Ralph. Not after what's happened."

He nodded and looked away, tears in his eyes. "Who would want to kill my ol' da in such a way, sir?"

"Did your father argue with anyone, Ralph? Is there anyone you think might have had something against him?"

He closed his eyes. "No, sir. No one."

I looked around the cottage. "Your mother died last year, didn't she, Ralph, and your sister is married and living away? It's just you and your father?"

"Aye, sir," he sobbed. "And now...it's just me."

I left him to his grief.

Johannes had told me that it was likely that the man had been dead for two or more hours when we'd found him, for he was not yet stiffening, not even in the jaw, which is the first place which shows the rigour. I needed to find out if anyone had seen Roger that morning.

One thing puzzled me...nay two.

Why was Roger partially clothed?

And why was just one of the birds hooded—the bird called Gilda, with which I liked to hunt?

I walked about the small village for the rest of the day, talking to the villagers. Did any of them have an idea why Roger might have been attacked? None did. No one had seen the man that morning.

The reeve, Henry du May, a man in his forties with a bright red beard which covered his throat, shook his head.

"He was a very quiet man, m'lord. Most of these falconers are. Calm, quiet and keeps themselves to their work."

"Friends or enemies?"

"Oh no, sir. He didn't have any special friends. In boyhood, yes, Yves of Harbook. Boyhood friends they were, coming from the same place, but he certainly didn't have any enemies."

"He always seemed to me a man wedded to his birds, Henry. Especially when his wife..."

"Lison, sir."

"That was her name, wasn't it? When... Lison died."

"His is a sad story. Five sons. All but the youngest, dead."

I crossed myself. "Sad indeed, Henry."

Henry du May recounted for me the deaths of Roger's sons. One drowned accidentally at the age of six; one died in his twenties of a cut which went bad; one taken off by some kind of fit aged fifteen; and the fourth an infant death. Ralph was the only survivor.

"There is the one daughter…"

"Ah yes, Richildis. I remember."

"Yes, sir. She went off to be married. Lives in Ramsbury town."

"She's the wife of a merchant, isn't she? I don't know much about it."

"Yessir. They have a fine house on the High Street near the church…a new one. Not been married all that long."

"Hmm. You know of no quarrel that Master Hawkes may have had with anyone?"

The reeve pursed his lips. "No, sir. Nothing."

I turned to leave.

"Except…well…well, it was hardly a quarrel."

"Ah, yes?"

"It was over that marriage, m'lord."

"Who did Richildis marry, du May?"

"Master Mansur Grover. You know that he is a wealthy man, sir."

"I'm told that he owns a large iron forge in Ramsbury. I have never met him."

"Aye, sir. Iron smelting. Much money in that, I'm told."

"And he argued with Roger?"

"His daughter, sir, ran away with the man."

"I remember she was quite a good-looking girl, Henry."

"Oh, ah… sir. She could have had her pick. She picked ol' man Grover."

"And her father was not happy?"

"Wasn't much he could do about it, m'lord."

"Oh?"

"Well, it went like this, see…"

"I remember," said Hal suddenly. "The girl disappeared

one night, didn't she?"

"Yes and her father, Roger, pursued them to the town. He'd no idea this amour had been going on. His friend told him where they were, I believe. They thought it was going to be a rape marriage."

"But it wasn't?"

"Oh no, sir. Ol' Roger eventually caught up with them."

"But they were already married, weren't they?" said Hal.

"They were, and by then, the man Grover had had the girl's maidenhead," said the reeve.

"Too late to do anything about it then," said Hal with finality.

"And so this man Grover was not popular with our dead falconer, du May?"

The man shook his head. "But the girl seemed happy enough, and Roger had to accept it. So, like I say, it wasn't really a quarrel."

"Hmm. Seems like a good reason to hate a man, all the same."

"But if that's so, sir," said Hal, "why is it that it's the *falconer* who's dead? Surely ol' Hawkes would want to widow his daughter, not the other way round."

"Perhaps they fought and this was the result?"

Johannes shook his head. "I don't see any evidence of a fight...certainly not in here, and this, I think, *is* where he bled to death." He pointed to the bloodstain.

"So if this is where he fell, why is he lying against the wall?"

"Crawled there, I s'pose?" said Hal, sadly.

"Hmm. And what we want to know is why did Hawkes dislike this fellow so much in the first place? Now, in that answer, we might find some bones, ol' Hal."

"Bones, m'lord? Meat and gravy, sir, meat and gravy!"

I needed to find and inquire of the other people involved in this tale. Before the coroner had come and gone and his jury of twelve men over fourteen had pronounced it murder, I sent a runner back to Durley to tell my wife Lydia that I would be staying at Bedwyn that night.

Off I went to Ramsbury with Hal in tow early the next day. My first call was to the forges worked by this wealthy man, Grover.

These were special forges in which the pulverised rocks holding the iron ore, brought from Seend, near Devizes, were heated to allow the metal to be released and melted.

Hal and I clopped down the main street, which ran parallel to the River Kennet. About two-thirds of the way down the long main street and not far from the church, we heard the sound of the workings and passed into a stockaded yard, about which many men bustled.

A man came to take our horses and gestured to a long, low building at the edge of the workings.

We scratched on the door and called out.

"Enter."

A young man with sparse brown hair and a small beard of the same colour rose from behind a table. He wore a brown capuchon hood and a short brown tunic and sported a tanned face. It seemed he was all brown. His face was smiling and showed a jolly disposition.

"Good day to you. Might I be speaking to Master Grover?"

The man chuckled under his breath.

"Ah, no, sir." He scratched his forehead with a rather dirty finger. "The master isn't here yet."

"I am Sir Aumary Belvoir, warden of the Forest of Savernake. I am also the constable of the county, and I am come about the death of my falconer, Roger Hawkes."

The man bowed low. "Ah, yessir. We heard that he'd...died."

"How did you hear? It's scarce a moment since the coroner made his pronouncement."

"Someone from Bedwyn came, sir, and spoke to Mistress Grover last evening about her father's death. It's hard to keep that sort of news silent after that."

"You are?"

"John of Burridge, sir." He bowed again. "I am the overseer of the men here."

"Well, John, is the mistress at home?"

"She is, sir. The house is the first by the church - you will not miss it, it's..."

"Tell me, John of Burridge, did you ever see my man Roger Hawkes here at the workings?"

"No, sir. Never."

"You know him then, how he seems?"

"Aye, my lord. You know how it is round here. Everyone is related to everyone else. I knew Roger. He's...he was...my sister's husband's uncle."

I turned that relationship around in my head.

I heard Hal chuckle softly in his beard behind me.

"The man was stabbed in the throat."

"Oh!" John of Burridge blinked a few times. "We heard that his birds killed him."

"Then whoever came from Bedwyn to tell you that he was dead told you awry, for it's murder."

The man swallowed.

"And I am investigating, as is my task as constable of this county."

The man fiddled with his fingers, nervously massaging his thumbs.

"I can't tell you anything about it, sir."

"Where do the men who work for you live, Master Burridge?"

"Most of them are Ramsbury men, m'lord."

"The rest?"

"Here and there around about."

"Any from Bedwyn? Free men?" I asked.

"A couple, sir."

"Then I'd like to speak to them. Now, please."

Burridge scurried around the end of the table. "I'll see if I can find them, sir."

The man left us, wiping his brow with the back of his hand.

Hal and I looked at each other.

"Jittery sod, i'n't he?" said Hal.

"Ah, well. Murder makes some folk nervous, Hal."

"S'pose it does. Whereas you and me, we'm used to it," he said philosophically.

I chuckled at him. "Sadly."

I looked down at the table. There was a pair of pincers lying on the surface. I picked them up.

"Expect to find that sorta thing, wouldn't you?" said Hal. I nodded as I replaced them.

I looked over the table-top again and noted, amongst other things, a long sample of iron shaped like a spearhead. Then, I picked up a dried piece of what looked like turf. I turned it over in my hand.

"What's this...? Ah, yes, see how the iron ore glistens. It's trapped in the moss-rich, red soil of some areas."

Hal looked over my shoulder.

"Is that the stuff they make this iron from then?"

"I heard that sometimes it can be found in abundance in bogs, Hal. If I'm not much mistaken, this stuff is known as bog iron."

"Iron found in bogs? Nah, go on, you're 'avin me on, sir."

"No, Hal. In some places, that is where it's found. In bogs."

"You are quite right, sir," said a deep and resonant voice from the doorway.

I put down the peaty sample and brushed my hands together.

We both turned as one and Hal took in a quick breath.

The man came into the building, out of the sunlight, ducking his head as he moved under the lintel.

"Sir Aumary Belvoir, isn't it? Warden of the forest."

I nodded. "And constable of the county."

Hal had his mouth open and was staring.

I smiled.

"Master Grover?"

"I am Mansur Grover, sir," he bowed, "Ironmaster."

I took a deep breath.

"I am pleased to meet you, sir."

The man before me was black of skin. Not tanned with wind and weather as some of the forest folk were, but dark, as if he had been painted with a black dye.

Hal cleared his throat. He whispered,

"Devils and demons."

Grover chuckled.

"Yes, my good man," he said smiling, "And the black goes all the way through." And he waved his hand down his body.

ALYSOUN WILL BE OUT SOON!

The Savernake Forest Series
Susanna M. Newstead

Belvoir's Promise
She Moved Through the Fair
Down By the Salley Gardens
I Will Give My Love an Apple
Black is the Colour of My True Love's Hair
Long Lankyn
One Misty Moisty Morning
The Unquiet Grave
The Lark in the Morning
A Parcel of Rogues
Bushes & Briars
Though I Live Not Where I Love
Wynter Wakeneth
Worldes Blis
Alysoun

Other Historical Fiction

I Am Henry - **Jan Hendrik Verstraten & Massimo Barbato**
The Sebastian Foxley Series - **Toni Mount**
The Death Collector - **Toni Mount**
The Falcon's Rise & The Falcon's Flight - **Natalia Richards**
The Reversible Mask - **Loretta Goldberg**

History Colouring Books

The Mary, Queen of Scots Colouring Book - **Roland Hui**
The Life of Anne Boleyn Colouring Book - **Claire Ridgway**
The Wars of the Roses Colouring Book - **Debra Bayani**
The Tudor Colouring Book - **Ainhoa Modenes**

PLEASE LEAVE A REVIEW

If you enjoyed this book, *please* leave a review at the book seller where you purchased it. There is no better way to thank the author and it really does make a huge difference!
Thank you in advance.

Printed in Great Britain
by Amazon